CHOOSING LIFE

JULIA TANNENBAUM

This book is dedicated to my parents. Thank you for being there for me no matter what. I love you.

Tannenbaum, Julia

Choosing Life / by Julia Tannenbaum

Summary: One year after spiraling into mental illness, a high school senior must overcome new challenges to stay in recovery and achieve her long-term goals.

ISBN: 978-1-7325554-4-0

Wicked Whale Publishing
P.O. Box 264
Sagamore Beach, MA 02562-9998

www.WickedWhalePublishing.com

Published in the United States of America

It happens sometime around midnight. I'm immersed in a dream about skydiving—or perhaps it's bungee jumping—when I abruptly wake up to an unfamiliar creaking sound. I look around in the dark, trying to figure out where the strange noise is coming from, but by the time I do, it's too late. With my hands gripping my mattress and my body tangled up in my sheets, I feel the entire right side of my bed sink through the frame and collapse onto the floor. I scream.

By the time Mom bursts into my room, I've managed to untangle myself and am sitting on my rug with my legs clutched to my chest. She flips on the light switch, and her jaw drops.

"Oh my goodness, Grace. What happened?"

Before I can respond, her boyfriend Kevin appears beside her. "Grace? Are you all right?"

"I'm fine—" I start to say when my sibling Jamie joins Mom and Kevin.

"Why are you yelling? I'm trying to sleep."

I don't know if it's the sight of them standing there looking frazzled in their pajamas, the fact that I'm running on two hours of sleep, or simply the absurdity of the situation, but I start to laugh.

"Maybe I should lay off the carbs," I joke.

"Not funny," Mom says, but I can tell by the small smile on her face that she's amused as well. "Come on, let's get you to bed."

The damage to my bed is pretty bad, so Mom and Kevin drag an old air mattress down from the attic and set it up on the floor. What is meant to be a temporary solution, however, results in me waking up the next morning with a dreadful back-ache, because the mattress had deflated while I was asleep.

Since then, I've taken to sleeping on the beige couch in the TV room. It's not ideal, but it's the best option while I'm waiting for my new bed to be delivered. The largest downside to the couch—other than the loose spring under the second cushion—is that I have to wear earplugs so I don't wake up when Mom comes downstairs at five o'clock to prepare for work. I'm unaware of how noisy she is the first morning and am jerked awake to the deafening sound of the coffee grinder.

I throw off my blanket and trudge into the kitchen, where she's standing at the counter on her phone. She looks up when she hears me, and we both ask at the same time, "What are you doing here?"

"Going to work," she says.

"At five AM?"

"Early shift. You?"

I point to the TV room. "I'm sleeping."

"Oh, so you were serious about the air mattress."

"Why wouldn't I be? That thing is a piece of crap."

The toaster oven dings. Mom takes out an everything bagel and begins to slather it with cream cheese. As she's wrapping the bagel in aluminum foil to take with her, she says, "You'll have to figure something out. Your new bed isn't coming until Friday, and I'm working an early shift every day this week." She places the bagel in her purse, grabs her keys, and plants a quick kiss on my cheek. "I'll see you for lunch."

I return to the TV room and flop face-first onto the couch. My eyes have just closed when the door reopens and she exclaims, "Forgot my coffee!"

From that point on, earplugs become my saving grace.

Friday morning isn't an exception. I rise at my normal time of eight thirty to a quiet house—minus the sound of the washer spinning in the basement—and stumble into the bathroom. I splash water on my face to snub my lingering drowsiness, comb my disheveled hair, and apply deodorant to my armpits. I usually skip the latter, but my friend Lou and I are going to the Center later today, and I want to smell nice. Then I flush the toilet and walk into the kitchen to prepare breakfast.

Breakfast has become a trusted meal between Mom and me. After some reassurance from my nutritionist and plenty of convincing on my end, she agreed that on the mornings when she wasn't around, I could eat breakfast independently. Although she was hesitant at first—to the point where she'd make me send before and after pictures of what I ate—she backed off relatively quickly. She said it was because I'd earned her trust, but I had a sneaking suspicion that she was just enjoying not having to wait on me as much. If I had to spend an entire year constantly supervising someone, like she'd done for me when I was unwell, I'd relish freedom too.

I hear her voice in my head—*volume, Grace*—as I shake a reasonable amount of Rice Krispies into a bowl. I add half a banana and a splash of milk on top and pour a glass of cranberry juice. At the table, I move Jamie's computer to the side and sit down with my cereal. As I eat, I admire the array of stickers adhered to the computer's shiny surface: a green flipflop, a pawprint, a pineapple. Below an intricate dreamcatcher is a yellow-white-purple-and-black striped flag that Jamie ordered during Pride Month.

"That's pretty," Mom remarked when the sticker arrived in the mail. "What's it for?"

Jamie snuck a sideways glance at me. I was standing behind Mom opening an envelope from the DMV. I stopped when the room fell silent and watched as Jamie took a deep breath.

"It's the non-binary flag, Mom. You know what non-binary means, right?" When she remained quiet, Jamie shakily continued, "It's, um, well, it's when someone doesn't identify as a boy or girl, and, um—many people don't by the way—and sometimes —*most* times—they use other pronouns, like they/them. That's the most common one. And I . . ." Jamie's hazel eyes suddenly welled with tears. "I . . ."

Before Jamie could finish speaking, Mom stepped forward and embraced my sibling in a fierce hug. "It's all right," she said. "I accept you."

Those three small words—*I accept you*—brought a smile to Jamie's face. Those words made everything—at least for that moment—okay.

It's almost nine o'clock by the time I finish eating breakfast. I place my bowl and glass in the dishwasher and head upstairs to get dressed. On my way out of the kitchen, I pass the giant calendar Mom has taped to the pantry door and sigh. In three days, vacation will be over, and I'll have to return to school. And while I'm excited that this is my last year at Chuck L Everett (aka Chuckles) High School, one-hundred-and-eighty-four school days is still a long way to go until graduation.

In my room, I open the top drawer of my dresser and

rummage through it for my navy Hollister t-shirt. I'm wriggling the t-shirt over my head when my phone goes off, so I quickly yank my arms through the sleeves and answer on the third ring.

"Hey, Mom. What's up?"

"Mr. Gomez called to let me know that he's heading over now," she says. "I'll try to be home when he arrives, but if I'm not, you can let him in."

"Mr. Gomez?" I ask.

"The man who's replacing your bed. Grace, we've been over this several times—including last night at dinner. The fact that you've already forgotten is a little concerning."

"Sorry. I'm bad with names."

"Uh-huh. So, you'll let him in?"

"Obviously. You think I want to spend my last year at home sleeping on the couch?"

"All right, all right. Point taken. I'll see you soon, okay?"

"Okay. Bye, Mom."

I end the call with another sigh and pull on a pair of denim shorts. As I'm redoing my ponytail in the mirror, I realize that my shirt is inside out. Before I remove it, I turn away from my reflection so I'm not troubled by the sight of my stomach. With that time of the month approaching, I've been feeling uncomfortably bloated all week. In the past, symptoms of PMS would send my mind into a full-blown panic, and I'd often revert to restricting food, resulting in me losing a pound or two when my cycle ended. Now, however, I've accepted that this is just part of being a female. Sure, I didn't have to deal with it when I was at my lowest weight, but I had much worse things to contend with than bloating and cramps then; things I never want to relive.

Once my shirt is on properly, I tuck a loose strand of hair behind my ear and apply a coat of mint ChapStick to my lips. I hear the rumble of a vehicle pulling up to the house and look out my window. A white van with *Frankie's Furniture* printed in capital letters on the side is backing into the driveway.

"It's about time," I say under my breath.

After one week of putting up with loose springs, stiff pillows, and ear-splitting coffee grinders, I could use a good night's sleep.

"I CAN'T BELIEVE we've only got one more year," Lou says.

She takes a long lick of her rocky road ice cream while I nibble on my strawberry, which has begun to drip down the sides of my waffle cone. With the temperature in the high eighties and the sweltering sun beating down overhead, I would have preferred to eat inside King Cone, but all the tables were taken.

"I know, right?" Now my ice cream is melting onto my hands. Since I'd forgotten to grab a napkin, my only option is to wipe my sticky fingers on my shorts. "It seems like yesterday when we were freshmen."

"Yeah, with my bright pink hair and overalls." Lou laughs. "What the hell was I thinking?"

"And I had that stupid choker I'd wear every day," I say, cringing at the memory. "We thought we were so cool."

"Ha! That lasted about a week." Lou polishes off her ice cream and tosses the white-and-blue-striped wrapper into a trashcan. "Speaking of cool . . ."

She gestures across the street where Bianca Santos and Tiffany Frasier are strolling down the sidewalk. Both wear crop tops and distressed denim shorts that barely cover their underwear. We watch them pause at a busy crosswalk with two joggers and a woman walking a dog. While Bianca casually leans against a lamppost, Tiffany impatiently presses the Walk button several times. Even from where I'm standing, I can hear Bianca's high-pitched laugh.

"Did you know that Jess is out of the hospital?" Lou asks.

I shake my head. "Where did you hear that?"

"I saw her on Heather's Instagram story. Then again, it might have been an old picture."

"Oh."

Jessica Bishops, Bianca and Tiffany's best friend, was involved in a car accident in June. The local news station ran a brief story about it, but Jess' family kept most of the details private. In the weeks that followed, rumors and speculations spread like wildfire. Since there was a power-outage in Jess' neighborhood that night—not to mention that the roads near her house are very winding—many assumed that she simply couldn't see properly. A select few claimed that the entire situation was a setup to distract the public from recent sexual harassment allegations against Mr. Bishops, who's our town's deputy mayor. Some kids at school even went as far as to say that it was karma that caused the accident.

Although I always thought Jess was spoiled and obnoxious, I still felt badly when Bianca told me what really happened to her: that Jess had too much to drink at Matt Durham's end-of-the-year party and swerved off the road driving home. I've never been in a car accident, but I know from experience how miserable being in the hospital for an extended period of time is. I guess I'll find out soon enough if Jess is actually back or if that too is nothing more than a rumor.

Lou and I spend the next hour aimlessly wandering through the Center. She rambles on about her disastrous two-week vacation in the Bahamas, where her luggage was stolen at the airport and she had an allergic reaction to papaya.

"My face swelled up like a balloon!" Lou exclaims. "I couldn't see anything!"

Having heard this story many times before, I merely nod and say, "That sucks."

"Damn right, it does."

"At least you actually went somewhere. Other than my writing program, all I did was sit around my house and watch Netflix and try not to die from this insane heat."

"You got your permit," she points out.

"Yeah, and now I have to wait months to get my license. That means I'll probably have to take more lessons with Mr. Ren." I sigh. "But whatever. You want to head back? I'm tired."

"Good idea. We're gonna need our energy for tomorrow. Last year, baby!" Lou slings her arm around my shoulder and begins to skip towards the parking structure near the library, dragging me along beside her.

When we reach the structure, we take an escalator to the third level and walk to her car, which is poorly parked between two sedans. She unlocks the door and climbs into the driver's seat. "God, it's hot in here. Let me turn on the AC."

With the air condition blowing, Lou navigates out of the narrow structure and turns onto the main road. Fifteen minutes later, she pulls up to my house and parks next to the curb. "Looks like Kevin is here," she remarks upon seeing his silver Kia in the driveway.

"Kevin is always here." I unbuckle my seatbelt and open the door. When I step onto my lawn, the overgrown grass tickles my bare ankles. "See you tomorrow."

"One more year," Lou reminds me.

I smile. "Yeah. One more year."

2

Mademoiselle Rousseau's lavender blouse is see-through. I try not to stare at her frumpy grey bra as she passes around rulebooks, but I can't tear my gaze away. To my right, Liam Fisher seems to have also taken notice of our advisor's atrocious outfit, his expression conveying both amusement and disgust. We make eye contact and he mouths, "oh my god."

"Here you are, Miss Edwards." Mademoiselle bends down to hand me my rulebook; now I can see her cleavage as well.

"Thanks," I mumble.

Liam snorts.

"Is something funny, Mr. Fisher?"

"No, Mademoiselle," he responds. He waits until she's out of earshot to whisper to me, "I don't think I'll ever be able to unsee that."

"Same," I say. "I hate advisory."

"You and me both," he mumbles.

Nodding my head, I avert my attention to the front of the

room, where Mademoiselle is loading a PowerPoint presentation onto the Smartboard. Using a grey remote, she clicks past the title page and stops at the first slide: dress code.

The frustration filling the room is palpable. Four years at this school, and my classmates and I are still required to review the same monotonous rules that were drilled into our brains when we were freshmen.

One more year, I remind myself. *You just have to survive one more year.*

When the bell finally rings, interrupting Mademoiselle's spiel on the consequences of vaping on school grounds, I grab my bookbag and follow everyone into the crowded hall. Liam hurries to my side as I'm walking through the language wing to the back staircase.

"Thank God that's over. I thought I was gonna die of boredom."

"I know the feeling," I say. "What class do you have next?"

"Something called Voices of Our Generation. You?"

"Same."

Liam's blue eyes widen with surprise. "You know that's a public speaking class, right?"

"It's more than just public speaking," I respond. "The course description said we'll be doing a lot of writing too. And plus, public speaking is a good skill to have. It might even help me improve my confidence." I tilt my head towards him. "Why are you taking it? You seem plenty confident as is."

"Because my only other option was British Lit, and after taking Intro to Theater last year, I'm so over Shakespeare."

"You took Intro to Theater?"

Liam nods. "It was a mistake, okay?"

I bite my lip to keep from laughing. "If you say so."

We walk through the cafeteria, where students are milling

around in groups or scarfing down breakfast at the bench tables, and enter the G-Wing. G-104 is located at the end of a long hallway across from a janitor's closet. I follow Liam through the door, and we find two empty desks in the back of the room. While he replies to a text on his phone, I glance around me in intrigue.

The room is on the smaller side, which would explain why the twenty-something desks are so close to each other. On the yellow walls is an array of colorful posters—some professionally made, others the works of rushed students—and three clocks, two of which are broken. To the left of the teacher's desk is a supply closet, while to the right is a podium with a small microphone.

I watch as a youngish woman drops a mint green bag onto the desk and stands in front of the whiteboard, patiently waiting for my classmate's chatter to cease. She's dressed in black jeans and a bumblebee-patterned shirt and has a sparkly clip in her curly brown hair.

"Good morning," she greets us when the room is quiet. "Welcome to Voices of Our Generation. My name is Miss Bacon—" This elicits several snickers, which she dismisses with a smile —"and this is my first year at Everett. I relocated from Chicago over the summer, where I taught public speaking for two years. While this course involves public speaking, we'll also explore storytelling, collaboration, different styles of writing, and much more. You with the Ronaldo jersey," she points at Matt Durham, "come help me pass these out."

She hands Matt half of a pile of stapled packets and walks to the back of the classroom, while he distributes them to the students sitting up front. I flip through the double-sided pages, skimming over general information like rubrics and due dates to get to a detailed course outline. Of the four main projects, one for each quarter, the latter particularly catches my attention: *Narratives*.

For your final project, you will write and present a piece about a period of personal growth in your life. This can include overcoming a setback, coming to terms with identity, or another topic that relates to the prompt. You may use any writing style of your choice, but your final copy must be seven to ten minutes long when spoken. You will present your piece from memory to your family and friends at the end of the year.

Although the end of the year seems like an eternity from now, the thought of having to deliver a speech—and a personal one at that—to a large audience from memory terrifies me. I think back to my Spanish final last year, where we were required to present a two-minute story about a made-up vacation to the class. I was so nervous that I thought I was going to throw up. If it weren't for the antianxiety medication I was on at that time, I doubt I would have survived the final.

Part of me is tempted to go see my guidance counselor Miss Dixon after this period and switch classes. But then I remember what I told Liam about improving my confidence. Like my therapist Anna says, change doesn't happen on its own; it requires exposure, risk-taking, and pushing myself outside of my comfort zone. It requires courage.

On the wall, the small hand on the one working clock has just reached the nine. Several minutes later, the bell rings, and class is dismissed. Guidance is on the way to my second period—Women's Literature—but I quicken my pace and walk past the entrance without looking twice.

Anna would be proud of me.

THE FIRST WEEK of school crawls by at the pace of a snail. From three assemblies—all of which were related to college—to entire periods spent reviewing syllabuses and assigning seats, it's a miracle that I've managed to stay awake. Lou, who sits in front of me in AP government, isn't as fortunate.

On Friday morning as Mr. McCarthy is explaining separation of powers, her head abruptly slumps against her desk. I lean forward and poke her back with my pencil. When she doesn't react, I poke her a little harder.

Lou finally lifts her head. She turns around and shoots me a sour look. "Fuck off," she mouths, then averts her attention to the front of the room, where Mr. McCarthy is drawing a chart on the whiteboard.

"To ensure that neither branch of government would become too powerful, the framers of the Constitution designed a system of checks and balances," Mr. McCarthy says. "I hope you're taking notes. This is important."

checks and balances, I scribble onto a lined sheet of paper. When I glance up from my notes, Lou is asleep again, her face nestled in the crook of her arm. Only this time, I don't bother to wake her.

After class ends, I meet Lou in the hall. "How come you're so tired?" I ask.

Lou pauses by a water fountain to adjust her shorts, which have ridden up her thighs. "I'm not. I'm just bored out of my fucking mind."

"Me too." I wait until she's situated to start walking towards the science wing. "I wish we were studying current events. All this eighteenth-century crap is giving me a headache."

Lou grabs my arm. "Where are you going? Your statistics class isn't that way."

"Jamie forgot lunch, so I promised I'd lend them money," I explain. "Their locker is near Ms. Lloyd's room."

"Right. Damn, I forgot freshmen eat so early."

"I know, right? It's no wonder Jamie is starving when they get home."

"Look at you, mastering your pronouns," Lou remarks. "How's your mom managing?"

"Fine, I guess. She's getting the hang of it. Believe it or not, Kevin is actually super chill with the whole situation. I don't think I've heard him mess up Jamie's pronouns once."

"That dude is full of surprises," Lou muses, shaking her head. "I hate to say it, but he's not so bad."

"Yeah, well, don't forget about the twins." I make a face. "They're coming over this weekend and not leaving until Monday. And as if an extra day with them isn't bad enough, they're bringing their tubas too."

"I still think that's hilarious." Lou laughs. "Of all the instruments in the world, they both picked the tuba. It can't get much better than that."

"You should see them lug their enormous cases around," I say. "Those things probably weigh as much as they do."

"My cousin used to play the tuba," Lou says. "Then she dropped it on her foot in band practice and broke her big toe. She quit after that."

"I wish they'd drop it on their big toes," I mutter.

Lou smirks. "You're evil."

"Good. You're here." Jamie, with their bulky blue backpack slung over one shoulder, hurries to my side. "Do you have the money?"

"Yes. Your shoe is untied." While Jamie bends down to tie the white laces, I rummage through the front pocket of my bookbag for a five-dollar bill. "Here. Don't spend it all on junk."

"Whatever, Mom. Can I go now? If I'm late, there won't be any cinnamon rolls left."

"No need to thank me or anything," I mumble as Jamie takes off towards the cafeteria.

"Save me a cinnamon roll," Lou calls. "Think they heard me?"

I roll my eyes. "I'm going to class. Later."

Abandoning Lou in the middle of the hall, I leave the science wing and speed walk upstairs to C-207. I slip into the room and claim my assigned seat in the second row from the front just as the bell rings. Mrs. Hall, a middle-aged woman with blonde hair who always looks like she hasn't slept in days, waits until the talking has ceased to make her way to the whiteboard.

"I hope you all had a good first week," she says. "Take out your homework so we can go over it. And please don't hesitate to ask questions. I know some of the material can be challenging."

She's not wrong; last night, it took me nearly ten minutes to simply remember the equation for the first problem. By the fourth, I had to ask Kevin, who studied statistics in college, for assistance. While I was reluctant at first, he ended up being pretty helpful. I suppose Lou was right: that dude is full of surprises.

Mrs. Hall spends fifteen minutes reviewing the homework—most of which I did relatively well on—then ten more answering questions about data distribution. Class is only halfway over when we finish, but unlike my other teachers, who pass the time with lectures and busywork, Mrs. Hall lets us start our homework.

"You should be able to finish most of it if you use your time wisely," she says. "You've worked hard this week. You deserve a break."

For some reason, I have a sneaking suspicion that maybe math won't be completely unbearable this year. Maybe.

I only have two problems remaining when the bell rings, ending both the period and, thanks to my part-time schedule, my school day. I slip the sheet in my homework folder, grab my bookbag, and head to the front entrance. I walk outside and sit on the brick ledge overlooking the sidewalk, picking at a hangnail while I wait for my ride.

A few minutes later, Kevin's Kia whips into the pick-up lane. He rolls down his window. "Hey, Grace. You ready to go?"

"Yes." I open the door and climb into his car, which reeks of coffee and garlic bagels. "Get me away from here."

Kevin chuckles. "Will do."

"So, how's the hospital?" I ask as he turns onto the main road.

"Busy. I still have six more patients to see this afternoon." Kevin sighs. "And how about you? Did anything memorable happen at school?"

I roll my eyes. "As if. I don't know why I thought senior year would be interesting. All anyone ever talks about is college. College applications, college scholarships, college deadlines. That one is the worst."

"Do you know when your applications are due?"

"I'm applying to two schools early action. Southern Boston University is my number one, and Buckner is my safety. The deadlines are both at the end of October."

"Then you have plenty of time. I never understood why high schools are always in such a rush. Shouldn't they have learned by now that most of you will do everything at the last minute?"

"Yeah, right. They'll never learn." I roll my eyes again. "Oh well. It's not like I can do anything to change it. As long as I keep my GPA up, I should be fine. I finished last year with a 3.7, which I guess is all right."

"I was accepted into my number one school with a 3.5 GPA," he says. "Colleges look at more than just grades when they're considering your application."

"I know." He pulls into the driveway, and I unbuckle my seatbelt, waiting for him to fully turn off the engine to step out of the car. "You're staying for lunch, right?"

Kevin nods. "What are you having?"

"Not sure." In the kitchen, I drop my bookbag onto the floor and open the refrigerator, scanning the shelves while I consider what I want. I ultimately decide on a sandwich and take soy deli meat, hummus, lettuce, and a tomato out of their respective drawers. "Do you know if Mom bought more grapes? She said she would, but I don't see them."

"I'm not sure. I can open a cantaloupe if you'd like."

"Okay." I reach behind several single-serving yogurt cups and hand him the melon. "Here."

Once I've assembled my sandwich and he's cut the melon and reheated a slice of leftover pizza, we sit down at the table to begin eating. I nibble around the crust while he sips from a tall glass of water, neither of us sure what to say.

After a minute or two of silence, I break the ice. "Are you gonna eat your pizza?"

"I was waiting for it to cool down." He picks up the slice and takes a tentative bite. "Next time, I won't put it in the microwave as long. How's the cantaloupe?"

I wrinkle my nose. "Not great. I think it needed another day to ripen."

"My mistake. There's a pineapple in there too. I can try that if you—"

"Don't bother," I interrupt. "It's not a big deal."

Before he can respond, my phone lights up with a text from Lou. She writes: *guess whos back? back again? jess is back. tell a friend.*

I'm laughing as I reply: *how do u know?*

Lou: she showed up in british lit. she looks good. tan too.

Grace: weird. guess shes been out of the hospital then.

Lou: guess so.

Kevin clears his throat. "Who are you texting, Grace?"

"No one." I turn off my phone and take another bite of the cantaloupe, making a face as I chew. "I can't eat this. It's too hard."

"Perhaps you should replace it with something else," Kevin suggests. "That's what your mom likes you to do, isn't it?"

"It's just fruit," I respond. "I'll be fine."

Kevin and I finish our lunches in silence. "I'll do the dishes," he offers and carries my plate to the sink. "Do you need anything?"

"No," I say and leave the kitchen without another word.

On my way to my room, I stop by Mom's office and unplug her computer. For our first Voices assignment, Miss Bacon instructed us to choose a picture of a special memory from when we were younger and write a few paragraphs explaining its significance. The deadline for the final drafts is a week from Monday.

While my computer only contains recent pictures that I've transferred from my phone, Mom's is loaded with photos dating back to my birth. With her computer on my lap, I log on and open her File Explorer. Under Pictures, I find a folder labeled *All* and double-click on it, which leads me to more folders, each from a specific period of time. I skip *Year One* to *Year Six*, as I was too young to remember anything that happened that long ago, and open *Year Seven* to begin my virtual walk down memory lane.

It feels strange to reflect on my childhood and to think about how much has changed over the past seventeen years. *Year Ten*, the year after my father left, is especially painful to look through. There aren't as many pictures as there were in the previous folders—not that I'm surprised. Mom was pretty withdrawn that year; some days, she wouldn't even leave her room. In the few pictures she has saved, she looks sad and depleted, as if she'd given up altogether.

That was also the year we moved to Connecticut. I don't know which was harder: losing my childhood home or losing the hope that Dad would one day come back to us.

The sound of a door slamming shut jerks me out of my thoughts. Through my window, I watch Kevin try to get in his car without spilling the mug of coffee in his hands. Just as he's about to, the mug tips too far to the right, and a couple of drops slosh onto his light blue dress shirt. He mouths "dammit" and throws his arms in the air, which causes more coffee to spill.

I realize that I'm laughing and bite my tongue to stop. I continue to watch him as he backs out of the driveway, my eyes honing in on the *Coexist* bumper sticker below his license plate. There's no denying that Kevin is a good man—easily the best of my mother's boyfriends. He's empathetic and generous and strangely accepting of our dysfunctional family. He's been Mom's rock during tough times and Jamie's friend when my sibling had none. Even Lou, the most judgmental person I know, thinks he's "not so bad." To an extent, I agree with her.

Kevin is a good man. But he'll never be my father.

3

There are many things that I don't like about living in New England, but my biggest dissatisfaction by far is how quickly the weather changes. When I went for a walk on Saturday, it was sixty-eight degrees and sunny. I wore denim capris and a flowy long-sleeved shirt, which I'd rolled up to my elbows by the time I returned home. Mom was outside hacking away at an overgrown lingonberry bush in an old Guns 'N Roses t-shirt.

"I wish it would stay like this forever," I said.

"It's only September," she responded. "You can count on nice weather for at least another few weeks."

But Mom couldn't be more wrong. When I wake up on Monday morning to my seven fifteen alarm, I'm freezing cold. With my blanket wrapped around my shoulders, I open the weather app on my phone, and my heart sinks. In front of a cloudy grey background is a depressing 46°. Factor in the wind chill, and the temperature drops to the low forties.

Dismissing the airy off-the-shoulder shirt I'd laid out on my nightstand before I fell asleep, I shimmy into a sweater and black jeans. In my closet, I rummage through a plastic bin packed with cold-weather clothing for fleece socks. The first pair I find has a hole near the ankle, but since I'm running low on time, I pull them on and head downstairs. Mom is sitting at the table with her phone in one hand and a mug of coffee in the other, while Jamie is pouring a glass of orange juice at the counter.

"Hard time getting out of bed?" Mom asks.

"Uh-huh." I open the cereal cabinet and grab a box of Cinnamon Life. "You said it wouldn't get so cold yet."

"Believe me, hon, I'm just as surprised. It's supposed to go up to the fifties in a couple of days if that makes you feel better."

"It doesn't." I fill three-quarters of a bowl with cereal, add some milk, and sit across from her. "I hate New England! Why did we have to leave California?"

"Grace, we've been over this."

"I know, I know. I still think it sucks."

"Are you going to be like this all winter?" When I nod, she sighs and says, "I guess I'm in for it, huh?"

"It's gonna be a fun six months," I tease.

"Can't wait," she responds sarcastically.

Ten minutes later, as I slurping down cinnamon-infused milk at the bottom of the bowl, I ask, "Do you have that picture I asked you to print in color? The one of Jamie and me at Disneyland?"

"What picture?" Jamie asks, but Mom ignores them.

"Shoot, I forgot. I'm sorry, Grace."

"But I need that picture today," I insist. "It's part of my Voice's assignment."

"Can you print it in black and white for now, and I can get you the colored one later? I'll put a reminder on my phone."

"Fine." With a sigh, I stand up and place my bowl in the sink. "It's not like I have a choice."

"Put the bowl in the dishwasher please."

Another exasperated sigh escapes my lips. I pick up the bowl, cram it in the packed dishwasher, then dramatically slam the door shut. Once I've rinsed my hands, I retrieve Mom's computer from her office, find the picture in the *Year Eight* folder, and send it to the printer.

The picture is slightly blurry and would undoubtedly look better in color, but it makes me smile nevertheless. Captured nine years ago, Jamie and I are posing outside of the entrance to our favorite Disney ride at the time: Pirates of the Caribbean. I'm wearing a red Minnie Mouse t-shirt that Dad bought me at a gift shop earlier that day, while Jamie is holding a melting vanilla soft serve. Both of us are beaming.

"Grace? Are you ready to go?"

I fold the picture in quarters and slip it in my bookbag, leaving Mom's computer on top of the printer. Then I pull a fleece jacket over my sweater and follow Mom and Jamie outside. Tiny drops of mist dampen my face and hair as I climb into the passenger's seat and buckle up. She starts the engine and backs out of the driveway while I fiddle with the radio. I settle on an alternative rock station, raise the volume from eight to twelve, and stare out the window until we arrive at Chuckles.

Mumbling "goodbye" to Mom, I close the door and follow an ill-dressed girl wearing a t-shirt and denim shorts inside. I navigate through the crowded halls to Voices and sit next to Liam, who's listening to music, in the back of the room.

When Liam sees me, he removes his AirPods. "Hey."

"Hey," I say. "What'd you think of the assignment?"

Liam's dark eyebrows crinkle. "Assignment?"

"The one where we had to pick a picture and write something about it?" When he continues to look confused, I say, "You did do it, right?"

"Oh, that assignment!" He shakes his head. "It completely slipped my mind. Is it due today?"

"Uh-huh."

"Shit."

"Good morning, class." Miss Bacon walks into the classroom wearing a fuzzy white turtleneck and khakis, which she's paired with black mid-calf boots. She places her bag on her desk and takes out a granola bar and a bottle of apple juice. "I hope you don't mind if I eat. I had to bring my cat to the vet and didn't have time for breakfast. Poor kitty has ringworm." She stops and shakes her head, causing her curls to bounce. "Sorry. You didn't need to know that. Anyway, please take out your assignments. I'll check them for completion while you answer today's prompt."

On Mondays and Thursdays, Miss Bacon starts class by assigning a short writing prompt. She uncaps a red Expo marker and scribbles on the whiteboard: *Tomorrow is the first day of fall. What does fall mean to you?*

"We'll regroup in five minutes."

While she begins walking around the room, I take my notebook out of my bookbag and flip to a blank page. I stare at the thin lines, my pencil clutched between my index and middle finger, and mull over her question.

What does fall mean to me?

It seems like every year, fall means something a little different. In California, it meant raiding the local Trader Joe's for as many pumpkin spice-flavored foods I could get my hands on. When we moved to Connecticut, it meant stocking up on wool sweaters and fleece-lined pants to prepare for the inevitable cold. And raiding Trader Joe's.

This year, fall feels sadder than usual. After all, it was around this time last year when I started to struggle with eating. The memories are still crystal clear in my mind: hiding food in my pockets, lying about how much I'd eaten, and exercising to the point where I could barely stand, to name a few. And then there were the numbers: on the nutrition labels, on the scale in Lou's house, in the journal where I'd diligently track how many calories I consumed. Back then, it was those numbers that decided how good I was. Now that I'm in a better headspace, however, I realize that everything I did, every disordered behavior I acted on and sneaky trick I pulled off, that I thought meant I was good was only making me sicker.

There was a time when fall was my favorite season, I scribble into my notebook. *A time when it brought me joy, not sorrow, and peace, not anguish.* I reread my writing, then shake my head and erase everything. *Fall represents*

"All right, pencils down," Miss Bacon announces. "Thank you to those of you who completed your assignments on time. Your grades will be in PowerSchool by Friday. I was planning to add a speaking element, but because we're tight on time, I think we'll skip it and jump right into our first quarter project. Please take out your rubrics."

She waits until everyone has their rubric on their desk to proceed. "For your project, you must choose a moment or event in your life that impacted you in some way. It can be anything you want so long as you can explain the significance. Your written draft is due in two weeks, and we'll begin oral presentations shortly after that. Now flip over your rubrics so we can review how you'll be graded."

While Miss Bacon explains the grading scale, I stare blankly at the paragraph summarizing the project. The longer I look, the fuzzier the letters become until they're just a blur. Sometimes, I feel like my life is blurry; like I'm seeing the world through a pair of smudged glasses.

Blinking my eyes, I reopen my notebook and write: *Fall represents change. It reminds me that life is constantly evolving and that nothing is permanent. It's kind of like walking through a forest and coming across two very different paths. One leads to a dead-end that will keep me trapped in perpetual darkness. The other will take me to a better, happier place. It should be an easy decision, but it's not. Because fall also represents comfort. And darkness is comfort.*

FOR THE SEVENTH day in a row, I wake up to dark clouds dominating the sky. I peer out my window, scanning the horizon for any hint of sunlight, but all I see is grey. It's becoming harder and harder just to get out of bed.

The morning seems to last an eternity. I keep staring at the clock, as if somehow that will make time move quicker. My head feels heavy, and more than once, I catch myself zoning out. No matter how hard I try to stay alert and present, fatigue and inattentiveness continue to get the best of me.

I briefly consider checking in with Miss Dixon, but I decide not to. Everyone has bad days—or, in my case, a bad week. It's like Bono says in Mom's favorite U2 song: *It's just a moment. This time will pass.*

By my one fifteen appointment with Anna, however, that horrible feeling of dread that I woke up with hasn't passed. Instead, it's only gotten worse. Mom drops me off at Anna's office building, and I trudge inside, my feet dragging against the damp pavement. I take a seat in the waiting room and scroll through my Instagram explore page until Anna is ready to see me. After she's recorded my weight, she takes a seat in her chair while I sit cross-legged on the couch.

"You look comfortable today."

I glance down at my outfit: an oversized grey sweatshirt and black leggings paired with beige moccasins. "I was going to wear something lighter, but it was in the forties when I got up. Again."

"Well, it is almost October."

"I hate October," I say.

"Because of the cold?"

"Because of a lot of things. It's just . . . it's hard to explain."

Anna leans forward, resting her elbows on her knees. "Try me."

I sigh. "Last October, I was in a bad place. I was restricting food and hurting myself and feeling hopeless, like I had nothing to live for. It was also the first time I went to the hospital." The thought alone sends a chill down my spine. "And although I'm doing better, the memories are still so vivid and constant. Like yesterday, Mom had on the radio, and a song I used to listen to when I was sick came on. Suddenly, all I could think about was lying in my bed and crying myself to sleep to those lyrics. It's more annoying than anything else, really. I mean, something so small shouldn't be able to mess with my head like that."

"And yet, it does," Anna responds. "When someone has gone through a traumatic experience, it's common for certain things to trigger unpleasant memories. But what you have to remember is that you're not in that place anymore. Who you were then is not who you are now. Does that make sense?"

"I guess so." I stare out Anna's window, watching as a single orange leaf floats to the ground. "I just wish there was a way to forget."

4

Presentations for our Voices project begin at the start of class on Monday. The lineup, which Miss Bacon had randomized on her computer last week, placed me sixteenth out of the twenty students enrolled in the course. That means I probably won't go until at least Thursday—maybe even Friday if I'm lucky. The further I can put off my presentation, the better.

Deanna Sherman is first. She stands at the front of the room and neatly places her essay on the podium. "My piece is titled *New Beginnings*," she says in a shaky voice. "Okay, here goes. When I was twelve years old, my sister tried to end her life."

I abruptly raise my head from my desk. This isn't at all what I'd expected to hear from Deanna, who's one of the most optimistic people I know. I glance around the room to gauge how my peers are reacting, but everyone else seems oddly unfazed. I can't be the only one taken aback. I'd written about the summer I vacationed in Reykjavík after all.

"My sister was my hero," Deanna continues. "Growing up, I

always wanted to be just like her. I didn't believe my mother at first when she told me what Emilia had done. I thought there was no way that someone so smart and successful and outwardly happy could be fighting a war inside. It didn't make sense, but then again, mental illness rarely does."

The more Deanna reads, the more uncomfortable I feel. She delves into the details of Emilia's mental health struggles and when she describes "the sullen, empty look on my sister's pale face as she sat in a small hospital room with grey walls," my mind instantly evokes the haunting memories from my stint in the Emergency Room. Even though I hadn't attempted suicide, the hours I spent there were the darkest and scariest of my entire life—not to mention the loneliest. It didn't matter that most of the rooms were occupied or that the hall was filled with doctors and nurses; I still felt completely alone.

"If Emilia has taught me anything," Deanna concludes, "it's that life and the lives of the people closest to us are precious. Cherish them. Celebrate them. And most importantly, don't be afraid to live." She glances at Miss Bacon, who's sitting at a table in the back of the room. "I'm done."

Miss Bacon begins to clap, and after a brief pause, everyone joins in. I weakly slap my hands together under my desk, still recovering from the shock of Deanna's harrowing piece. I don't know who I'm more upset with: Deanna for making me remember such an awful time in my life or Miss Bacon for letting her share that kind of content without so much as a single trigger warning.

At the front of the room, Tracey Amaro has taken Deanna's place behind the podium. She tucks a strand of her long blonde hair behind her ear and straightens the black leather jacket she's layered over a skintight grey shirt. Tracey moved here from Manhattan two years ago and instantly became one of the coolest girls in the school. In no time at all, she had a large group of friends and several thousand Instagram followers. Even I was intrigued by her. After all, she was everything I wanted to be back then: stylish, confident, popular. Sometimes she still is.

Tracey waits until the room is quiet to begin. "It was a rainy Saturday afternoon. My mom and I were sitting on my bed. I could hear the raindrops pounding against the window, and I could hear my heart pounding inside my chest. I was about to tell her the secret I'd been hiding from her and everyone else for months: that I had an eating disorder."

No sooner have the words left her lips that my discomfort returns. Under my desk, I anxiously tug on my cuticles until tiny beads of blood appear. I wish I could stand up and walk out the door or—better yet—simply disappear into thin air. But I stay in my seat, my fingers bloodied and my nailbeds raw, and painstakingly listen to Tracey recall the temporary joy of fitting into double-zero jeans.

Several drawn-out minutes later, Tracey ends her piece with a cliché conclusion and returns to her seat. As Curtis Guthrie walks to the podium, I approach Miss Bacon. "Can I use the bathroom?" I ask quietly.

She nods. "Go ahead."

Grabbing my bookbag, I hurry out of the room and ascend the staircase. My chest feels tight, as if I'm wearing a too-small sports bra, and my breathing is so uneven that by the time I arrive at Guidance, I'm practically breathless. Mrs. Hawkins, the administrative assistant, isn't at her desk, so I walk right past it and down the narrow hall to Miss Dixon's room. Behind her semi-ajar door, she's typing into her computer. A half-eaten blueberry muffin is next to the mouse.

"Miss Dixon?" I ask. "Is this an okay time to talk?"

Miss Dixon looks up from the screen. Removing her

rectangular reading glasses, she says, "Of course, Grace. Come on in."

I close the door and take a seat in the chair across from her desk. I glance around her office—at the watercolor paintings on the walls and the ceramic animal figurines on her bookshelf—and realize how much has changed since the last time I was here. Although it's only been a few months, between the new décor and the lingering fumes from a recent paint job, it seems like much longer.

"It's good to see you, Grace," she says. "How are you?"

"Not so great," I admit.

"What's troubling you?"

"It's one of my classes—Voices of Our Generation. We're doing a project where we have to write and present a piece about an important moment in our life, and some of them are, like, super triggering. One girl wrote about her eating disorder, and she was describing clothing sizes and bad behaviors, and it was just a lot to process, you know?" I sigh. "I knew I should have switched after the first week. What the hell was I thinking taking a public speaking class? I'm the most anxious person I know."

"It's good to push yourself outside of your comfort zone," Miss Dixon says.

"That's what I thought, but after hearing those pieces . . ." I sigh again. "This time of the year is already hard enough without having to listen to other people talk about their issues. I know that sounds selfish, but it's true."

"Well, it's your decision," Miss Dixon says. "If you really want to switch classes, I'm sure we can work that out with Miss Bacon. However, I'd encourage you to stick with Voices. From what I've heard from other students, I'm optimistic that it will end up being a good experience for you."

I stare at the framed Friedrich Nietzsche quote on her desk: *That which does not kill us makes us stronger.*

"I'll think about it." The bell rings, and I ask, "Do you mind telling Miss Bacon that I was with you? She was kind of under the impression that I went to the bathroom."

Miss Dixon nods. "I'd be happy to. Shoot me an email if you need anything. And, Grace?"

"Yeah?"

"If you decide to switch, it's better to do it sooner than later. I imagine most classes are already full by now."

"Okay. I'll let you know." Slinging my bookbag over my shoulder, I leave her office and walk back down the hallway. I'm surprised to see Lou talking to her guidance counselor Mrs. Schneider in the waiting area. "What are you doing here?" I ask when Lou turns around.

"Dumb college stuff," she responds. "You?"

"Same," I lie as I follow her out the door.

"Oh, Aisha told me that Tommy Kershaw's parents are going away over Halloween weekend, and he's throwing a party. You should come."

"Lou, you know how I feel about parties."

"When was the last time you went to a party?" When I shrug, she exclaims, "See! How do you know you don't like something if you won't even try it?"

"Fine, I'll talk to Mom," I agree. "No guarantees though."

Lou grins. "I knew you'd say yes."

"I didn't say tha—" I start to respond, but she quickens her pace before I can finish. "Hey, will you wait up?" I adjust my bookbag and hurry after her. "Lou! For God's sake!"

"You're the best!" Lou blows me a kiss, then disappears behind a tall boy.

I sigh. When I thought today couldn't get any more complicated, it just did.

The rest of the morning is a blur. I spend seventy-percent of class time mulling over what I'm going to do about Voices and the other thirty-percent brainstorming ways to convince Mom to let me attend Tommy's party.

I wait until after lunch when we're cleaning up the kitchen to casually mention the party. "So, uh, this guy at school is having a Halloween thing in a couple of weeks. Is it cool if I go with Lou?"

Mom stops washing dishes long enough to give me a skeptical look. "What kind of 'thing'?"

"A party," I clarify, "but it shouldn't be too big, and I promise I'll be back before my curfew."

"And will his parents be home?"

"I'm not sure. Lou didn't say."

Mom, still eyeing me skeptically, starts to tap her index finger against her chin—a telltale sign that she's deep in thought. "Do I need to lecture you about drinking?" she asks finally.

I shake my head. "Too many calories. That, and you know I like to be in control."

"Yes, I do." The tapping resumes for several more seconds. "All right, you can go," she says, "under one condition."

"What's that?"

"You have to promise you'll call me if you need a ride home. I don't want you getting in a car with anyone—and that includes Lou—who's had even a sip of alcohol, understand?"

"I promise," I respond emphatically. "Thank you, Mom."

"You're welcome."

Mom picks up the sudsy sponge and continues to scrub the dishes, which I assume means our conversation is over. I'm about to head upstairs to start my homework when something dawns on me. "Oh crap," I say. "I'm gonna need a costume."

"I'VE DECIDED I'm not switching classes."

Miss Dixon flinches when she hears my voice. "Oh, Grace. I didn't see you there."

I continue to hover in her doorway, rocking back and forth on my heels. "Sorry. I just figured I should let you know. I thought about it a lot, and I decided it might be good for me to stick with Voices. Plus, all the other presentations this week have been better. Well, there was one about self-harm that was sort of triggering, but otherwise, I've managed fine."

"I'm glad you've come to that decision," Miss Dixon says. "When are you presenting?"

"Today." I make a face. "I'm so nervous, I barely slept last night. I've practiced almost every day, but I still don't feel prepared."

"You're going to do great," she assures me. "I know it's nerve-wracking, but you've obviously worked hard. I'm sure it will pay off."

"I hope you're right," I respond as the first bell rings. "Well, I should get to class. I'll see you around."

"You too, Grace. Good luck."

"Thanks," I say. "I'm gonna need it."

Despite Miss Dixon's reassurance, the second I step into the room, I'm overcome with anxiety. I rush to my seat and place my head flat against my desk, inhaling the scents of lead and sweat that are lodged into the wood. Liam, who presented a piece about a fishing trip with his dad on Friday, taps my shoulder.

"Are you all right?"

"Fine," I mumble without looking up.

"You sure? You don't look so good."

"I'm fine, Liam," I reiterate. The final bell rings, and I open my bookbag, rummaging through my cluttered homework folder for my spoken draft. "I'm just tired—that's all."

Liam arches his eyebrows skeptically. "If you say so . . ."

"Grace?" Miss Bacon asks. "Are you ready?"

Nodding numbly, I stand up and shakily walk to the front of the room. I position myself behind the podium and exhale deeply. "My piece is called *A Summer I'll Never Forget*," I say. "*Velkominn í land elds og íss*. In Icelandic, that means 'welcome to the land of fire and ice.' When I was eight years old, my family spent an entire summer in Iceland. My father's college friend Amundi was from a small port town called Akranes, which is outside of Reykjavík. My father and Amundi met their freshman year when they were staying in the same suite. One day, my father set fire to a pan of ravioli in the communal kitchen, and Amundi helped him put it out. They were inseparable ever since."

In my mind, I can see Dad sitting at the dinner table at our home in California and theatrically sharing the amusing story of how he and Amundi became friends. He had a habit of laughing with his mouth full of food. I remember it drove Mom crazy.

"William, you're going to choke," she'd say. "Slow down, okay?"

"Yes, dear," was Dad's classic response. He'd wait until she looked away to cross his eyes or stick a carrot up his nose or some other childish reaction of that sort.

It took every ounce of willpower I had not to laugh. Sometimes, it felt like he was more of my big brother than my father: someone who made sure I knew how to stand up for myself; someone who took my side no matter what; someone who always tried to fix my problems with a joke or an anecdote even when all I wanted him to do was listen. He used to describe himself as "young at heart." Mom disagreed, insisting that he was "a big baby in a grown man's body."

"Vacation always goes by too quickly, but that summer seemed shorter than usual," I continue. "When we boarded the plane to go home, I felt a dreadful heaviness in my chest. In ten hours, my relaxing fairytale vacation would be over, and I'd be forced to return to my quick-paced suburban lifestyle. Leaving Iceland and knowing that I might not come back was a bitter pill to swallow, but no matter how many years go by, I'll never forget the best summer of my life."

I realize I'm gripping the podium and unclench my sweaty hands. Wiping them on my jeans, I fold my paper in half and return to my seat while everyone politely applauds. Liam flashes me a thumbs up.

"Nailed it."

I laugh awkwardly. "Thanks."

"Well done, Grace," Miss Bacon says. "I'm officially adding visiting Iceland to my bucket list. Becky, it's your turn."

Becky, a tall brunette with an obvious fake tan, takes my place at the podium. Unlike me, she doesn't seem at all nervous. She's even smiling as she smooths out her paper, her teeth blindingly white against her orangey skin. "My piece is titled *The Perfect Promposal*."

Liam and I make eye-contact and share an amused grin. Then we revert our attention to Becky, who's begun to describe her prom dress in excess detail. I realize as I'm listening to her ramble on about the "silky chiffon fabric" and the "sparkly turquoise sequins" that I'm glad I didn't change courses. One year ago, I doubt I would have been able to push through my insecurities and triggers and stick with Voices. And although I might come to regret my decision in a week or two, at this moment, I'm pretty proud of myself.

The rest of the morning is an emotional rollercoaster. My excitement from conquering my fear of public speaking is subdued by a disheartening C- on a psychology quiz, then revived by a near-perfect grade on a government essay. By fifth period statistics, I'm so mentally worn out that I can barely concentrate on Mrs. Hall's lesson. So naturally, when she distributes the homework, I have no idea what I'm doing.

With the worksheet in my hands, I approach Mrs. Hall's desk. "I need help," I say.

"What's confusing you?" she asks.

"Everything."

"All right. Pull over a chair, and I'll see what I can do."

I grab an empty chair near the whiteboard and carry it to her desk. I then place the sheet on top of a stack of loose-leaf paper, while she takes out her reading glasses and a blue pen. She peers at the first problem with her thin eyebrows furrowed.

1. A sample consists of four observations: 1, 3, 5, 7. What is the standard deviation?

"Do you remember how to find standard deviation on your graphing calculator?"

I shake my head. "I'm sorry."

"Don't apologize. I'll show you."

Mrs. Hall takes my graphing calculator from me and guides me through the steps, starting with inputting the data into L_1 and ending when the calculator computes a standard deviation of 2.58. Then she has me try while she watches and gently corrects me whenever I make a mistake. By the fourth equation, I'm able to find the standard deviation all on my own.

This is the first time in years that I don't feel entirely incom-

petent at math. I finish computing the answer for the fifth equation and glance at Mrs. Hall, who smiles and pats my shoulder.

"See? It's not so hard, is it?"

"I guess I was wrong," I say. "Thanks, Mrs. Hall."

Mrs. Hall's kind smile broadens. "You're welcome, Grace."

When the bell rings, I retrieve my bookbag from my desk
and make my way to the front of the school. Mom's car is
nowhere to be seen in the parking lot, so I send her a quick text:
where r u? im cold. Barely ten seconds have passed when she pulls
into the pick-up lane.

"Well, you're awfully impatient."

"Hello to you too," I respond sarcastically and get in.

"I'm sorry," Mom says. "How was your presentation?"

I shrug. "Okay, I guess. I didn't pass out, so that's good."

"Oh, you're always so dramatic. Ready to go to Panera?"

"Uh-huh."

Instead of going home, Mom and I decided this morning to
have lunch at Panera and then stop by the Spooky Store—a local
Halloween outlet—so I can find a costume for Tommy's party.
Since both are in the same vicinity, it was a convenient alternative to our usual schedule.

We arrive at Panera fifteen minutes later. I skip the long line
of customers waiting at the counter and beeline to the row of
kiosks by the coffee machines. I enter my order—a Mediter-
ranean veggie sandwich and creamy tomato soup—into the
machine while Mom scans the overhead menu. I've just finished
subtracting onions from my sandwich when she taps my arm.

"Caprese sandwich and autumn squash soup."

I add her selection to the cart and proceed to the checkout
before she notices that her order is nearly two hundred calories
more than mine. Once the kiosk has processed her credit card, I
grab a buzzer, and we claim an empty table next to a large

window. I make her sit on the left so the sun isn't shining in my eyes.

Mom and I make small talk about our mornings until the buzzer loudly goes off. "I'll get it," I say and stand up, accidentally bumping my knee into the table. Mom grabs her cup of water in the nick of time. "Sorry."

"No worries." She hands me the buzzer. "Don't forget to return this."

"Okay." Taking the buzzer, I navigate through the crowded bistro and drop it in a metal basket. I then precariously carry two plastic trays back to the table and place them at our respective seats. "Here you go."

"Thank you," Mom says. She picks up her sandwich and takes a bite. "When was the last time we went out to lunch?"

"I dunno. It's been a while." I begin to transfer the soggy croutons on top of my soup onto my tray with my spoon. When Mom shoots me a disapproving look, I say, "What? You know I don't like croutons."

"Since when?" she mumbles, just loudly enough for me to hear her.

"Um, we started reading *The Handmaid's Tale* in Women's Lit," I say in an attempt to change the subject. "It's good, but the writing is kind of hard to follow. When I write a book, I'm definitely gonna avoid stream of consciousness."

"Oh, yeah? And what will your book be about?"

"Not sure. But I have some ideas."

"You're not going to tell me, are you?"

I shake my head. "No way. It's a secret."

"You and your secrets," she muses. "Even when you were a kid, you kept so much to yourself. I could never tell what was on your mind." She takes another bite of her sandwich, causing several drops of pesto to ooze onto the table. "Crap."

I bite my lip to refrain from laughing. "Smooth."

Mom and I finish our lunches—thankfully without any more spillage—and then we clear our dishes and return to the car to drive across the street to the Spooky Store. During the other eleven months of the year, the Spooky Store is simply a vacant warehouse sandwiched between Bed Bath & Beyond and Trader Joe's, but with Halloween quickly approaching, it's been transformed into a Party-City-meets-haunted-house combination. The second Mom and I step inside, we're greeted by an eight-foot-tall animated werewolf. Mom gasps as the hairy prop lurches towards her.

"Scared?" I tease.

Mom rolls her eyes. "Come on, we have shopping to do. And this store," she glances around us at the dozens of aisles packed with costumes, accessories, and decorations, "has a lot to choose from."

"I'll be quick." I begin to walk towards the costumes, but I stop next to a levitating ghost with blinking red eyes when I realize that Mom is following me. "I can go on my own."

"Right. Text me when you're done, and I'll meet you at the checkout."

So, while she disappears behind a woman and two young boys, I wander through the store in search of a costume. In the vampire section, a silver necklace with a ruby pendant catches my eye. I place it in my shopping basket as a consideration and head into the next aisle, which is skeleton-themed. I sift through several shirts hanging from a rack, but none of them are in my size.

"Dammit," I mumble.

"Can I help you, miss?" an employee—a brown-haired boy who doesn't look much older than me—asks.

"Do you have this in a smaller size?" I grab a black t-shirt with a rainbow-colored ribcage and show it to him.

"Unfortunately, we don't, however those shirts run small, so you could try a size up."

"Oh. Thanks."

I wait until he's looking away to return the shirt to the rack. That's when another costume, this one neatly packaged in a sealed bag, catches my eye. "Um, excuse me?"

The employee turns around. "Yes?"

"Is there a dressing room?"

"Yes, off of aisle thirteen."

After thanking him again, I add the bag to my cart and make my way to the back of the store. The dressing room is hidden behind a rack of scary-looking masks. A female employee hands me a tag with 2 printed on the front, and I lock myself in a small room with a dusty mirror crookedly nailed to the wall. I remove my sweatshirt, carefully open the bag, and shimmy into a black dress. The silky fabric stops just above my knees, and the skeleton design glistens when I turn. There's even a hood to pull over my head. It's slim-fit but not bodycon and feminine but not promiscuous.

In the mirror, I watch my lips lift into a pleased smile. "Perfect."

Ten minutes later, all of which I spend browsing decorations, I meet Mom at the checkout with my dress, gel blood splatters, and a roll of *Enter If You Dare* caution tape. She places her card in the chip reader, politely declining when the cashier asks if she'd like to donate to cancer research, and after her payment has processed, we leave The Spooky Store.

"Can we stop at Trader Joe's?" I ask. "I want to get Pumpkin O's."

"Sure."

Despite it being the middle of a weekday, Trader Joe's is packed with shoppers. Mom and I squeeze past a cluster of women inconsiderately chatting in front of the automatic doors and walk inside. While she browses the produce section, I beeline to the cereal aisle. I find the Pumpkin O's in a matter of seconds and tuck two boxes under my arm. Then I wander through the rows of food, keeping an eye out for seasonal products. I grab a jar of pumpkin butter off a shelf stocked with jams and spreads and continue my search.

In the frozen dessert section, I notice several pints of pumpkin ice cream. I pick up the one on top and turn it over to analyze the nutrition facts. My eyes widen at the number of calories, which is significantly higher than the brands of ice cream Mom buys me.

I hear someone clear their throat and turn around. A woman stands behind me with her hands on her hips. "Are you almost done?" she asks impatiently.

"Sorry."

I return the ice cream to the freezer and scamper away, almost colliding with another shopper in my haste. I end up in the back of the store near the bathrooms and lean my head against the wall as another intense wave of anxiety washes over me. I wish I understood why this is so hard for me; why something I once loved to do at somewhere I once loved to be now fills me with discomfort and dread.

Up until last year, going to Trader Joe's to buy pumpkin spice-flavored foods was one of my favorite fall traditions. I'd fill the cart with pumpkin cereal, pumpkin butter, pumpkin granola bars, pumpkin ice cream—once, I tried pumpkin pasta sauce, which was surprisingly tasty. Even Jamie, who doesn't share my love of pumpkin whatsoever, agreed that it was good.

But like I told Anna, everything changed when I got sick. I

no longer enjoyed seasonal foods; on the contrary, I dreaded them. Last year in mid-October, about a week before I was admitted to the hospital, Mom bought me pumpkin spice ginger snaps. She was so excited when she showed me the bag—"look, Grace, you'll never believe what was on sale"—but I refused to even try them. While she ate four snaps with a glass of milk, I sat across the table from her and nibbled on a small apple. When I finally gathered the nerve to look at her, I thought she'd surely be upset. But instead, she just looked sad.

"Find anything?"

When I turn around, Mom is standing behind me. I hand her the cereal and the pumpkin butter, and she places them in her handcart with a head of iceberg lettuce. "Yep."

"I think I know what you're having for breakfast tomorrow," Mom remarks as we slowly make our way to the checkout. She scans the cash registers for the shortest line, and after realizing that they're all equally long, gets behind a woman with a full cart. "Carla? Is that you?"

When she sees Mom, the woman's bright red lips lift into a smile. "Kira!" she exclaims. "Oh, it's lovely running into you. How have you been?"

"Not too bad. And you?"

"Good, good." Carla pushes her cart up to the cashier, who begins to scan her groceries. "Katie is home right now, but she'll start school at Southern Boston University in January. She's majoring in screenwriting."

"Katie Brinkley?" I ask.

Carla nods. "You must be Grace. I've heard so much about you."

"Oh, uh, okay." As Carla pays the cashier, I nudge Mom and whisper, "How do you know Ms. Brinkley?"

"We met in January. We were in—"

"Well, I'd better get going," Carla says. "I have to pick up Alex from soccer practice. But we should meet up sometime, Kira. Grab a cup of coffee maybe."

Mom smiles. "I'd like that. It's good seeing you, Carla."

"You too." Carla begins to wheel her cart towards the exit, calling over her shoulder, "Nice to meet you, Grace!"

"Same," I respond hesitantly. "Mom, you were saying . . ."

"Carla and I were in a support group for parents with kids with eating disorders," she explains. "I went twice a week while you were in your residential program."

"I didn't know that."

"Oh. I thought I told you."

"Well, you didn't. So, Katie has an eating disorder?"

"Yes." Mom hands the cashier a red tote so she won't have to pay ten cents for a bag. "I didn't realize you two were close."

"We're not. We just played soccer together."

I think back one year ago to my first practice with the Varsity soccer team. As I stood on the outskirts of the huddle, feeling like I didn't belong, Katie smiled at me. It was that small gesture that gave me the strength to press on despite my insecurities. We might not have been close in the way that best friends are, but out of the sixteen girls on the team, she was the only one who I knew had my back.

If she was struggling then, I had no idea. Katie always seemed so strong and self-assured, like she had everything all figured out. I admired that about her. I looked up to her.

As Mom drives home, taking backroads to avoid traffic, I stare out my window at the decorated houses we're passing. An inflatable Dracula sways in the wind. Several black bats dangle from the thin branches of a dogwood tree. One house has a giant spider hanging over the front door.

"We still have Lester, right?" I ask, referring to the hanging skeleton with a tattered white cloak that Mom bought at Target three years ago. Jamie, who was ten at the time, had named him Lester, and it stuck.

"I think so. I'll check the attic when we get home."

"Cool."

"It's nice to see you enjoying Halloween again," she continues. "You weren't in the spirit last year."

"Yeah, well, it was hard to get excited about anything last year."

"Yes, it was," she agrees. "I'm glad that's behind us now."

With my gaze still trained on the houses, I nod. "So am I."

5

I've always been an excellent procrastinator. Mom used to say it was my superpower; that I could save everything for the last minute and still finish on time. While she relies on to-do lists and color-coded calendars to punctually complete tasks, it's impending deadlines and my fear of failure that incentivizes me.

On Friday afternoon, three days before my college applications are due, I calmly sit in front of my computer and fill out my CommonApp profile. Even though my anxiety is relatively low, I can tell by the dampness of my palms and the fact that I've misspelled my middle name twice that the nerves are lurking nearby.

Once my profile is complete and I've double-checked the spelling, I move on to the dreaded *Family* tab. Filling out the family section of any form always makes me a little sad. I try not to get too much in my head as I select *Separated* from the drop-down menu under *Parents' marital status* and *Parent 1* from *With whom do you make your permanent home?* When I open the second tab to input Parent 1 (aka Mom's) information and see the dozen or so boxes, most of which have tiny red asterisks next to them, my sadness quickly becomes frustration.

I groan. "This is stupid."

"What's stupid is you saving everything for the last minute," Mom responds predictably. She's standing at the stove waiting for the kettle to boil. "You're just stressing yourself out more."

"The application isn't due until next week," I say. "Technically that's not last minute." I finish entering her contact information and scroll to the questions about her education. "What degree did you get from UCLA?"

"Bachelor of Science."

"And what year was that?"

"1998."

"Dad too?" I ask as I move on to Parent 2.

"No, he received his one year before me."

I select 1997 under *Year Received* and fill out the rest of the questions about Dad. I then begin inputting Jamie's information. The options under *Relationship* only include brother and sister, so I select the former.

"Christ, now they want to know about my education," I gripe. "There are, like, seven tabs too!"

Mom laughs. "Still glad you waited this long?"

"Whatever. It's not like I've got anything better to do."

With a deep sigh, I expand the first tab, which is labeled *Current Secondary/High School*, and type *Chuck L Everrett* into the search bar, accidentally adding an extra 'r.' A second sigh escapes my lips. This sucks.

Forty-five minutes later, I've finally finished filling out not only my CommonApp profile but the application questions for Southern Boston University as well. I upload my essay and carefully review my submission.

"I'm gonna do it," I say.

Mom hurries to the table with her phone. She stands behind me and starts to take pictures while I place my cursor over *Submit*. I take a deep breath and count down from five in my head.

Five . . . four . . . three . . . two . . . one . . .

I click.

Mom takes one final picture and wraps her arms around my shoulders. "You did it. How does it feel?"

"I don't know," I say. "Can you get off me? You're smothering me."

She loosens her grip. "I'm sorry. I'm just so excited for you—that's all."

"Right. Well, um, I guess I should check Gmail. You know, to make sure my submission went through." I open a new tab and type 'g' into the search bar. "Then I'll submit to Buckner."

"Sounds like a plan. Let me know when you're about to, so I can take more pictures."

"Okay, I will."

While I wait for a confirmation email, I open Instagram and scroll through my feed. Liam has posted an album with three photos of him and Jess in his kitchen. In the first one, they're flattening a brown dough with a rolling pin; in the second, they're holding up a plate of cookies that vaguely resemble pumpkins; in the third, he's seductively licking a batter-covered spoon while she stands next to him with an amused look on her face.

His caption is a simple *spooky szn* followed by a Jack-O-Lantern emoji.

Weirdly enough, I don't feel jealous looking at the photos; instead, I'm curious. I'm not one to gossip, but I'm itching to know the truth behind Jess' three-month disappearance. If she wasn't in the hospital all summer, where was she? What happened to her?

Temporarily dismissing my curiosity, I put down my phone and refresh Gmail. When the page finishes loading, there's an email from CommonApp in my inbox confirming my submission. *Here we go again,* I think as I return to the CommonApp homepage.

"Mom! I'm about to submit!"

Mom dashes back into the kitchen. "Where did I put my phone? Oh, there it is." She grabs her phone off the counter, nearly dropping it on the floor in her haste.

"Don't get too excited," I mumble sarcastically.

"I'm sorry," Mom apologizes again. "I don't mean to over-whelm you. It's just that, well, for a while, I wasn't sure that this day would come. I'm so proud of you, Grace."

I turn to thank her at the exact same time she snaps another picture, momentarily blinding me with the flash. Blinking furiously, I rub my eyes and say, "It's not over yet. I still have to get in."

"And you will," she responds without a trace of doubt in her voice. "I know it."

WE NEED A NEW VACUUM CLEANER. It's something that Mom has been saying for months, but she has yet to find a replace-ment. Instead, she's stuck with our old vacuum, which is not only clunky and cumbersome but also incredibly loud.

Now, as I stand in my room preparing for Tommy's Halloween party, I hear the familiar rumble and raise the volume on my earbuds to drown out the sound. I hum along to a Halloween-themed playlist and wriggle into a pair of old opaque leggings. Once I've removed a couple of loose strings from the waistband and adjusted my wedgie, I take the skeleton dress out of the package and run my hand over the fabric, mesmerized by the rainbow shimmer it gives off in the dim early-evening lighting. Then I slide my arms through the skintight sleeves and pull it over my head. The dress feels tighter than it did in the Spooky Store, which puzzles me. Just two days ago, Anna said I was down half a pound.

You're delusional, I tell myself.

Turning off the music, I leave my earbuds on my nightstand and walk to the bathroom to apply my makeup: sparkly silver eyeshadow and red lipstick. Downstairs in the kitchen, Mom has finally finished vacuuming. She leans the vacuum against the counter and begins filling a pot with water.

"The dress looks great, Grace."

"Are you sure?" I stare at myself in the metallic reflection of the refrigerator, turning my body from left to right. "It doesn't seem too tight to you, does it?"

"No, it's perfect." She transfers the pot to the stovetop and turns the back-right burner to High. "When I was your age, my best friend and I went up to her lake house for Halloween. She invited some of the local teens to join us for the night, and, well, they weren't the nicest crowd to say the least. Things got so out of hand that I actually had to call my mom to come get me."

"Was she upset with you?"

"She wasn't too thrilled to have to drive to Rhode Island at midnight, but she was glad I asked for help. I want you to remember that you always have that option. You shouldn't stay in a situation if it's making you uncomfortable."

"I know that. Where's Jamie?"

"In their room. I'm driving them to Sara's house after dinner for a monster movie marathon or something of that sort. I can't remember exactly what Jamie said." Mom dumps a box of spaghetti into the boiling water and stirs it around with a wooden spoon. "You're having dinner at the party, right?"

"Yeah, Lou said there's going to be pizza. I mean, it's not ideal, but I'll make it work."

"You can always eat before you go," Mom says. "Dinner will be ready in ten minutes."

"Thanks, but I think I'll—" I start to say when the doorbell rings. "That must be Lou."

Sure enough, when I open the door, Lou is standing on the porch. She's dressed completely in black—from her cropped sweatshirt to her leggings to her sneakers—and she's shoved a headband with sheep ears over her wavy hair. Her eyes are hidden behind a pair of oversized sunglasses.

"What are you supposed to be?" I ask.

"A black sheep." She removes her glasses and hangs them in her collar. "Ready to go?"

"One sec." I slide on my navy Converse and grab a fleece jacket from the closet. Even though the weather is milder today, it's still in the low forties—and dropping quickly. "Mom!" I call. "Lou and I are leaving!"

"Be home by eleven!" Mom yells back.

Rolling my eyes, I close the door and follow Lou to her car. Once we're both seated, she turns the key, and LL Cool J's *Mama Said Knock You Out* blasts through the speakers. I quickly lower the volume.

"Why do you always play your music so loud?"

"If you think that's loud, you're gonna hate where we're going," she responds as she follows a FedEx truck onto the main road. "Nice dress by the way."

I adjust the hem, which has begun to inch up my crossed thighs. "Thanks."

Four '90s rap songs later, Lou turns onto Tommy's street. Although the party only started half an hour ago, cars are already filling the driveway and lining the narrow road. Lou parks behind a silver sedan, and we cut across the Kershaw's leaf-covered lawn. We follow Elena Russel, a girl I take statistics with, through the front door and into my personal hell.

A couple dozen rowdy teenagers are packed into the living room, dancing and talking loudly over the trippy techno song blaring through a Bluetooth speaker on the mantle. Even more teens file in and out of the kitchen with red Solo cups and paper plates piled high with pizza and chips.

"Oh, there's Aisha." Lou points at Aisha, who's standing next to the mantle dressed in a floor-length black gown. The blood-red brooch below the gown's puritan collar matches her hijab. "I'm gonna say hi."

"Lou!" I call, but the deafening music drowns out my voice. "LOU! WAIT UP!"

I watch in dismay as Lou vanishes behind a person in a gorilla mask. I try to quicken my pace, and in doing so, bump into Heather Maiden. The cup in her right hand tilts, sloshing beer all over her skintight white shirt. Behind her golden masquerade mask, Heather's eyes widen in horror.

"What the fuck!" she exclaims.

"I'm so sorry," I apologize. "I'll get a napkin."

"Don't bother."

Heather walks away, grumbling under her breath, while I inch closer to the wall. I can feel my cheeks burning from humiliation. I've been here for barely five minutes, and I'm already a nervous wreck. I knew I should have stayed home.

I close my eyes, rest my head against the wall, and attempt to block out the laughter, the chatter, and, most of all, the music.

For a second or two, I manage to find peace amid the chaos, but then someone taps my shoulder, and I'm jerked back to reality.

"Having fun?" Liam's grinning face fades into focus. He's dressed in a Hawaiian t-shirt, bright orange shorts, and black flipflops, the cheap kind that you find at Ocean State Job Lot. A tan visor with a shark logo is shoved over his dark hair.

"Surfer dude?" I guess.

Liam nods. "Not bad, huh? So, how are you liking the party?"

"I'm not. I wish I'd just stayed home."

"Oh, come on. What's so bad about it?"

"It's loud," I say, "and crowded, and everyone is drunk."

"I'm not drunk," he says, showing me the dark liquid in his cup. "See? Just Coke."

"Really?" For some reason, him not drinking surprises me. "And why might that be?"

"Designated driver. Plus, you don't know what my mom would do if I came home wasted."

"Oh, I think I have an idea."

Liam laughs. "Right. Well, here's an idea for you. Let's go outside."

Before I can respond, he grabs my arm and guides me to an exit near the back of the room. He holds open the door for me, and I step onto the Kershaw's well-lit patio. The chilling October wind would normally bother me, however in comparison to the stuffy house, it's refreshing.

Liam hugs his arms to his chest, goosebumps surfacing on his bare skin. "Better?"

"Much." I place my hands on the wooden railing and gaze at the starry sky. "It's a full moon," I observe, instantly regretting how stupid I must sound.

"It is."

An awkward silence settles between us. I try to think of

something to say to lessen the tension, but what I ultimately come up with only makes it worse. "So, um, how's Jess?"

Liam shoots me a confused look. "Huh?"

"Jess," I repeat. "A few days ago, you posted a picture of you and her at your house. You were baking cookies or something."

"Oh, yeah. We made vegan pumpkin spice cookies—her idea. They actually weren't that bad."

"So . . . she's better then?"

Liam shrugs. "More or less."

I'm eager to ask him for details, but I hold my tongue. "That's good."

"Yeah." After a brief hesitation, he says, "We're not dating by the way. We're just friends."

"Right," I say, unsure of what to make of this news. "But, like, if you were, it would be fine."

"I know. But we're not." The uncomfortable silence returns. This time, Liam is the first one to speak up. "What'd you do last Halloween? Matt threw a party sort of like this, but I don't remember seeing you there."

"I, um . . ." I clear my throat. "I was in the hospital."

"Oh. Shit."

"Uh-huh. So, I guess this isn't so bad in comparison."

Liam and I fall quiet for several more seconds. Finally, he clears his throat. "What was it like?"

"The hospital?"

"Yeah. I had a friend in Florida who was in a psych hospital for a few weeks. I always wanted to ask her what it was like, but I could tell she didn't want to talk about it. You don't have to either if it makes you uncomfortable. I'm just curious—that's all."

"The hospital is like . . ." I close my eyes, and for a second, I see the bleak walls; feel my scars itch under my long sleeves; hear the endless ticking of the clock in the Rec Room as the minutes crawled by. Tick, tock. Tick, tock. "It's like being in a bubble. The real world doesn't exist. You don't have to deal with school • or work or relationships or anything really. And there's no concept of time either because every day is basically the same. You go to groups and take your meds and eat enough to keep the nurses happy. You're not dead, but you're not alive either. You're stuck in between if that makes any sense."

"Were you scared?"

"I was in the beginning," I admit, "but then you get used to it, and after a while, it doesn't seem that bad. If I'm being honest, it was kind of nice to have an escape. I know that sounds messed up, but that's how it felt at the time."

"How do you feel now?"

I consider this. "I feel a lot of things. Sadness, anger, nostalgia, shame. I definitely don't want to go back—that much I'm sure of." A huge gust of wind blows our way, and I shiver. "I think I'm gonna head inside. I'm cold."

"Me too. I'll come with you."

I pause with my hand on the doorknob and look at him. "You won't tell anyone, right? About what I said about the hospital?"

"Of course not."

"Thanks," I say.

Liam places his hand on top of mine. His skin, while as cold as ice, is softer than I'd expected, and when he smiles, his teeth glisten in the darkness. "You're welcome."

6

Lou got a haircut. Her thick shoulder-length waves, which she's had since ninth grade, have been entirely restyled into a sleek layered look that stops just short of her earlobes.

When I see her, I do a double-take. "Whoa. When did you do that?"

"After school. I got home from the barber, like, half an hour ago. It was a last-minute thing." Lou invites me into her room and stands in front of her mirror to admire her new hairdo. "Do you like it?"

"Totally," I respond, trying my best to sound genuine. "It's really cool, Lou."

"Thanks, girl. You should have heard Ma: 'Louisiana, what in God's name have you done?'" Lou laughs. "It was fucking hilarious."

"So, why did you cut it anyway?" When she shrugs, I urge, "Come on, Lou. Tell me."

"This is gonna sound super petty, but I thought if I changed my hair, Cassie might notice me." Lou shakes her head. "Is that not the most pathetic thing you've ever heard?"

I frown. Lou and her girlfriend Cassie, who moved to Vermont for college in late August, are by far the most compatible and committed teen couple I know. "What makes you think she doesn't notice you?"

"I dunno. Nothing really. It's just that she's been distant lately. She'll take ages to reply to my texts, and when she does, it's usually one-word responses or emojis. And then there's the Instagram story thing."

"Instagram story thing?"

"On Halloween, she was posting pictures and videos on her story from some party she was at, which is fine—except for Manon."

"Who's Manon?"

"Some French chick." Lou opens Instagram on her phone and shows me a photo of an attractive girl with long brown hair posing with Cassie and several other girls in a dorm room. She's wearing a white button-down shirt, knee-high socks, and sunglasses: a homage to *Risky Business*. "She was on Cassie's story a lot."

"So? I'm on your story all the time, and we're just friends."

"Yeah, but we don't kiss on the cheek and grind with each other. Plus, Manon has a rainbow flag in her bio. She hasn't approved my follower request, and I don't want to make assumptions, but it all seems a little suspect, you know?" Lou turns off her phone with a heavy sigh. "Whatever. I'm probably just being paranoid."

"You're *definitely* being paranoid."

"Uh-huh. Speaking of Halloween . . ." Lou's dark eyes twinkle mischievously. "Aisha told me she saw you and Liam out on the porch."

"And?"

"And . . . did anything happen?"

I shake my head. "It's not like that with Liam and me. You don't have to believe me, but it's the honest truth."

Lou arches an eyebrow. "For real?"

"I'm serious. I mean, he's cute and all, but I'm not attracted to him—not romantically at least. It was like that with Isaac too actually. I think I liked the idea of having a boyfriend so much that I went along with it even though I didn't feel the same way he felt about me."

"So, what are you saying? Are you ace?"

"I'm not asexual," I say. "At least I don't think I am. I'm just not ready for a relationship right now."

"Good. Relationships are a pain."

I pat Lou's hand. "It'll be okay. You and Cassie have already been through so much together. I'm sure you can work this out."

"I hope you're right."

I'm about to respond when my phone lights up with a text from Mom. She says: *stop&shop is out of breyers strawberry. theres fudge twirl, mint choc chip, black raspberry, cookie dough, and cherry vanilla. any of those sound good?*

"I'll try to Facetime her tonight," Lou continues. "I really hope she likes my hair. Are you sure it's not too short? Grace? Did you hear me?"

I stop googling Breyers ice cream calories long enough to say, "Huh?"

"My hair. Is it too short?"

"No, I already told you I like it." I finish my search and text Mom: *cherry vanilla plz.* "Cassie would be crazy not to."

"Thanks. Do you think I should ask her about Manon?"

Mom: sounds good.

"Who are you texting?"

"Mom," I respond, turning off my phone. "My favorite ice cream flavor is out, so I had to pick another one, and there are, like, a ton of different options. You know how stressed I get about those kinds of things." I laugh awkwardly. "Did you say something?"

"Never mind. It's not important."

"Oh. Okay."

"Do you want a snack?" she asks. "Ma hasn't gone shopping in a few weeks, but I think there are some chips in the pantry."

"I'll pass. But if you want to get something, that's fine."

She shrugs. "Maybe later. I'm not hungry right now."

"You're not?" I can't remember the last time Lou turned down junk food. "Well, in that case, do you want to watch TV or play a game or—"

"TV," she interrupts. "I'm too braindead for a game. School is literally sucking all the mental energy out of me. Plus, I have a late shift at Plantain Nation tonight, which means I'll probably be stuck there until at least eleven. I'm gonna be a zombie tomorrow."

"That sucks."

"I know, right? Even Ma gets more sleep than I do."

I'm tempted to ask Lou how her mother is—especially since she was in the hospital last week undergoing another round of chemotherapy—but before I can, my own mom texts me again: *new special k cereal. chocolatey strawberry. wanna try it out?*

"Oh, for God's sake," I mumble.

"What's wrong now?" Lou peers over my shoulder, watching as I open safari and type *special k chocolatey strawberry calories* into the search bar. "Seriously? You're still doing that? Isn't that, like, disordered behavior or something?"

I don't respond. I know she has a point: that obsessively fixating on calories only compromises the progress I'm making.

But since I'm not in the mood to have this conversation with her, I merely shrug.

"Yeah. Something like that."

I'M DREAMING about the hospital again. This time, I'm at Connecticut Treatment Center, sitting in a small, dimly-lit room by myself. On the table in front of me is a paper plate consisting of a stack of pancakes and syrup. The pancakes are as hard as rocks, and the syrup is cold and lumpy. I don't know how long I've been here. I don't know when I'll be allowed to leave. I don't know anything, other than that I really want to go home.

Moving as if I'm in a trance, I stand up and walk to the door. I grab hold of the knob and twist it as forcefully as I can, but it won't budge. So, I sit back down and draw a smiley face on a pancake with the tines of my fork. And I wait. And wait. And wait some more. Outside of the room, I hear footsteps padding across the tiled floor followed by the click of a lock. With my heart racing and my empty stomach in knots, I watch as the knob slowly turns and the door creaks open.

"Hello?" I say. "Who's there?"

"It's me, Gracie," a familiar voice responds. "It's Dad."

I wake up in a pool of sweat. My phone says it's only seven twenty-two, but since I'm already wide awake, I figure that there's no point in staying in bed—even if it is Saturday. So, I toss aside my blanket, throw on a navy shirt and grey sweatpants, and wander downstairs. Mom is in the TV room watching CNN while she holds a side plank.

"What are you doing?" I ask.

"Oh, Grace!" She quickly lowers herself and sits cross-legged on the floor, facing me. "You're up early."

"Yeah. Since when do you work out?"

"I'm doing some core exercises. My doctor recommended them." She mutes the television and stands up. "I'll get started on breakfast. How do pancakes sound?"

I'm suddenly reminded of my distressing dream. "Not pancakes. Anything but pancakes."

Mom peers at me skeptically. "All right then. I'll make eggs instead."

"Thanks," I say, taking a seat on the couch. I grab the remote and flip to TBS, where a *Brooklyn Nine-Nine* season five rerun has just started.

"Can you help me?"

With my eyes glued to the screen, I ask, "Do I have to?"

"I guess not. I'll let you know when the eggs are almost ready so you can at least set the table, okay?" When I shrug, she tries again. "Okay, Grace?"

"Okay, okay. I heard you the first time."

"Next time, try responding. It's polite."

Visibly frustrated, she leaves the room, while I revert my attention to the show. With the sounds of a sizzling frying pan and the repetitive opening and closing of the refrigerator in the background, I recline into the sofa and immerse myself in Andy Samberg's shenanigans.

I'm three-quarters through the episode when Mom calls my name. "Grace! Two minutes until breakfast!"

I turn off the television and join her in the kitchen. There, I lazily arrange four placemats, four napkins, and four forks on the table. "Should I wake up Kevin and Jamie or—"

Before I can finish speaking, Kevin walks into the room. He places his hands on Mom's waist and peers over her shoulder. "Smells delicious."

Mom flips the last egg, then turns around and plants a kiss on his lips. "Good morning to you too."

"Can I help with anything?"

"You can pour the drinks. Coffee for us, water for Grace, and juice for Jamie. But hold off on Jamie's drink until he's awake."

"They," Kevin calmly corrects. "Until *they* are awake."

Mom nods. "My mistake."

While they're talking, I sit down in my chair and rest my head against the table, suddenly very tired. If I'm still low on energy after breakfast, I rationalize, I'll take a nap. It is the weekend after all.

"Rough sleep?" Kevin asks.

I keep my eyes closed, because I know if I look at him, there's a chance that I'll see my father instead. It wouldn't be the first time that's happened. "Bad dreams—that's all."

"Me too." He sits next to me and takes a sip of his coffee. "I had this bizarre one about a cancer patient I'm treating. She was in surgery, and, well, things weren't going to plan."

"Were you in the hospital?"

"I think so. Why? Was that what your dream was about?"

I shake my head. "I don't remember. It's all a blur now."

This, of course, is a lie, but the last person I want to share my dream with is Kevin. He wouldn't understand. Even I don't fully understand why putting my past behind me is so challenging. Maybe there's a part of me that isn't ready to let go; a part that still perceives my disorder as my identity.

Mom nudges my arm, and I reluctantly raise my head. She hands me a plate consisting of one over easy egg, two strips of soy bacon, a toasted English Muffin, and sliced strawberries. As I stare at the food, not really wanting to eat it, I wonder to myself if that part will ever go away. I wonder if I'll ever be able to truly move on.

7

Therapy sucks. That's the one thought on my mind as Mom drives me home from my appointment with Anna. I rest my head against the window, my eyes half-closed, and try to dismiss the lingering frustration from my substandard session.

"You seem upset," Anna said after my weigh-in. "What's bothering you?"

"Nothing is bothering me," I responded. "Really. I'm good."

"And how is eating going? Have you changed your diet?"

"I'm eating the same amount of food as usual," I said, which, aside from replacing chips with fruit at lunch, was true. "Why are you asking?"

"Because it's my job to. If something is wrong, we should talk about it."

"Well, nothing is wrong. I'm fine. Everything is fine for fuck's sake."

The session only went downhill from there. Anna was like a detective, trying to figure out why I was so noncommunicative, and I was like a suspect, denying her accusations and insisting that I was A-OK. It literally felt like an interrogation.

Although I'd survived Anna's relentless questioning, I'm still in a sour mood when Mom and I return home. The second we walk inside, I notice a plate of yellowish cookies with small brown specks on top on the counter.

"What are those?" I ask.

"Snickerdoodles. I made them while you were with Anna. I hope you'll have some with me."

As much as I'm tempted to refuse, I don't want to start an argument with Mom. "All right."

Mom sets four cookies aside and begins to transfer the rest into a Tupperware container. When she's finished, she evenly distributes them between us and pours a cup of coffee while I fill a glass with water. I wait until she's added milk and a spoonful of sugar to her coffee to take a seat at the table.

"They're not bad, huh?" Mom says, referring to the cookies.

I wipe a crumb off my lip with my napkin. "They're okay."

She dunks a piece into her coffee. "Rough day?"

"What makes you say that?"

"Oh, nothing. You just seem a little down."

"Now you sound like Anna," I say. "I'm fine, Mom—I promise." When she continues to look skeptical, I change the subject. "Can we play a game?"

"Sure. But first, finish your cookie."

I pop the last bite of my second snickerdoodle in my mouth, then wash down the sugary taste with a sip of water. "Do you want to play Scrabble?"

Mom shakes her head. "No, I'm not in the mood for that. How about Knock Rummy?"

"Okay. I'll get the cards."

Pushing back my chair, I stand up and walk into the TV

room. Next to the television is a small green chest where we keep our board games. I find a deck of playing cards buried under a beat-up Monopoly box and toss it to Mom.

"You shuffle."

She slides the cards onto the table and splits the deck in half. As she's shuffling, she says, "By the way, Kevin won't be home for dinner. Stacy fell off a ladder and broke her wrist. He's helping out with the twins."

"What was Stacy doing on a ladder?" I ask.

"Set decoration, I believe. The twins' school is having a Thanksgiving gala."

"Of course they are," I mumble.

"Speaking of Thanksgiving," Mom continues, "Kevin's parents invited us over to their house for a feast. What are your thoughts on that?"

"I dunno. How many people will be there?"

"I know Kevin's sister is flying in from San Francisco, and his aunt and uncle live locally, but other than them, I'm not sure who's coming. You can ask Kevin."

"You mean when he isn't busy with his other family?"

"Grace . . ." Mom warns.

"Sorry. I shouldn't have said that."

She starts dealing the cards. "It's all right."

I wait until she's finished to pick up my cards and fan them out in my hand. Other than a seven, eight, and nine of diamonds run, they're mismatched. I glance at the card in the middle—a jack of spades—and shake my head. "I don't want it."

"Me neither," Mom says.

So, I take the card off the top of the pile—a two of diamonds —and exchange it with my queen of hearts. Behind Mom, my eyes hone in on the large November calendar she's taped to the pantry door. On the square reserved for the 26th, Jamie has stuck a sticker of a cartoon turkey.

"Do I have to go?" I ask Mom.

"Huh?"

"To Thanksgiving. Is it cool if I stay home?"

"No, it's not cool," Mom responds firmly. She examines a new card, then places it face-up on the discard pile. "If we decide to go, you're coming with us. And it's your turn."

"Okay, okay," I grumble as I exchange her rejected ten of spades with my ace of clubs. "It was worth a try."

"Grace, I understand how you feel about Kevin—"

"Mom, I don't want to have this conversation," I interrupt. "Just leave it."

"No, we should talk about this," she insists. "You were the one who started it."

"Then I'll be the one who ends it." I slam my cards onto the table and abruptly stand up. "Gin. I win."

"Where are you going?" she calls as I storm out of the kitchen.

"Away!" I respond sharply.

Before she can say another word, I charge upstairs and close the door to my room. I flop onto my bed and clutch my pillow to my chest, blinking tears from my eyes. I know it's foolish to get this worked up over a stupid holiday, but I can't help myself. It's more than just Thanksgiving I'm upset about. Ever since Kevin moved in, nothing has been the same. I've tried to convince myself that it will get better; that eventually, all this change won't seem so unwelcome. But the more time passes, the more I wonder if that's simply wishful thinking.

Ding!

I reach for my phone and open a text from Lou. She writes: *found out were going to my aunt and uncles for thanksgiving. last time i saw them was a disaster. i dont think i can do it again. can i spend the day with ur fam? pretty plz?*

Grace: sorry. going to kevins parents house. looks like were both in for it :(

Lou: at least theyre not batshit crazy bible thumping republicans ... are they?

Grace: no idea. never met them.

Lou: ugh. were so fucked.

Grace: tell me about it.

I wait a minute for her to reply, and when she doesn't, I leave iMessage and log onto Facebook. I type *Daniel Osborne* into the search engine, then when dozens of profiles pop up, I try his wife's less traditional name: *Willa Osborne*. Bingo. I click on an older woman originally from Lawrence, Kansas and enlarge her profile picture. She has reddish hair and rosy cheeks, and her grey eyes are hidden behind large, black-rimmed glasses, sort of like the ones my grandmother wears in the few photos I've seen of her.

Willa Osborne's last post is an album from July geotagged in San Francisco. It mostly consists of photos of her, her husband, and Kevin's older sister Aurora visiting tourist traps, going on hikes, and lounging in a studio apartment that I assume belongs to Aurora.

Neither Mr. or Mrs. Osborne look like the cranky old people I'd thought—and lowkey hoped—they would. Instead, they look . . . nice.

Although it annoys Mom when I text her while we're both in the house, I can't be bothered to leave my bed, so I open iMessage and write: *fine. we can go.*

"Thank you, Grace!" she yells several seconds later.

Rolling my eyes, I turn off my phone and stare at the ceiling with my hands behind my head. My mind is in overdrive, my thoughts swirling around it like an unruly tornado. I know there are ways to stop it; coping skills that I can use to distract myself from, well, myself. But I don't move. I don't watch a funny YouTube video or listen to a song or go downstairs and challenge Mom to a Knock Rummy rematch.

I stay where I am, my body completely still, and let the thoughts wash over me, as if I'm lying on a beach and the tide has just rolled in. The next thing I know, I'm thinking about how I wish I was at the beach, and then I'm remembering the crashing of waves the sound machine outside my therapist's office at my residential program, The Center for Healthy Living, would project.

"What is it that you want, Grace?" she asked during one of our sessions. We were talking about my goals—or, rather, lack thereof.

I thought about this for a minute. Several things came to my mind, but what I eventually settled on was something I'd wanted since I was ten years old. "To know that I'll be okay."

"It's okay, babe. Just take a deep breath."

"This is ridiculous," Kevin complains as we wait behind a van at a red light. We're driving to his parent's house—or at least we're trying to. With so much traffic on the main road, we're doing more sitting than anything else. "I checked Maps one hour ago, and it was only a forty-five-minute drive!"

"Everyone must be traveling for Thanksgiving," Mom says, stroking his arm. "Dinner doesn't start until five. I'm sure we'll make it by then."

Kevin glances at the dashboard: four thirty-eight. "We'd better. My mom used to teach middle school, so she's a stickler for punctuality. 'Early is on time, on time is late, and late is unacceptable' was her favorite quote when I was growing up."

"Who said that?" Jamie asks.

"No idea, but it stuck." Kevin sighs. "What the hell is wrong with this light? It should be green by now."

"Be patient, Kev," Mom says. "There's nothing you can do about the traffic."

Kevin doesn't respond, and when the light changes, he switches lanes and zooms past the van. Next to him, Mom is biting her lip. I can tell she wants to comment on his aggressive driving, but she holds her tongue. We all do.

We arrive at Mr. and Mrs. Osborne's house at six minutes to five. Kevin parallel parks between a black sedan and a Toyota with a New York license plate, and we hurry up the driveway, passing a massive inflatable turkey as we ascend a small staircase to the door.

"You can open it," Kevin says. "It should be unlocked."

Sure enough, it is. Once Mom has twisted the knob, the door opens, and we step into an elegant foyer. To our right is a wooden table covered in a festive red cloth; to our left is an ajar closet. A colorful array of winter coats hang from metal hangers. As Kevin squeezes ours between a magenta parka and a black jacket with a fur-lined hood, I follow the sound of chatter to a spacious living room. Dozens of people stand in groups talking and eating hors d'oeuvres. Jamie immediately zips over to a plate of deviled eggs, while I remain by the door, trying to make sense of how I'm feeling.

Part of me wants to turn around and flee; another wants to stay for the sake of Mom and Jamie, who I know were looking forward to this. But no amount of selflessness, nor rational thinking, can dismiss the anxiety I feel from being around so many people and so much food.

"Are you all right, Grace?" Kevin asks, coming to my side.

"Where's my mom?" I ask.

"She had to take a call."

"Oh."

"Come on," he says. "I'll introduce you to everyone."

"That's okay, I think I'll wait for Mom," I respond.

"At least let me introduce you to my sister. She's been looking forward to finally meeting you and Jamie."

I sigh. "Fine. Then I'm finding my mom."

"Deal. Hey, Jamie?" Kevin beckons over my sibling, who has whipped egg on their cheek, and we navigate through the crowd to the fireplace. He taps a tall woman on the back. "Aurora? I have some people I'd like you to meet."

Aurora places her champagne glass on the mantel and turns around. Aside from the Facebook photos, this is the first time I'm truly seeing Kevin's older sister. She's wearing a dark grey pantsuit paired with an ivory blazer and black pumps. Her tanned face is natural other than her lips, which are a deep shade of red.

"You must be Grace," she says to me in a husky voice. "I've heard so much about you."

"Nice to meet you," I say politely. As Aurora turns to Jamie, towering over their five-foot-four frame, a realization dawns on me. "Oh wow."

"Did you say something?" Kevin asks.

"Never mind."

"Kevin tells me that you're from California," Aurora says.

"Pasadena," I specify. "You live in San Francisco, right?"

She nods. "I moved there when I was nineteen. Quit community college and up-and-left. You remember that, don't you, Kevin?"

Kevin chuckles. "Mom and Dad were so angry."

"Oh, you know they were secretly relieved. If it was you, on the other hand . . ." Aurora shakes her head at the thought. "Kevin was always the good child. Straight As, star athlete—he did theater too."

"You did theater?" Jamie asks.

"We don't need to talk about that," Kevin says, but Aurora ignores him.

"For years. He was Romeo in our school's production of *Romeo and Juliet* and Pugsley in *The Addams Family*. The pictures from that one are especially amus—"

"All right, that's enough about me," Kevin interrupts. "Aurora, why don't you tell Grace about your new project. She's interested in writing."

"Ah, yes. I recently created a website called Anonymous Authors. It's a place for young people to share and receive feedback on their writing in a safe and supportive environment."

"Cool," I say. "Where'd you come up with the idea for something like that?"

Aurora opens her mouth to respond when Mr. Osborne loudly claps his hands. "Who's ready for dinner?"

"I'll tell you later," Aurora says. "Let's get in line before my family takes all the good stuff."

I force myself to laugh. "I'm gonna wait for my mom. You go ahead."

"All right. Oh, and one word of advice: don't sit anywhere near the man wearing the bright red tie. He's my cousin from Alabama, and he has some, um, strong opinions if you catch my drift."

"I do. Thanks for the heads up."

"No problem."

While Aurora joins the swarm of guests flooding into the

kitchen, I find Mom on her phone in the foyer. "Is everything okay?"

She holds up her index finger. "Thanks, Sam. I'll talk to you later." She ends the call with a sigh and slips it in her pocket. "Just some confusion at the hospital. How are you?"

"Fine," I respond instinctively. "I mean, I'm a little nervous, but I expected that."

"Well, I appreciate that you're being flexible. I know you would have preferred to stay at home, but this means a lot to Kevin."

"It's not like I had a choice," I say. "I met his sister by the way."

"Yeah? I'll have to introduce myself later. She sounds lovely."

"Um . . ." I clear my throat. "Not that it's a big deal or anything, but did you know Aurora was transgender?"

"I did," Mom says. "Kevin told me a while ago."

"Do you think that's why he's so good with Jamie?"

"I think that's part of it. It could also be that Kevin is just a good person. I know you don't like to give him any credit, but maybe—"

"Maybe we shouldn't talk about this," I interrupt. "Now isn't a good time."

"It's never a good time for you," Mom says, and I can tell by the tone of her voice that she's irked. "Ready to eat?"

I shrug. "I guess."

I follow Mom into the packed kitchen, grab a glass plate off the stack next to the sink, and join the line of people crowded around the island. The closer we get to the food, the tighter the knot in my stomach becomes. I start to feel dizzy and force myself to breathe deeply.

You can do this, I tell myself. *It's just one meal. It won't kill you.*

I tentatively fill my plate with salad, cauliflower, a slice of pumpkin bread, a scoop of roasted potatoes, and cranberry sauce even though I doubt I'll like the latter. Of the remaining options, it's the healthiest.

In the dining room, the table is quickly filling up. Towards the middle, Mrs. Osborne is arguing with the man with the red tie, the one Aurora warned me about. Now he's wearing a camo baseball cap with a gun symbol and the words *Come and Take It* printed across the front.

"Why do I have to take it off?"

"Because it's my house, and these are my rules."

He sulks into the hall, mumbling something about Mrs. Osborne being "racist against whites." I glance at Mom, who has a slightly amused, slightly concerned look on her face.

"Let's sit up here," I say.

She nods. "Good idea."

We claim the two empty chairs between Kevin's uncle and younger cousin; a girl with messily braided hair and turquoise braces. While I nibble on my cauliflower, she shoves a heaping spoonful of mashed potatoes in her mouth and washes it down with a swig of apple cider.

I take a sip of my sparkling water and place the glass on the off-yellow table cloth. The girl is now noshing on a thick slice of pumpkin bread, the crumbs adhering to her smudged lipstick. She notices me watching her and smiles bashfully.

"Sorry. I can't help myself around all this food."

"Don't worry about it," I respond. "I'm Grace."

Her grey eyes widen. "My name is Grace too."

Looking at Grace, with her frizzy hair and metallic teeth and cat-patterned blouse, I feel like I'm looking at a younger version of myself. It makes me kind of sad to think that just a few years ago, I too eagerly anticipated occasions where I could eat large amounts of food and no one would care. Not my parents, not my doctor, not the skinny, pretty girls at school—most importantly, not me.

"Are you all right?" Grace asks. "You don't look so good."

This is the third time this evening someone has asked me that question. And, for the third time, I fake a smile and say, "I'm fine."

8

I skipped snack again. For the fourth day in a row, my Clif Bar, which I routinely eat during psychology, has remained untouched at the bottom of my bookbag. When I discharged from CHL and returned to school last year, I always ate my bar with Miss Dixon. Back then, I was just starting to regain trust with Mom, who was convinced that I wouldn't eat it if I was left to my own devices. Although I'd never admit it, she was probably right.

But I'm in a better place this year—or at least I thought I was. Lately, however, I've felt so sad and alone. All my ambition and motivation have faded away, and no matter what I do, I can't seem to get them back. I can't seem to shake myself out of this funk I'm in.

I got rejected from my safety school on Saturday night. Even though I haven't heard back from Southern Boston University, it was a tough pill to swallow. This was the college I thought I'd have no problem getting into, but I was wrong. And if a school with a sixty-five-percent acceptance rate denies my application, who's to say SBU won't as well?

I spent all of Sunday isolating in my room. The only times I emerged were for meals, where I sat at the table and picked at my food in silence. I was too ashamed to tell anyone what was wrong, but of course Mom figured it out on her own. She kept asking me if I wanted to talk about it. I kept saying I would later. But I never did.

It's been five days since then. Five days of nodding off in class, moping around the house, and restricting food whenever I can get away with it. I know what I'm doing is wrong, and that I should stop or at least tell someone I trust, but I can't. Once I get in this kind of mindset, it's like a switch goes off in my brain, and suddenly, I'm on autopilot. I lose all control.

At the front of the room, Dr. Green is talking about the human brain. "The brain is a powerful tool," she says. "Use it wisely."

She then scribbles the homework—a multiple-choice packet —on the whiteboard and gives us the last few minutes of class to start working on it. I'm writing my name at the top of the first page when Lou nudges my arm.

"What's up with you?"

"What do you mean?" I ask.

"I dunno. You're acting weird. And you're wearing a lot of black too."

I glance down at my outfit: black skinny jeans and an oversized black sweater. Even my socks, minus the purple soles, are black. "I don't know what you're talking about."

"Fine, don't tell me then. It's not like I'm your best friend or anything."

"What's your problem, Lou?" I snap. "I'm fine. If anyone is acting weird, it's you."

Before Lou has a chance to respond, the bell rings. "Whatever, Grace." She slings her backpack over her shoulder and briskly leaves the room.

Rolling my eyes, I stuff my homework folder in my bookbag and follow my peers into the hall, tossing my bar in the trash on my way out the door. Then I pull my hood over my head, shove my hands in the pockets of my jeans, and trudge to government.

Lou is already in her seat when I enter the classroom. I avoid making eye-contact with her as I walk past her and slump in my chair. Heather, who sits next to me, is watching me in her periphery with a small smirk on her face.

"What are you looking at?" I ask.

Heather's smirk broadens slightly. "Oh, nothing," she responds and returns her attention to her phone without another word.

Ninety minutes and two painfully boring periods later, I meet Mom in the parking lot, and we drive home. She has to return to work after lunch, but before she goes, she makes a point of asking me if I'll be able to have snack on my own.

"Of course," I say. "I wish you'd stop worrying so much."

"I'm a mother," she responds. "Worrying is what I do best."

Grabbing her keys off the counter, she kisses my forehead and walks outside. I wait until she's gone to wander into the TV room, collapse onto the couch, and pull a grey fleece blanket over my head. I'm asleep in seconds.

I AWAKEN two hours later to the sound of the door swinging open. "Grace!" Jamie bellows. "Grace, are you home?"

"Jesus Christ, Jamie, I'm sleeping," I say. "Can you keep it down?"

"Sorry," Jamie says, not sounding at all apologetic. They sit on the arm of the couch and flick my foot. "Why are you sleeping anyway? You went to bed at, like, nine last night."

"I have a cold," I lie, "and unless you want to get it too, you should leave me alone."

"Okay, okay. I'm going." Jamie pauses in the doorway and turns to face me again. "Can I, like, get you anything? When I'm sick, Mom makes me drink a lot of juice."

I shake my head. "I'm fine. But you can close the curtains. The sunlight is hurting my head."

Jamie walks to the window and pulls the burgundy curtains over the smudged glass. "Better?"

"Yeah. Thanks, Jamie."

"You're welcome, Grace."

As Jamie's footsteps fade into the distance, I unlock my phone and set an alarm for five thirty, figuring that will give me enough time to get myself together before Mom comes home. With the harsh wind rapping against the window and the soft hum of the boiler in the basement, I drift back into oblivion.

"YOU LOST WEIGHT."

I listlessly pick at my cuticles on my middle finger until beads of blood surround my shredded skin. Then I wrap my black shirt around the wound to stop the bleeding and move on to my pinky. I can feel Anna watching me from across the room, but I refuse to look her in the eyes.

You lost weight.

One year later, and I still don't know how those words make me feel.

"Grace? Did you hear me?"

Now a thin stream of blood is trickling down my pinky. "I heard you."

"And? Do you know how that happened?"

"No," I lie.

"Okay, well, have you been restricting?"

"I've been really stressed lately," I say, "and sometimes when there's a lot on my mind, I forget to eat enough. It's not like I do it on purpose. It just happens."

"Then that's something we have to work on. I understand that extenuating circumstances may pose challenges for you, however your health must always be your priority. If you feel like you have too much on your plate, take a step back. It's okay to give yourself breaks every so often."

"I know. I promise I'll do better."

"I trust you, Grace." Anna glances at my chart. "You fell out of your range, so you're going to need to gain a couple of pounds. How would you like to proceed with that?"

"I don't know," I mumble.

"You don't have any ideas?"

"No." I suddenly feel angry, as if all the frustration I've been suppressing for the last few weeks is surfacing inside me like bubbles in a shaken soda can. "Why do I have to gain weight anyway? It's not like if I lose a pound or two I'm gonna drop dead. And can you explain to me why everyone is so obsessed with my body? I mean, it's *my* body. Shouldn't *I* be in charge of what I do with it?"

Behind her glasses, Anna's hazel eyes are wide with surprise. "What's going on, Grace? This isn't like you."

"I got rejected from my safety school," I mumble. "Sixty-five-percent acceptance, and I didn't even get waitlisted."

"I'm sorry. Have you heard anything from SBU?"

I shake my head. "No, but I doubt I'll get in. I thought

having a good GPA would help me, but obviously colleges can't see past my half-day schedule or that I missed so much school last year. They just don't want to deal with someone with my problems. I can't say I blame them."

"Grace, you know that isn't true. I've worked with many seniors who said the same thing, and most of them got into a college they liked. You're smart, you're determined, and most importantly, you've learned how to overcome setbacks. Those are excellent qualities to have. Whatever college you end up going to will be lucky to have you."

"We'll see about that," I say.

"Yes, we will," she responds. "In the meantime, you still haven't told me how you plan to gain back the weight. I'm sure you already know this, but undereating has a huge impact on your mood too."

"Uh . . . I could drink more, I guess," I suggest. "Mom bought chocolate milk for Jamie. I could probably have a glass once a day or something."

"Twice a day," Anna corrects firmly. When I groan, she says, "I know it's not fun, however if you continue to lose weight, I'll have no choice but to talk to your mom."

"Okay, okay. Two glasses. Please don't tell my mom."

"Follow the plan, and I won't have to. It's up to you."

"No pressure," I mumble.

"You can do this," Anna says, smiling kindly. "Would you mind if I invited your mother in for the last few minutes? I won't tell her about your weight, but it might be good for her to know some of what we discussed today so she can support you."

"She's not here," I say. "Kevin is picking me up."

"Okay. Will you tell her yourself?"

"I don't know. I'll see how I feel."

Anna nods. "Fair enough. Just promise me you'll keep in

mind that we're all here for you. No one will judge you if you have a bad day or need a little extra support. You do know that, right?"

"Yeah, I know." I glance at the clock—four fifty-nine—then begin to put on my coat and boots. "Should I come back in one week or stick with two?"

"Let's do one. Does three o'clock work for you?"

"Three is fine. So, I guess I'll see you then."

"See you then," she says. "You've got this."

"Uh-huh." I leave Anna's office, closing the door behind me, and walk down the staircase and outside. Kevin is waiting in his car next to the curb with his eyes glued to his phone. When I yank open the door, he flinches. "Sorry."

"No worries. It's my fault for losing track of time." Kevin turns the keys, and the engine roars to life. "How was your session?"

"Fine," I lie and raise the volume on the radio before he can ask me anything else. With a new wave eighties song blasting through the car, I press my forehead against the glass and stare out the window at the darkening sky until we're home.

Because Mom's five o'clock meeting runs late, dinner is postponed until six thirty. I'm a little hungry from skipping both my morning and afternoon snack, so I eat a clementine to hold me over. While she boils a pot of water for pasta on the stove, I start working on my salad.

"How did it go with Anna?" she asks.

I open the refrigerator and take out a red pepper and a container of cherry tomatoes. "Fine. I'm seeing her next week by the way. Three o'clock."

"I thought you usually do two weeks," Mom says. "Are you sure everything is okay?"

"Yes, Mom. How many times do I have to tell you for you to

believe me?" I realize I'm yelling again and quickly lower my voice. "It was her idea anyway."

I expect Mom to be annoyed or at least surprised by my outburst. But when I glance at her, she looks more worn out than anything else. "Linguine or penne?"

"Huh?"

Mom holds up two boxes of pasta. "Linguine or penne? Your choice."

"Um, penne."

"Penne it is."

I watch her shake the box into the boiling water, then turn the dial down to Medium. She adds a pinch of salt and gently stirs the pasta with a wooden spoon.

"I'm sorry for yelling," I say.

Without looking away from the pot, Mom nods. "Thank you."

Dinner tonight seems even more uncomfortable than usual. While Jamie and Kevin make small talk about their days, Mom watches me like a hawk. Only when I'm finished eating my pasta does she avert her attention to my sibling, who's griping about a lame musical number the band teacher had assigned them.

"I don't understand why I have to take regular band when I'm in the jazz band," Jamie whines. "It's such a waste of time."

"Because otherwise, the band would be awful," Kevin responds. "I played the trumpet when I was your age, and if it weren't for the jazz band kids, we would have been booed off the stage."

"They deserve to be booed off the stage."

"That's a little harsh," Mom remarks.

"I don't care. Everyone in that class is so annoying—especially the brass section. No offense, Kevin."

Kevin laughs. "None taken."

"But whatever. It's still better than gym."

"Did something happen?" Mom asks. "Because if Coach Berger is giving you grief about the locker room again—"

"Nothing happened, Mom. I just don't like volleyball—that's all."

Before Mom can respond, I stand up. "I'm going to my room. I have homework."

Without bothering to push in my chair, I discard my sauce-stained plate in the sink and leave the kitchen. Upstairs, I sit at my desk and take out my psychology packet. I hadn't paid attention to Dr. Green's lesson, so I end up googling most of the answers.

Around eight o'clock, as I'm circling letter C on the last question, my mind begins to drift from my schoolwork. I leave the packet and pencil on my desk and crawl into bed with my computer to watch *Atypical*. I'm partway through an episode when my phone buzzes.

Lou: sorry for being a dick the other day. can u stop ignoring me now?

My thumb hovers over the keyboard. Part of me wants to stay angry with her. Part of me knows I should grow up and move on. But before I can commit to either, there's a knock on my door.

"Go away, Mom!"

"I just got off the phone with Anna," Mom says in a muffled voice. "Can I come in so we can tal—"

"I don't want to hear it," I interrupt. "Just leave me alone, okay?"

I hear a deep sigh, followed by the sound of her footsteps fading into the distance. Rolling my eyes, I adjust my earbuds and resume *Atypical*. I finish the episode a couple of minutes later and move on to the season finale. I'm just past the opening credits when the show unexpectedly freezes. I exit Netflix, wait ten seconds, and reopen it, which usually resolves the problem. But it does the exact opposite, as now Netflix won't load either.

"What the hell?" I mumble.

With an exasperated groan, I turn off my computer and reach for my phone. I open Instagram, but since it's a school night, and I only follow two-hundred-and-twelve accounts, there's not much content to keep me entertained. I'm too tired to text Lou and too uninterested to check my primarily political Twitter feed, so out of sheer boredom, I go onto my photos app and begin to scroll through the hundreds of pictures, looking for ones to delete. I select unflattering selfies, blurry shots of Lou and me, and diagrams of the human ear that I'd screenshotted for a psychology assignment a month ago. I'm an eighth of the way through the album when I get to the bad photos; the ones from when I was sick. I stare, as if I'm in a trance, at a picture of me in my underwear standing in front of the bathroom mirror. My collar bones and ribcage are shockingly prominent, and the morning sunlight shines through the gap between my thighs.

The sound of my phone buzzing jerks me back to reality. It's another text from Lou: *wtf grace? i know u saw my message. if ur gonna be a baby about this maybe we shouldnt talk. i cant deal with ur negativity rn.*

Letting out another frustrated groan, I impulsively hurl my phone across the room. It collides with the strip of wall between my door and closet and falls onto the floor with an audible *thunk*. I leap off my bed to assess the damage, which, to my dismay, is worse than I'd anticipated. Not only is the screen cracked; now my phone won't even turn on.

With my back against the wall, I sink to the floor and bury my face in my hands. "Shit."

THE NEXT MORNING, Mom and I drive to the Apple Store to fix my phone. With the holidays quickly approaching, the mall is even busier than usual. Mom finds an empty spot towards the back of the crowded parking lot, and we hurry to the Macy's entrance, eager to escape the frigid weather. We walk through the store, which has been decorated with twinkling Christmas trees and sparkly silver baubles that dangle from the ceiling, and enter the second floor of the mall.

"Do you know where we're going?" I ask.

"Yes, it's this way." As we pass store after store, Mom asks, "Have you thought about getting a job here? A lot of these places are looking for some extra help for the holidays."

"You mean in retail?" I shake my head. "No way. I could never deal with all those shoppers. I mean, I barely survived being around Kevin's family for three hours on Thanksgiving."

"It does take a great deal of socializing," she says, "and that's not exactly your strong suit."

"You don't have to rub it in," I snap.

"Grace . . ."

"Mom."

She sighs. "Never mind. We're here."

Like the rest of the mall, the Apple Store is buzzing with customers. Mom and I wait in a long line to talk to an employee, neither of us speaking to each other. I wish I had my phone, but since it's broken, I end up reading the backs of newly released Blu-ray movies to pass the time.

Twenty minutes later, we finally reach the counter. "My daughter dropped her phone down the stairs," Mom says to a woman named Delilah, which is what I told her when she asked what happened. "It won't turn on. Is there anything you can do to help us?"

Delilah takes the phone from Mom and begins inspecting it.

While we're waiting, I stare across the mall at a popular clothing store. Shoppers flood in and out of the door: some taking their time to browse the selection, others in a mad dash to find what they're looking for. A young employee stands at the entrance greeting customers. Although the smile on her face never wavers, her fatigue is evident.

"Grace will need a new phone," Delilah informs Mom. "Unfortunately this one is irreparable."

"Dammit," Mom grumbles. Checking her watch, she says, "I have to be at the hospital in thirty minutes. We'll come back over the weekend and buy one then."

"But that's in—" I start to protest when she cuts me off.

"Two days. I'm sure you'll survive. Come on, let's go."

"It can be like an early holiday gift," I say as we're leaving the store. I try to sound optimistic, but she doesn't reciprocate. Instead, the scowl on her face only broadens.

"Merry Christmas to me," she responds sarcastically.

I follow her back through the mall, which seems to have doubled in population while we were with Delilah. Every direction I look there are shoppers. My stomach feels kind of funny, though I can't tell if it's from anxiety or the sickly smell of French fries wafting out of a fast-food joint.

"Hey, Mom?"

"Yes?"

"I, um . . ." I shake my head, unable to articulate the whirlwind of emotions I'm feeling. "Never mind. Just thank you. For the phone, I mean."

"Let's not talk about it, okay?" She still sounds annoyed, but her voice is no longer as hostile.

I nod. "Okay. I won't say another word."

9

Eight-hundred-and-fifty-dollars. That's how much my new phone costs—and it isn't even the most recent version. Had I known how insanely expensive phones are to replace, I would have thought twice before I hurled mine at the wall. At least now I understand why Mom was so upset with me.

"I promise I'll be super careful," I said. It was Saturday afternoon, and we'd just spent an hour at the Apple Store with Delilah completing the transaction and syncing my data to my new phone.

"You'd better be," Mom responded. "Next time, it's coming out of your bank account."

Whereas the tension between Mom and me persisted through the rest of the weekend, at least I was able to resolve my conflict with Lou. We made up on Sunday morning over the phone, and when we came back to school on Monday, it was like nothing had happened.

"I'm still surprised your mom bought that stairs lie," Lou says as we sit in psychology waiting for class to start. "I drop my phone down the stairs all the time, and it's always fine. Well, there was this one time when the case cracked, but I have, like, five extras just lying around, so it wasn't a big deal."

"Okay, rich kid," I say, rolling my eyes.

"I work hard for my money," Lou protests. "Do you know how much working in retail sucks? On Saturday, some lady was trying to return a pair of heels that she'd obviously worn before, and when I explained to her why she couldn't do that, the bitch had a total meltdown and threw one at my head."

"Jeez. How come you're still working there?"

"Easy: money. I mean, eleven dollars an hour is too low considering all the shit I have to deal with, but at least it's something."

I'm about to respond when the bell rings. Dr. Green rises from her desk and stands at the front of the room, her tall frame casting a shadow against the projector screen. "Good morning, scholars. I hope you all read Module Nine over the weekend because we're having a pop quiz." She ignores the collective groan from the class. "Move your materials to the floor. I had someone try to cheat during first period, and let's just say they'll be spending a lot of time with me this week."

"Ten bucks Matt cheated off Eli," Lou whispers.

"My money is on Tommy," I respond quietly and lock pinkies with her under the desk.

When school ends, I meet Mom outside, and we drive home to have lunch. After I've finished my bagel sandwich and she's polished off a slice of leftover pizza, she clears our dishes and begins to put her heels and jacket back on.

"How long will you be?" I ask.

"A while, so you can go ahead and eat dinner without me. Kevin will be home around six, all right?"

"Uh-huh."

"I bought peppermint ice cream if you'd like to have it for your night snack," she says on her way out the door. "Or this afternoon. Whatever you want."

I wait until she's gone to open the freezer and take out the carton of ice cream. With the door still open, I turn it over and analyze the nutrition facts. It's relatively healthy compared to some of the other brands that offer seasonal flavors, which I imagine is the reason Mom chose it.

Great. Now I've got my mother fixated on calories too.

Beep! Beep! Beep!

"Oh, be quiet." I put the ice cream away, close the freezer door, and sit down at the table to get started on my statistics homework. I'm halfway through the first page when my phone buzzes.

Lou: u were right. tommy cheated :(

Grace: haha, looks like someone owes me $

Lou: ur a bitch.

Shaking my head in amusement, I turn off my phone and return my attention to my homework. I finish at three twenty and put the sheet in my folder with the rubric for my second quarter Voices project. With a single-serving carton of banana yogurt in my hands, I amble into the TV room and load Netflix to start season three of *Atypical*.

I'm almost through the first episode when Jamie comes home. "I thought you were staying late for that band thing," I call from the couch.

"It was a clarinet workshop, and I didn't feel like it," Jamie says. I hear rummaging around in the kitchen, and twenty seconds later, my sibling joins me in the TV room with a bag of barbecue potato chips. "What are you watching?"

"Just a show." I reach for the remote on the coffee table and turn off the television. "How was school?"

Jamie ignores my question. "You're so lucky Mom picks you up. Walking home in this weather sucks. I'd even take the bus if the closest stop weren't, like, a mile away."

"I told you to ask Lou for a ride," I respond. "She'd have no problem driving you. And anyway, aren't you carpooling with Sara Fisher?"

"Sara stays after school for volleyball. The season started a week ago."

"Oh." I frown. "Look, if you're too shy to ask Lou, I'll do it for you. I can text her right now."

I start to unlock my phone when Jamie holds their greasy hand over the screen. "Don't bother. I'll walk."

"Your call, weirdo," I say, which elicits a scowl from Jamie. "Let me know if you change your mind, okay?"

Jamie polishes off the bag of chips and stands up. "I have homework. Later."

"Later. Oh, mind tossing this for me?" I hold out the yogurt carton.

Jamie takes the carton from me and leaves the room without another word. I wait until they're gone to turn the television back on and resume my show. Two episodes later, I hear the rumble of the garage opening, then the slam of a car door.

I'm on my feet when Kevin bustles inside, bringing a gust of cold air with him. He places his briefcase on the counter and removes his brown loafers, revealing mismatched socks. "Hi, Grace."

"You're early," I remark.

Kevin glances at the clock: five twenty-two. "My last patient canceled. I was thinking I'd make risotto for dinner. How does that sound?"

"Doesn't risotto take a while?"

"We have time. Where does your mom keep the vegetable stock?"

"Pantry, I think. Try the second shelf." I watch him open the pantry and rummage through the vast assortment of nonperishables. "What else goes in risotto?"

"Rice, of course. Butter, cheese. I usually add onions too, but I know you don't like those. Ah, here it is." He triumphantly holds up the vegetable stock. "Do you want to help me?"

I shake my head. "I'll pass. When do you think it'll be ready?"

"Give me forty minutes, okay?"

"Fine."

While he warms up the stove, I return to the couch and open Safari on my phone. *calories in risotto* I type into the search engine. Each website gives a different number, however all of them—aside from a low-fat recipe on a blog called Nourish—are very high. By the time I've finished my search, so is my anxiety.

"Grace! Jamie! Dinner is ready!"

When I enter the kitchen, Kevin hands me a large bowl of risotto and a wooden spoon. I place them on the table and serve myself a small amount of the light yellow rice and some salad. I wait until both Kevin and Jamie are seated and served to tentatively take a bite. The risotto, while better than Mom's past attempts, is overcooked and too cheesy, and when I swallow, those scary numbers are the only thought on my mind. Under the table, my foot starts to tap against the floor. I don't want to eat anymore. One more bite, and I think I'll be sick.

I wipe wisps of cheese off my fork with my napkin and move on to my salad. By the time I'm chewing on my final forkful of lettuce, Jamie is helping themselves to a second serving of risotto. Then Kevin shares an anecdote about a misunderstanding between two of his coworkers, and Jamie bursts out laughing.

"That's hilarious."

While they continue to chat, I quietly push a clump of cheesy risotto around my plate and wish I could just disappear. Now Jamie is ranting about a "totally stupid, completely pointless" science project that's due next week. When I glance up, Kevin is watching me out of the corner of his eye.

He waits until Jamie has finished venting to clear his throat. "You know, the risotto won't taste as good if it's cold."

I methodically separate individual grains of rice from the clump with my fork. "You cooked it for too long. The rice is hard."

"No, it's not," Jamie disagrees. "I think the rice is just right."

"Well, I think it tastes like dried-out glue."

"You've had dried-out glue?"

No longer able to contain my frustration, I abruptly push back my chair and stand up. I can feel Jamie and Kevin's eyes on me as I storm out of the kitchen and hurry upstairs. In my room, I slam the door and dramatically collapse onto my bed. I wait with my face buried in my pillow for one of them to check on me, but after several minutes pass, I realize that they're not going to. I should feel relieved, considering that all I've wanted for the past month is to be left alone, but for reasons I can't explain, the solitude makes me melancholic.

I raise my head and gaze into the smudged mirror mounted on my wall. My eyes look sadder than they have in a long while, almost empty. I take a deep breath, then slowly exhale, then repeat the cycle twice more. In my periphery, I notice a Gmail notification from CommonApp appear on my lock screen. I eagerly reach for my phone to read the message, but it's just an ad promoting a new feature.

I scoff at my stupidity. What was I expecting to happen? Haven't I learned by now not to get my hopes up?

I spend the next hour staring at my ceiling and listening to sad songs, neither of which improves my mood whatsoever. Around eight o'clock, there's a knock on my door. "What?"

"Can I come in?" Mom asks.

I remove my earbuds with the music still playing. "All right."

Mom sits on the edge of my bed, her khaki pants cinching at the knees. "Kevin told me about the risotto."

"Of course he did," I say.

"You could have made something else. I know you don't like leftovers, but we have corndogs and soy burgers and soup bowls. I bought more Spring Onion yesterday. That's your favorite, isn't it?" When I don't respond, she continues, "All I'm saying is that you had choices. And you chose to not eat."

I roll my eyes. "Why does everything have to be such a big deal with you? It's one meal, Mom! I'm not gonna die 'cause I didn't eat some shitty risotto. Jeez."

"It's one meal," she repeats. "That's what you said last year days before you were admitted to the hospital. One meal might not seem like much to you, but if there's something I've learned from all of this it's that any bad behavior, no matter how small, incites your eating disorder. And I won't stand for that."

I avert my gaze to my fuzzy black socks, unable to look into her eyes. "I don't know what you want me to say."

"You don't have to say anything. You just have to do better."

"And what if I don't?"

"Do you really need me to spell it out for you?"

"No," I mumble, knowing full-well what she means. "So, Anna told you everything, huh?"

"It wasn't anything I didn't already know." Mom places her hand on my slumped shoulders. "You need to tell me when you're having a hard time, Grace. I'm here for you, okay? Let me help you."

"Okay."

"Okay?"

I nod. "Okay. I guess I can try to be more open with you."

"I'd like that. Now, what do you say we go have some soup?"

I glance at the clock on my nightstand. "You know it's bad for your body if you eat after eight, right?"

"Grace . . ."

Even though I really don't want to eat right now, the thought of having to return to the hospital is more than enough incentive. "What the hell? I call dibs on Spring Onion."

Mom nods. "Deal."

In the kitchen, Mom takes two instant soups—Spring Onion and Lemongrass & Chili—out of the pantry and hands the former to me. We dump the uncooked rice noodles and seasoning packets into bowls and add hot water. Once the noodles are cooked, we sit across from each other at the table. Mom rolls up the sleeves of her maroon sweater, while I pull the hood of my black sweatshirt over my greasy hair.

"Well, this looks good," she says.

"Yeah." I blow on my soup, then attempt to down a spoonful of the aromatic broth. My tongue immediately reacts. "Crap! That's hot!"

Mom chuckles. "What were you expecting?"

"I dunno." I wrap my ice-cold hands around the bowl, embracing the warmth as I wait for the soup to cool. "Sorry I was a dick to your boyfriend by the way."

"It's all right," she reassures me. "We don't take it personally."

"Good." I blow on my soup and try again. "Nope. Still too hot."

"Anna said that you and she set a plan to gain back the weight?"

I can't tell by Mom's phrasing if this is a question or a statement. "Sort of."

"Sort of?" she repeats skeptically. "Grace, I hope you're taking this seriously—"

"Of course I'm taking it seriously," I interrupt. "Do you think I like this? 'Cause I don't."

"I know this isn't easy—" she starts to say, but once again, I cut her off.

"No, you don't. You don't know crap, so quit pretending like you do."

"Who's pretending? Grace, I've been your caretaker for the last year. If anyone should at least have some understanding of what you're dealing with, it's me."

I'm about to respond when my phone lights up with another email—this one from SBU. *Dear Ms. Edwards, I am pleased to inform you* . . . The preview stops there, but my racing heart is only getting started. With Mom watching me closely, I enter my password and open the email.

Dear Ms. Edwards,

I am pleased to inform you that you have been accepted into Southern Boston University. On behalf of the faculty and staff at SBU, I congratulate you on this outstanding achievement and welcome you to our community. To begin the road to academic success, there are a few steps you need to follow to complete your enrollment . . .

The email goes on for three more paragraphs, but I'm too excited—and jittery—to read another word.

"Grace?" Mom reaches across the table and nudges my forearm. "Put your phone away. We're in the middle of a conversation."

"Sorry," I apologize. "It's just that . . . holy crap. I can't believe it."

"What can't you believe?"

I glance at the email again, then back at Mom, who now looks more curious than anything else. "I got in, Mom," I say in a whisper. "I'm going to SBU."

LATER THAT NIGHT, I lie in my bed, unable to sleep, and reflect on the chaotic day I've had. I know I should be happy that I was accepted into my number one school, but I'm not. I don't feel happy or relieved about college, nor do I feel upset or scared that I'm still a few skipped meals away from going back to the hospital.

Truth be told, I don't feel anything at all.

To CELEBRATE my acceptance into Southern Boston University, after lunch on Thursday, Mom lets me order forty dollars' worth of merchandise from the school's online shop. I feel somewhat guilty for spending more of her money, but she seems oddly okay with it, even agreeing to let me exceed my budget by five dollars.

"You'd better be committed to going there," she jokes as the website processes her card. "I'm not buying you all this merch for nothing."

"It's my number one school," I respond. "Obviously I'm going."

"I'm just teasing you. I'm really proud of you, you know that?"

"Yeah, Mom, I know. Do you want me to forward you the receipt?"

"Yes." She places her card on the counter and sits across from me. "Grace, don't take this the wrong way, but did you eat enough for lunch? Because it didn't seem like it to me."

"I don't know what you're talking about. I ate the same amount of food as usual."

"But you should be eating more, right? So you can gain back the weight you lost?"

I groan in frustration. "Oh my god, Mom. Why are you doing this?"

"I'm doing this for you, Grace. I know how badly you want to get out of here. You only tell me every day." She rolls her eyes. "But I also know that if you're unable to feed yourself properly at college, you'll fail. And I know you know it too."

Mom is right: from the moment I decided I wanted to go to college, it's become obvious to me that it's either my disorder or my degree. I can't have both.

Sighing dramatically, I close my computer, stand up, and open the refrigerator. I grab a quart of one-percent milk and pour approximately eight ounces into a cup. I then add a squirt of chocolate syrup and return to the table, where Mom is watching me with a neutral look on her face.

"You can smile," I say. "This is what you want, isn't it?"

"I want it to be what you want too," she responds.

I take a small sip of the milk and swallow. "It is."

"Good." She reaches behind her and hands me a napkin. "You have a milk mustache."

"Thanks." I pat my upper lip with the napkin, then continue to slowly drink my milk. "I know it might not seem like it at times, but I really am trying. I promise."

"I know." Mom places her hand on top of mine, her lips finally lifting into a small smile. "So am I."

10

I can't remember the last time I was this nervous before a therapy session. Sitting in Anna's waiting room, listening to the repetitive chirping of birds coming from the sound machine outside her door, my stomach is twisted into knots. I take out my phone to pass the time, but upon realizing that it's at four percent, put it back in my pocket and pick up a picture book on the circular end table to my left called *All Dogs Have ADHD*.

I smile thinking about how easily distracted my old Labrador was. Sometimes, a simple walk around the block could take up to thirty minutes. From the abundance of wildlife to the other dog walkers to the hum of lawnmowers or the whirring of sprinklers, it was impossible to keep Tiana's attention for an extended period of time.

"Hello, Grace." Anna's voice interrupts me from my thoughts. "Come on in."

I follow Anna into her office and kick off my moccasins next to the maroon couch. I then step backward on the scale so she can record my weight. Once I hear the familiar *beep*, I return to the couch and sit cross-legged with my elbows resting on my knees. Anna takes a seat across from me and digs my chart out of her filing cabinet.

"How are you?" she asks as she flips through the stapled pages.

"I'm okay," I say. "Better than last week anyway. I'm sorry I acted like that."

"It's all right. We all have bad days."

"No kidding. So, uh, how's my weight?" It's the question that's been literally weighing on my mind from the second Mom dropped me off.

"Better," she responds vaguely.

"Does that mean I'm back in my range?"

"Not yet, but you're headed in the right direction."

"Oh." I'm not sure how this makes me feel. "Good."

I spend the rest of the session rehashing my eventful week, from breaking my phone to getting into SBU to my conversation with Mom about independence to the risotto incident. "Kevin seemed sort of surprised when I apologized," I say. "I guess I've never done that before. Did you know his daughters are coming over today?" When Anna shakes her head, I make a face. "They have been coming for months now, but it's still so awkward. I'm beginning to think it'll always be."

"Have you noticed any improvement? Any at all?"

"Maybe a little. I'm not as bothered by the tubas."

Anna laughs. "Well, that's a start."

I shrug. "I guess it is."

After my session, I meet Mom in the parking lot to drive home. We arrive at the house shortly after four. Coincidentally, as I'm helping her unload groceries from the trunk, Kevin pulls into the driveway and parks behind us. He gets out with his daughters McKayla and McKenzie, who are dressed in their private school uniforms. Both girls carry matching pink duffle bags with smiley emoji keychains looped through the straps. Although their facial features are identical, McKayla's brown hair cascades past her elbows, whereas McKenzie's is shoulder length and has a blue streak on the right side.

McKayla is loudly complaining about a science test she did poorly on. "It's so unfair. I studied for, like, an hour last night, and there was literally nothing from the guide on the test. Miss Frickle is literally the worst teacher ever! Literally!"

If there's one thing I've learned about McKayla over the past six months, it's that her favorite word is "literally." She's much more talkative than her sister, who barely spoke a word to anyone the first few times the twins stayed over. Whereas Mom and Jamie made an effort to treat them with hospitality, I wanted as little to do with them as possible. It felt like they were intruders; like they didn't belong in our house with their preppy clothes and posh mannerisms and devious smiles that made them seem as if they were always up to trouble.

Maybe that makes me a bad person. Maybe I should have given them a chance. But it was hard enough getting used to Kevin—never mind his kids. Every time I see them, I start to wonder what would have happened if Dad hadn't run off, and instead, he and Mom had split up like most couples do. I wonder if I'd still see him on the weekends. I wonder if he'd find a new family too—a better family.

It wouldn't surprise me if he already has.

Mom pan-fries potato and cheese perogies for dinner, and afterward, the twins disappear into the guestroom to unpack. Once I've helped Mom clear the dishes, I return to the table to get started on my psychology homework. I'm skimming through

a passage in the textbook about narcolepsy when Jamie sits next
to me.

"What'cha doing?"

"Nothing interesting," I say. "Do you have homework?"

Jamie shakes their head. "No, I finished all of it at lunch."

"I thought you ate with Sara."

"She had a lunch detention. The worst part is that she didn't
even do anything wrong. Jack was the one who was drawing
dicks on the whiteboard."

"Do I want to know?" I ask.

"Probably not."

"Well, can you at least tell me why you're down here? You
always hole up in your room after dinner."

"I don't 'hole up,'" Jamie says. "It's just that the twins are
practicing their tubas, and if I hear *Walking in a Winter Wonder-
land* one more time, I'm gonna stick scissors in my ears."

I laugh. "Now you know how I feel."

"Very funny. Want some ice cream?"

"No. I finished the peppermint last night, and I don't like
cookies and cream. Mom said she'd get vanilla tomorrow."

"Bo-ring." Jamie stands up and opens the freezer, rummaging
through an abundance of frozen food for the carton. Once
they've located it, they scoop two heaping spoonfuls into a bowl.
"Mmm. I can't believe you don't like this."

"It's just not for me," I say. "Can you toss me the bag of
ginger snaps? I think they're in the snack cabinet."

Jamie finds the snaps and throws them at me a little too
forcefully. The bag soars through my hands and collides with my
chest. "Sorry."

"No worries." I take three cookies—one fewer than the
recommended serving size—out of the bag and place them on
the table. "Have you tried these? They're pretty good."

Jamie grabs a cookie, breaks it into small pieces, and vigorously mixes them into the ice cream. I have to hold my tongue to refrain from commenting on the bizarre combination. "Not bad," Jamie says as they're chewing. "You know, I heard McKayla talking about building a gingerbread house at their mom's house. Remember that time when we made one?"

"I do. That was a lot of fun. I mean, it looked like crap, and we basically destroyed the kitchen, but I'd still do it again."

"We should."

"I dunno. I think we're a little old for that."

"Oh, come on. If I'm not allowed to go trick-or-treating anymore because I'm in high school, at least let me make a gingerbread house."

I laugh. "All right. Add it to Mom's shopping list."

Jamie picks up a pencil and scribbles *gingerbread house* on the sheet of paper Mom had taped to the refrigerator. "But you have to help me."

"Fine," I agree. "I'll help you."

Jamie grins broadly. I realize it's been a long time since I've seen my sibling smile like that—too long. "I can't wait."

"HARDER, MAN! THROW IT HARDER!"

"Quit yelling at me! You're stressing me out!"

"Oh, you're stressed out? You're not the one who has to host a corporate gala in three days!"

Setting down my pencil, I walk to the kitchen window and watch as the melodramatic Hoffman brothers—two German guys who moved in across the street with their mother last year —attempt to string fairy lights around the pine tree in their front yard. Florian Hoffman stands at the top of a wobbly-looking ladder, while his younger brother Felix tries to toss the lights to him. Ms. Hoffman sits in a rocking chair on the porch knitting a red scarf, completely oblivious to the chaos.

I crack open the window so I can hear them better just as Florian exclaims, "For God's sake, Felix! You're throwing like a child!"

"Oh, yeah? I'd like to see you do better," Felix retorts.

"I'd come down and try, but someone is afraid of heights."

"Will you boys keep it down?" Ms. Hoffman says. "You're going to wake the neighbors."

"It's three in the afternoon, Mom!" Florian yells. "No one is sleeping! No one!"

Shaking my head in amusement, I close the window and return to the table to continue filling out a character chart for *The Handmaid's Tale*. I'm partway through summarizing Offred's traits when my phone rings.

"Hey, Mom," I say. "What's up?"

"Hi, Grace." She sounds more frazzled than usual. "Are you all right having snack by yourself? Something came up, and I won't be able to make it home on time."

"Why? What happened?"

"It's your sibling. They were caught vaping in a science lab with some other kids."

"Vaping?" I repeat. "That's ridiculous. Jamie would never do something like that."

"Either way, I'm meeting with Principal Meyers at three fifteen. That's why I can't come home. If you need me to call Kevin—"

"Don't bother. I'm fine eating on my own."

"Great. I'll see you at dinnertime. I hope pasta is okay."

"Pasta is fi—" I start to say, but she ends the call before I can finish.

With a sigh, I place my phone screen-down on the table and try to resume my work. But I can't concentrate. I keep picturing Jamie in that lab taking a drag from an e-cigarette. I know vaping is common among high schoolers—hell, Chuckles even had to close the upstairs bathrooms last year because it was such a problem—however this is Jamie; the kid who months earlier was deliberating whether to get a shirt with a dinosaur or a shark on the front. This is the kid who, to this day, begs Mom to buy m&ms when we walk through the candy aisle at the grocery store. This is the kid who spent most of their birthday money on Harry Potter merch and then made me take fifty pictures of them in a Hufflepuff cardigan holding an Elder Wand for Instagram.

Like the peanut butter and pickle sandwiches Lou regularly brought for lunch in middle school, it just doesn't seem right.

I'm not hungry by three o'clock, so instead of my usual weight restoration snack of an apple with Nutella and chocolate milk, I settle for a vanilla yogurt and a handful of green grapes. I doubt Mom would approve, but I figure if I eat fewer calories now, I won't complain when she inevitably serves me too much pasta at dinner.

Then again, if what Principal Meyers says is true, I'm sure me fussing over portion sizes will be the least of her worries.

Once I'm finished with snack, I rinse out the cup and toss it in the recycle bin. I've just logged onto Gmail to organize my cluttered inbox when the door opens, and Mom and Jamie walk into the kitchen. Both of their cheeks are bright red from the blustery weather.

"Hi," I say.

"Hi," Jamie echoes flatly, whereas Mom kicks off her heels, slams a tote bag onto the counter, and leaves the room without a single word. I notice a DIY gingerbread house kit poking out from the overflowing bag.

"She seems upset," I observe. "So, is it true then? Is my sibling a stoner?"

I'm joking of course, but Jamie doesn't crack a smile. "It was one time, and it wasn't even my Juul. She's totally overreacting."

"Sit with me, okay?" I gesture to the empty chair to my left, and Jamie reluctantly takes a seat. "Why did you do it? That stuff has always grossed you out."

Jamie shrugs. "I dunno."

"Does Sara vape?"

"No." When I shoot Jamie a knowing look, they sigh. "Okay, yes, but big deal. It's just vaping, Grace. Everyone does it."

"Everyone? So, what does that make me then?"

Jamie groans. "Oh my god! I knew you were gonna be like this!"

"Like what? Jamie, I'm just looking out for you. Was Sara there too? Was it her Juul?"

"So what if it was?" Jamie asks. "Sara is the only person at Chuckles who doesn't treat me like a freak. I'm not gonna stop being friends with her because she likes to get high sometimes."

"I never said you shouldn't be friends. Look, Jamie, I know you think I'm being overprotective, but the last thing I want is for you to end up like me. I wasn't able to talk about what I was going through, and that almost cost me everything."

"I'm nothing like you," Jamie says. "I'd never hurt myself on purpose."

"But you'll let others hurt you instead?" When Jamie remains quiet, I say, "I was bullied too, you know. I get it."

"No, you don't." The sudden animosity in Jamie's voice takes me by surprise. "You don't get it, Grace, so stop pretending like you do. People don't call you names or make fun of your clothes or whisper things about you when you walk down the hall. So a couple of girls were mean to you. Big deal. It's not like the whole goddamn school has it out for you."

"You don't have to yell at me," I snap. "I'm just trying to help."

"You wanted me to talk," Jamie retorts. "Well, I'm talking. Happy?" Jamie abruptly stands up and storms out of the kitchen. Their chair wobbles for a second or two before falling onto the floor with an audible *thunk*.

I sigh. "Couldn't be happier."

LOU HAS A FAKE TREE. In all the years I've known her, it's been a tradition for her family to go to the Christmas tree lot at the Old Maple Mill in early December and pick out the best-looking evergreen to proudly display in their living room. I remember how when I was younger I used to wish I could swap her tree with mine, which was not only difficult to assemble but also shed pine needles like a Golden Retriever sheds fur.

As I grew older and learned about the environmental benefits of having a fake tree, my opinion on the matter evolved. But I continued to admire the Jackson's real tree nevertheless. It gave me a feeling of joy; the kind you only get from Christmas spirit.

"So, are you an environmentalist now?" I ask, trying to be funny.

"Nah, it was just easier to order a fake one—or at least that's what Ma said. She didn't have to spend an hour putting it up. Look." Lou holds out her hand. Several pinkish scratches are engraved into her dark skin. "They were bleeding yesterday."

"Fake trees sure are a hassle." I take a seat on the shag rug, while she adjusts her position on the couch, sinking further into the crease between the pillows. Since the heater in her bedroom is broken, we're hanging out in the living room instead. "We were supposed to put ours up yesterday, but after the whole vaping thing, no one was in the mood. Mom and Jamie are barely speaking to each other."

"Yeah?"

I nod. "Honestly, I think it's ridiculous. I get that they're mad, but is the silent treatment really necessary? It's just creating a lot of tension, and I'm so not in the mood to deal with that right now. I've got enough stress in my life as it is."

"Like what?"

"Well, for one thing—" I start to say when Mrs. Jackson walks into the room. She's wearing baggy sweats and an olive-colored headscarf, and she looks more tired than usual. I can tell by the hollowness in her eyes. I wave. "Hey."

"Hi, Grace. I didn't know you were coming over."

"You were asleep," Lou responds. "I would have told you, but I know you don't like it when I wake you up."

Mrs. Jackson places her hand on the back of the couch, as if to steady herself. "Thank you for being so considerate," she says, sounding almost sarcastic. "Grace, do you need anything? Perhaps something to drink?"

"We're fine, Ma," Lou says before I have a chance to respond. "Can you give us some privacy for once?"

Mrs. Jackson sighs. "Fine. I'll be in the kitchen."

Visibly upset, she leaves the room. I wait until she's out of earshot to say to Lou, "That was a bit harsh, don't you think?"

"Whatever. It's not my fault she's so fucking nosy."

Sensing Lou's frustration, I change the subject. "So, um, Kevin's kids are visiting on Tuesday. It was a last-minute thing—

his ex is on a business trip in Chicago. I'm just glad they won't be here for Christmas. That would mess up everything."

"Yeah, your life really sucks."

I can't tell if she's being sarcastic or genuine, so I simply shrug. "I guess. This time of year is just so weird for me. Like, I try not to think about how things were last Christmas, but sometimes, I feel like a part of me never left that dark place." I shake my head. "That probably doesn't make sense to you."

"No, it does."

I wait for her to elaborate, but after several seconds of silence, I realize that she's not going to. "Well, the best thing I can do now is try to make new memories," I say. In the reflection of a shiny red ornament dangling from the tree, I watch my lips lift into a small smile. "Better memories."

11

I don't like dressing up. Regardless of the occasion—and Mom's incessant nagging—I try to avoid wearing fancy clothing if I can. But after caving in on Thanksgiving and our next-door neighbor's daughter's bat mitzvah over the summer and a luncheon at the country club in May, Mom insisted that I look presentable for Christmas dinner. To our collective surprise, I didn't argue otherwise. Mom and I have been on relatively good terms lately, and I'd like to keep it that way—at least until the holidays are over.

What I don't understand is why we're going out to dinner in the first place. We were never the type of family who ate out on Christmas Eve. Even though Kevin's parents invited us to an upscale restaurant—and offered to pay for the meal—Mom could have said no. She knows perfectly well that if there's one thing I hate more than dressing up, it's eating out. And yet, she agreed.

While I was eager to protest, in an effort to be more cooperative, I held my tongue once again. I figured the scowl on my face conveyed as much as my words ever could.

With ten minutes until departure, I stand in front of my closet staring at my scant collection of formal clothing. After some consideration, I settle on a simple black dress that stops just above my knees. I pair the dress with black leggings and a red button-up sweater (I figure I should try to look a little festive) and head downstairs, where Jamie is snacking on an angel-shaped sugar cookie in the kitchen.

"You know we're having dinner in, like, an hour, right?" I say.

Jamie wipes their hands on their navy dress pants. "So? I'm hungry now."

"Your prerogative." I sit on the floor and pull on a pair of black kitten heels that pinch my toes. "Where are Mom and Kevin?"

"Mom is upstairs, and Kevin is scraping ice off his car. I can't believe you haven't ridden in it yet. You're gonna think it's so cool."

"We'll see about that."

Last week, Kevin came home with a brand-new Acura MDX —a Christmas gift to himself, he said. Whereas Mom and Jamie were excited for him, I thought it was a waste of money. Kevin's old car was perfectly fine; so fine, even, that when I asked him if he was going to take it to CarMax, he shook his head.

"I'll keep it around for a while. Having an extra car could come in handy someday."

"Right." As much as I hated to admit it, Mom's conservative approach to spending money was starting to rub off on me.

"Wait until you see the inside," Jamie continues. "It has a sunroof and a huge touch screen and backseat butt warmers."

"Wow, that's so cool," I respond sarcastically. "Do tell me more."

Mom, who has just entered the kitchen, frowns. "Grace, that's enough. I know you're unhappy about dinner, but could you at least try to be polite?"

"No," I say and walk outside before she can respond.

Kevin unlocks the car, and I reluctantly get in the back with Jamie. The interior smells like nail polish remover, but I know Mom will snap at me if I mention anything, so I refrain. While she and Kevin chat up front and Jamie fiddles with their butt warmer, I text Lou: *going out to dinner with the fam. fml.* I add a facepalming emoji and send the message. Then I turn off my ringer and slip my phone in the pocket of my jacket.

Giancarlo's is an elegant Italian restaurant thirty minutes from my house in the wealthiest part of town. The two-story glass building is festively decorated with twinkling fairy lights and an inordinate number of wreaths, while inside, instrumental holiday music fills the grand foyer.

"I'll take your coats," a well-dressed middle-aged woman says. Her ruby lips are pursed, as if she's eaten a lemon. It's clear that we're not her usual customers.

I hand her my navy parka, immediately feeling out of place in my forty-dollar Marshall's dress and leggings, which I'd noticed on the ride over have a small hole above my left knee. The woman hangs my parka on the same hanger as Jamie's ski jacket and Mom's grey peacoat and places them behind an expensive-looking fur coat.

"Do you have a reservation?"

"Yes, but we're waiting for two more," Kevin says.

"I'll take you to your table. No need to wait here. What's the name?"

"Osborne."

"This way." The woman grabs six menus and briskly walks through a crowded seating area to a circular table near the restrooms. I bet they're the kind with fancy soap and breath mints. "Your waiter will be with you shortly."

I sit on a cushioned chair next to Jamie and open my menu. I hadn't had time to google it ahead of time, and the calories aren't listed anywhere—not that it would matter if they were. Most of the main courses I've never heard of in my life.

Under the table, my foot rapidly taps against the wooden floor. I wish more than anything else that I was at home right now eating store-bought tofurkey and gluey mashed potatoes and watching *The Polar Express* with Mom and Jamie, like we always do on Christmas Eve. That is, aside from last year.

"Sorry we're late," Mr. Osborne says.

He and his wife claim the two empty chairs between Kevin and Jamie. Unlike the four of us, his tailored suit and her mauve cocktail dress are much more suitable for this upscale environment. Mrs. Osborne kisses Kevin's cheek.

"Isn't this nice?" she says cheerfully.

"So nice," Mom responds, but I can tell by the strain in her voice that she's regretting coming here too. "I wonder where our waiter is. I'm getting thirsty."

As if on cue, a man with gelled black hair and a thin mustache suddenly appears behind Jamie, causing my sibling to flinch. "May I offer you something to drink?"

I scan the drink options. "Just water for me."

"I'll have lemonade," Jamie says.

Mom requests a glass of red wine, while Kevin and his father split a sangria and Mrs. Osborne orders a Cosmopolitan. Once the waiter has jotted everything down, he gives us a forced smile and speed walks away.

"What's his deal?" Jamie mumbles to me.

"No idea," I respond quietly, "but this place sucks."

Jamie steals a glance at Mom. She's talking to the Osbornes, paying zero attention to either of us. "Did you see that there's a drink called One Night Stand?"

"For real?" I flip over the menu, and sure enough, Jamie is right. "I think our waiter could use one of those."

Jamie and I burst out laughing, then quickly quiet down when a woman sitting at a nearby table shoots us an icy glare. "I hope we're not here too long. I want to have time for *The Polar Express*."

"Don't worry," I say. "I'm sure we'll be out within the hour. You know Mom hates overstaying at restaurants."

But I couldn't be more wrong. It takes the waiter nearly twenty minutes to prepare our drinks, then thirty more to bring us our appetizer: a gelatinous cream-colored soup with a pungent garlicky scent and mushy corn kernels on top. I take one bite and place my spoon on my saucer. At least I can say I tried.

There are only two vegetarian options out of the twenty or so main courses, and they both look equally unappetizing. I eventually settle on the beet and goat cheese salad—without the beets and the goat cheese—and assure Mom that I'll have a bread roll with butter to supplement.

"The salad shouldn't be that small," I say. "I mean, it costs forty dollars."

Mom, who's already on her second glass of wine, holds her finger to her lips. "Don't talk about prices, okay?"

"But—"

"Please, Grace," she interrupts. "I know this isn't ideal for you, but can you at least try to keep an open mind? You might be pleasantly surprised."

"Doubt that," I say as the waiter returns with our main courses.

He places a glass bowl modestly filled with arugula, sliced

cucumbers, whole grape tomatoes, and dried cherries in front of me. I wait until everyone else has been served to drizzle half of the thick blackish dressing onto my salad and take a small bite. It's mediocre at best, but I force myself to finish the entire serving. Then I reach for a bread roll and spread a thin layer of butter on top of the soft surface.

"Pass me one of those," Jamie says.

"Jamie, you've already had three rolls," Mom interjects. "Eat your meal."

Jamie stares down at the crab cakes on their plate. So far, they've only eaten one. "But I want the bread."

Mom takes a sip from her third glass of wine. "Fine."

That's when the waiter returns to ask if we're finding everything all right. I feel him looming over me, invading my personal space, and try to make eye contact with Mom, but she's staring at the wall. I reach to the left to tap her arm, and in doing so, accidentally knock her glass, causing it to tip. Wine spills all over the fancy table cloth.

When I glance at the waiter, he has a look of contempt on his face. I can't even begin to imagine what he's thinking of us right now. "I'll get a towel," he says in a pinched voice and hurries towards the kitchen.

"I—I'm sorry," I say. I'm so overwhelmed that I'm on the verge of tears. "I didn't mean to."

Mom must finally notice my distress, because she places her hand on my arm and, slurring her words, says, "I think it's time we wrapped this up, don't you, Kevin?"

Kevin nods. "I think that's a good idea."

"But what about dessert?" Mrs. Osborne asks.

"Oh, Willa, let them go," Mr. Osborne says. Then he turns to us. "Thank you for coming. As always, it was a pleasure seeing you all."

"You too," Mom responds at the same time Kevin says, "Merry Christmas, Mom and Dad."

"Merry Christmas," Mr. Osborne echoes, smiling kindly. "Stay warm. I hear it's going to snow tomorrow."

"We will."

After a few more parting words, we follow Kevin to the foyer, where the snotty woman hands us our coats. Mom lets Jamie sit up front with Kevin on the ride home. As we're pulling out of the parking lot, she pats my shoulder.

"It's over now," she says. "You survived."

"Let's never do that again," I respond.

Mom chuckles. "I can live with that."

"Kira? Grace? Do you mind if I turn on the radio?" Kevin asks.

"Fine with me," Mom says. "Grace?"

I shrug. "Sure."

Keeping his left hand on the wheel, Kevin uses his right to press the radio icon on the complex touchscreen. He waits until we're at a red light to pull up a lengthy list of stations and selects one called Holly.

They've got cars big as bars
They've got rivers of gold

As the familiar lyrics of The Pogues' *Fairytale of New York* fills the car, I rest my head against the window and gaze at my twinkling town as we drive through it: at the lively restaurants and the old cathedral and the pitch-black movie theater where I had my first kiss. That theater was the last place I heard this song.

In the blink of an eye, I see Isaac and me standing on the concrete stairs amid the falling snow. I hear his voice, as clear as the cathedral bells; "I'm so glad I met you."

He smiled at me. And I smiled back.

It was at that moment, after months of solitude and sadness, that I remembered what happiness felt like. I was so insecure that having someone in my life who was genuinely attracted to me in spite of my flaws seemed too good to be true. But it was true—at least for a short while. And even though we ultimately broke up, the confidence and security he restored in me were everlasting.

I wish I could have told him how much he meant to me at that time. I wish I could have thanked him for giving me the greatest holiday gift of all: hope.

I WAKE up at eight o'clock on Christmas morning to the familiar aroma of waffles wafting through the house. Outside my frost-covered window, tiny snowflakes fall from the sky. I dress in the most festive clothing I own—a navy sweater with *Ho Ho No* printed on the front in red and candy cane-patterned sweatpants —and head downstairs. In the kitchen, I'm surprised to find Kevin, not Mom, pouring batter into the waffle iron at the counter. He's wearing a pink *No Bitchin' in the Kitchen* apron that one of Mom's colleagues gave her for her birthday.

"Where's Mom?" I ask.

"Sleeping," he responds. "I thought I'd get a head start on breakfast. I heard you usually have waffles on Christmas."

"Uh-huh." My eyes hone in on the gooey butter wrapper to the left of the iron. "Did you use a whole stick?"

Kevin shakes his head. "No, there was only a third left. I'm sorry about last night by the way. I know that wasn't how you wanted to spend Christmas Eve."

"It's fine," I lie.

"I still feel badly. If I'd known where my parents were taking us, I would have suggested that we go somewhere else."

"Why? Are we not classy enough for Giancarlo's? Is Ruby Tuesday more our style?" Before he can respond, the iron beeps. "Never mind. Should I go wake up Mom and Jamie?"

Kevin nods. "That would be great. How do you feel about strawberries with your waffles?"

"Strawberries are fine." As he starts to rummage through the refrigerator for the berries, I turn around and walk upstairs. Jamie is face-first on their bed buried under a thick comforter. "Jamie," I say, gently shaking my sibling's shoulders. "Jamie, wake up."

Jamie's eyes flutter open. "Is it Christmas yet?"

I smile. "Sure is. Come on, Kevin is making waffles. And there are a ton of presents under the tree."

Suddenly, Jamie is wide awake. "Sick!"

"Careful," I say as Jamie stumbles out of bed. "Go help Kevin, okay? I'm gonna wake Mom." I tousle my sibling's disheveled hair and knock on Mom's closed door. "Mom? You up?"

"One sec." A few moments later, Mom steps into the hall wearing a white turtleneck and loose-fitting jeans. She gives me a quick hug. "Merry Christmas, hon."

"Merry Christmas. I can't believe you slept later than me."

"I needed it." She sniffs the air. "Did Kevin make breakfast?"

"Waffles. I think he might have used a whole stick of butter. He says he didn't, but I'm not so sure."

"Oh, Grace. When will you start trusting people again?" When I don't respond, she sighs. "I'm sure they taste great. Kevin knows what he's doing."

"Uh-huh."

"Funny sweater by the way. I don't think I've seen it before."

"It was a Christmas gift from Lou last year," I say, "but I was in the hospital, so you probably weren't around when I wore it."

I blink, and suddenly, the miserable memories of spending Christmas in the psych ward fill my mind. I see the minimal decorations on the walls; hear the squeaky wheels of the medication cart the nurses routinely pushed around; feel the palpable dread consuming the narrow hall as the other patients and I walked to the kitchen for breakfast. I remember that we had pancakes that morning. They tasted like cardboard.

After breakfast, we were allowed to use the phone for twenty minutes. I called Lou first, then when she didn't answer, Mom. I sat on the tiled floor in my sweats with my back against the wall and listened to the sound of her heavy breathing while we tried to think of something to say.

"I'm sorry," I whispered.

"It's okay," she responded, but we both knew that it wasn't. On the contrary, "okay" couldn't be further from the truth.

"I'm glad you're home." Mom's voice jerks me back to reality.

"I'm glad I'm home too," I say.

"Mom! Grace!" Jamie bellows. "Breakfast is ready!"

Mom chuckles. "Shall we?"

I nod. "After you."

Back in the kitchen, the table is set with festive placemats and neatly folded napkins. A platter of fluffy waffles is in the center with a bowl of sliced strawberries and bottles of syrup and honey. China plates with a decorative blue trim are at our designated seats.

"Very nice," Mom remarks. She stands next to Kevin and kisses his cheek. "You did all this?"

"Merry Christmas, Kira," Kevin responds, kissing her back. "Come on, let's eat. I don't know about you, but I'm famished."

He places the iron in the sink, and the four of us gather around the table. Jamie grabs a waffle off the top of the stack and drops it onto their plate. While they pour syrup over the golden-brown exterior, Mom uses her fork to distribute the remaining three. I spoon some strawberries onto my plate and wait until Jamie is finished with the syrup to add a modest drizzle. Then I divide one of the four sections into small pieces and take a bite.

It's a good waffle—easily the best one I've had in a long time. Once again, I think about those hospital pancakes; how hard and cold they were, like they'd been sitting in a refrigerator for weeks. A chill races down my spine.

It's in the past, I remind myself. *Move on.*

But if only it was that easy to forget.

Once our stomachs are chock-full of waffles, we clear our dishes and gather in the living room to open the presents under the tree. That's another thing I missed out on last year. Other than some clothing, like the sweater, I had to wait until my first home visit at the end of January to open most of my presents. Mom hung lights around the living room and baked cookies shaped like Santa hats to celebrate, but I wasn't feeling the Christmas spirit. I wasn't feeling much of anything due to the side effects of an antidepressant I'd started that same week.

I close my eyes, and when I reopen them, Mom, Kevin, and Jamie are all staring at me. "What?" I ask.

"Your stocking." Jamie waves a green stocking with a white *G* embroidered on the front in my face. A pack of peppermint chewing gum falls out. "Whoops."

I take the stocking from Jamie and shake the rest of the contents onto the floor: a deck of cards, a small journal, new shampoo, cheap hoop earrings, purple eyeshadow, and another pack of gum. Jamie opens a bag of chocolate-covered marshmallows that was in their stocking and pops one in their mouth.

"Yum!" Jamie says as they're chewing. "Grace, do you want one?"

"I don't eat gelatin," I respond. "You're up, Jamie. Youngest first."

Jamie scans the assortment of presents and selects a rectangular package covered in a reindeer-patterned wrapping paper. They tear off the paper, revealing a purple lava lamp inside of a partially see-through box. A fifteen-dollar Marshall's tag is stuck to the back.

"Awesome!" Jamie exclaims. "Thanks, Mom!"

"My turn," I say, suddenly eager to partake in the excitement. My first present is a grey beanie and matching gloves. "Mom, these are great. And I love the color."

"I'm glad you like them," Mom says. "Although you'll probably need something a little more durable in this weather."

I glance out the window next to the tree, where the snow has escalated from a light dusting to thick, dense flakes. At least two inches already coat the ground. "No kidding."

We spend the next hour opening presents. Even Mom and Kevin get in on the action, marveling at the *Life is Good* mugs I ordered for them online and the new frying pans Jamie bought from an appliance store in the Center.

As the tree is starting to look depressingly bare, Kevin hands me a small package. "This one's from me. Open it."

"Okay, I will." I tear off the red wrapping paper to reveal a small box. Inside the box is a black key. "I don't understand . . ."

"It's the key to the Kia," he explains. "When you get your license, you're going to need a car, and I thought this might be a good one to start with."

Suddenly, I wish I could take back all the snarky remarks I made about his new car. "I, um, I don't know what to say. But thank you."

Kevin smiles. "You're welcome, Grace."

Mom reaches over my shoulder and plucks the key out of my

hands. "I'll take that. First things first, you need to sign up for a road test. Maybe now you'll actually have some incentive to see it through."

I laugh. "I think I just might."

"Is it my turn now?" Jamie whines.

"Go ahead, sweetie," Mom responds.

There are only two more gifts under the tree, and both are for Jamie. Once they've unwrapped a pair of skinny jeans and a magenta backpack, Jamie disappears into the kitchen with Kevin to make hot chocolate, leaving Mom and me to clean the messy living room.

I'm picking crumpled wrapping paper up off the needle-covered floor when my phone buzzes. I stuff the paper in the recycle bin and check iMessage. Lou texts: *can i see u? i need to talk.*

Grace: sure. do u want me to come over?

Lou: no meet me at the end of ur block. and dress warmly.

Grace: ok ...

Lou: see u in 10.

"Mom, I'm going to hang out with Lou," I say.

"Okay. Do you need me to drive you to her house?"

"No, she wants to meet outside for some reason." I shrug. "Whatever. Is the winter clothing in the closet or the basement?"

"Closet. Have fun with Lou."

I find a large box labeled *SNOW CLOTHES* in the hallway closet and bundle up in a silver ski jacket, wool gloves, and a black hat. I pull on fleece socks and a brand-new pair of boots, but I don't bother with waterproof pants. It's not like we're going sledding.

Despite the temperature having risen above thirty-two degrees, it's still snowing when I step outside. I stand at the bottom of the driveway and bounce up and down to keep warm. Two minutes later, I see Lou, dressed in a vibrant pink parka and matching waterproof pants, trekking towards me.

"Are you gonna tell me what we're doing?" I ask. "Because it's, like, really cold out here."

"Come with me."

She quickens her pace, and I hurry to keep up. I realize that my boots are a size too big, but by then, we're already nearing the end of the block. Just when I think we're going to turn onto the main road, Lou continues straight and cuts across someone's lawn to reach the white picket fence encircling the golf course.

"Um, Lou? This is private property." I point at a faded metal sign that reads *No Trespassing* in capital letters.

"It's Christmas. You think anyone's gonna care?" Before I can respond, she ducks through the space between the second and third slat. "Come on."

With a sigh, I hop the fence and follow Lou onto the vacant golf course. The snow feels heavier than it did on the street as I trudge after her. She stops by a patch of evergreen trees and places her hands on her knees, gasping for breath.

"Now can you tell me why we're here?" I ask. I can feel the wet snow starting to seep through my jeans.

Lou lays down on the snowy ground and spreads her arm above her head, as if she's making a snow angel. She closes her eyes for a few seconds, and when she opens them, they're suspiciously wet. "I just needed to get away. Sit with me?"

Surrendering to the cold, I take a seat beside her and clutch my legs to my chest. "Is something wrong?" When she doesn't respond, I try again. "You can tell me, Lou. I'm here for you."

"Are you though?"

"What does that mean?"

"Don't get mad, but sometimes, I feel like you get so caught up in your own issues that they're all you can focus on. And I know you're dealing with a lot right now, so I understand why you do that, and of course I want to help you, but I'm dealing with shit too, and when everything is always about you, Grace, I can't talk about my problems because you don't think they're as important as yours or you just don't want to hear them."

"That's not true," I say. "When have I ever said your problems aren't important? Also, I listen to you complain all the time about how annoying your mom is and how you hate your job and—"

"I got fired from my job on Monday," she interrupts.

"What?"

"I was tired and hungover from a party I went to over the weekend, so when I got to work and realized I couldn't function, I took a nap under a desk in the break room. I just wish I'd remembered to set an alarm. My boss was pissed when he found out I'd been sleeping on the job for two hours and fired me. I was going to tell you sooner, but you were upset about what happened with Jamie, so I never got the chance to." Lou gazes at the sky, blinking tears from her eyes. "Then Ma wasn't feeling well last night, and we had to take her to the hospital. I tried to call you, but you didn't answer. I know you'd gone out to eat, and that makes you stressed, but I really needed your support. I needed you."

Part of me is tempted to deny Lou's accusations, however when I look at her, at the sadness in her eyes and the way her lower lip trembles when she speaks, I can't bring myself to do so. Maybe she has a point. Maybe I haven't been as good of a friend as I should be.

I hesitantly place my hand on Lou's shoulder. "I'm sorry."

With her gaze still trained on the sky, she nods. "Thanks."

"So, um . . . what now?"

"Now we sit," she says.

Silence settles between us as the snow continues to fall. Even though my jeans are soaked and I can't feel my face, I don't move. I stay by her side, my hand resting on the sleeve of her jacket, and stare straight ahead at the steep hills we used to sled down when we were younger. I can see us as plain as day with our cheek's bright red from the harsh wind and our teeth cold from smiling so widely. I can hear our rowdy laughter as we raced each other down the slope, eager to be the first one to reach the bottom. More often than not, Lou would win. But we both knew it was only because she had a better sled.

Then I blink, and the hills are empty again. I slowly exhale and watch my breath disappear into the wintry air. Next to me, Lou has started to cry; quietly, but in the stillness of our surroundings, I hear every tear she sheds. I wish there was something I could say to make her pain go away—at least for the moment—but I can't find the right words.

So, I say nothing at all.

12

As far as I'm concerned, the saddest time of the year is after the holidays. From the evergreen trees lying lifelessly on the roadsides to shop owners disassembling storefront decorations to the sudden absence of generosity and cordiality to the stress of the impending new year, the end of December is one big downer.

To make matters worse, an envelope addressed to Jamie and me arrives in the mail three days after Christmas. There's no return address, but I don't have to open it to know who the sender is. I recognize Dad's sloppy handwriting immediately.

"So, is this, like, a tradition now?" I ask Mom.

Dad had pulled the same stunt last Christmas after seven years with zero communication. I was a lot more fragile then, so the memories his gesture evoked, regardless of his intentions behind it, were so triggering that I came dangerously close to relapsing. I was readmitted to the hospital that same day.

Although I'm more capable of handling triggers now, my hands are still shaking as I carefully open the seal. Inside is a fifty-dollar bill—thirty dollars more than last time—and a card with two cartoon penguins in Santa hats on the front.

"You don't have to do this," Mom says.

"I know." I hand Jamie the money, take a deep breath, and read out loud, "Dearest Gracie and Jamison, I hope this finds you well. As another new year approaches, I find myself thinking about the two of you. Gracie, I imagine that this is an exciting time for you. You must be looking forward to graduating from high school and beginning this new chapter in your young life. Wherever your future takes you, I hope it is bright and opportunistic. And Jamison, my dear son, I cannot believe how quickly you're growing up. Thirteen is a challenging age, but I'm confident that it will serve you well. I wish you both all the best. Merry Christmas – Dad."

When I'm finished reading, I close the card and glance up. Both Mom and Jamie are watching me with worried looks on their faces. I feel their eyes following me as I walk to the recycle bin in the corner of the kitchen and drop the note on top of an empty cereal box.

"Screw you, Dad," I say and kick the bin.

"Grace—" Mom starts to say, but I interrupt her.

"It's okay, Mom. He can do what he wants. I don't care."

What once would have been a total lie now holds some truth to it. There's still a part of me that misses my father—there probably always will be—yet at the same time, I could care less for his pathetic attempts to reconnect with me. The more years go by, the more I realize that I'm not to blame for his decision to leave us. That's on him. All the hurt and disruption he caused is on him. He's the perpetrator in this situation, whereas I'm merely a witness to his crimes.

Nevertheless, I continue to think about the card to an unhealthy extent over the next few days. I don't tell Mom, as I know it'll only worry her, but the second Anna asks me how I am during our session on Friday, the truth comes spilling out.

"I can't imagine how challenging this is for you," Anna says once I'm finished venting. "That being said, you seem to be handling it well. I don't think you would have been able to demonstrate this level of maturity when I met you."

"I'm trying not to let things bother me as much," I say. "I can get in my head sometimes, and, well, you know how that goes."

Anna nods. "Yes, I do."

"Plus, the more preoccupied I am with my problems, the less time and patience I have for other people. That's what Lou said anyway."

"She did?"

"Uh-huh. I can see her point, but it still sucked to hear that. So, I've decided that I'm gonna try to be a better friend to her—and just a better person in general. It's my New Year's resolution."

"Have you told her that?"

"No, but I might the next time I see her. She's in New Orleans visiting her grandparents. She'll be there for another week. I would be jealous of her, but I know how much she hates them."

"Why does she hate them?"

"Well, for starters, they're super religious. Their house literally looks like a church. Check this out." I open my phone and show Anna a picture Lou had sent me of a life-sized Jesus statue in her grandparent's foyer. "Creepy, right? And then there's the fact that they're lowkey homophobes."

"Now I understand," Anna says. "That must be hard for her."

I glance at the photo again, then turn off my phone. "It is."

"And how is everything with your family?"

"Okay, I guess. Mom keeps saying I need to get out of the

house more. The problem is, there's nothing to do. I don't have a job, I'm not playing sports—I certainly don't want to come back to school for a stupid club. If you've got any suggestions, I'm listening."

Anna considers this. "Do you know Miss Kerr?"

"The teen librarian?" I nod. "What about her?"

"She oversees a writing group for high schoolers every other Wednesday afternoon. In the past, I've had clients who were part of the group, and they had wonderful things to say about it. I know you enjoy writing, so this could be something interesting —and social—for you to do."

"I dunno," I say. "A writing group sounds kind of lame."

"You won't know until you try," Anna responds. "How about you at least email Miss Kerr to see about joining? If you have questions, I'm sure she'd be happy to answer them. She's a lovely woman."

"I know."

When I was in middle school, I was obsessed with reading. I could go through two, sometimes three books a week. Mom was renovating the kitchen at that time and didn't feel comfortable with me being home alone with the workers, so I spent many afternoons at the library. Miss Kerr, who knew how much I loved to read, would often recommend new books for me to try. After I finished each one, I'd meet her in the Teen Room, and we'd share our thoughts on it. She was so impressed with my thoughtful critiques, she said I could be a professional book critic. I told her I'd rather be a librarian.

All of that changed when I started high school. Between my rigorous soccer schedule and my increased workload, I didn't have the time or energy for reading. I stopped visiting the library other than to check out an occasional DVD or use the colored printer. Then Mom finally signed us up for a Netflix subscription, and I became hooked on *Stranger Things, Black Mirror, Schitt's Creek, How to Get Away with Murder*—every time I finished one show, a new season or series had been released. It was endless, mindless entertainment. And, like most people, I couldn't get enough.

There wasn't a lot of access to streaming services at the Center for Healthy Living. In fact, the only times we were allowed to watch television was on weekend mornings, so on weekdays, I had little to do to keep busy between groups. When I complained to my therapist about how bored I was, she gave me a notebook and suggested that I write. I was reluctant at first, but once I sat down at the kitchen table and put my pencil to the paper, I couldn't stop.

Even though I was genuinely trying to be more transparent with my treatment team, I was still reluctant to talk about certain things. But with writing, I didn't have to hold back. It was a cathartic release for the thoughts I was too ashamed to share. It was a coping mechanism that didn't involve harming my body or my mind. To an extent, it was my voice.

Most of the short stories and poems I wrote at that time ended up at the bottom of the recycle bin in the kitchen. But not all of them. I still have that notebook on my bookshelf tucked between a book of crossword puzzles and a battered *Harry Potter and the Sorcerer's Stone*. I haven't looked at it since I discharged, but then, I haven't gotten rid of it either.

Other than my summer program and several Voices assignments, I've done very little writing of my own this past year. Perhaps it wouldn't be such a bad thing to pick it up again. With so much confusion and uncertainty in my life, revisiting a beloved hobby might do me some good.

"All right," I say. "I'll give it a try."

WE'RE SUPPOSED to return to school on Monday, but because of yet another brutal snowstorm, it's canceled the morning of. The same thing happens on Tuesday. On Wednesday, despite most of the snow having melted, the roads are still icy, so the town issues a ninety-minute delay.

Mom tries to act unbothered by this, but I can tell she's annoyed that she has to stay home and drive Jamie and me to school. The scowl on her face speaks volumes to her frustration.

"Have you looked into scheduling a road test yet?" she asks as we eat breakfast. "Or lessons?"

I shake my head. "I'm waiting until the weather gets better to commit to anything."

"You'll need to learn how to drive in bad weather at some point, Grace," she responds. "Like it or not, you do live in New England."

"And who's fault is that?" I swallow my last spoonful of soggy Special K flakes and stand up. "I'm gonna get dressed. What time do we have to leave?"

"Nine fifteen at the latest. Tell Jamie to get up, or else we're leaving without him."

I don't bother to correct her pronouns. "Okay." With one foot out of the kitchen, I turn around and say, "I will schedule the test. I promise."

"You'll just do it on your own time," she says.

I'm not sure if she's being sarcastic or not, so I merely nod and walk away. In my room, I dress warmly in a grey sweater Mom bought me for Christmas and fleece-lined leggings, and then I head to the bathroom to comb my hair and apply mascara to my stubby eyelashes. Before I return to the kitchen, I open Jamie's door and flick their forehead.

"Rise and shine, sleepyhead."

"Ouch! What the hell, Grace?"

Biting my lip to keep from laughing, I close the door and dash downstairs. "Jamie's up," I tell Mom as I rummage through the snack cabinet for a Clif Bar. "Where are all the Chocolate Chip?"

"Out. I'll pick up more when they go on sale."

"Fine. I'll take Brownie then." I've just placed the bar in the front pocket of my bookbag when Jamie ambles into the kitchen, still in their pajamas. "G'morning."

Jamie scowls. "My head hurts."

"Take an ibuprofen," Mom says, checking her phone for the umpteenth time. "You've got ten minutes, Jamie. Get a move on."

Jamie takes a new box of Cheerios out of the cereal cabinet and rips open the seal on the plastic bag, causing cereal to spill all over the counter. "Whoops."

Mom throws up her hands in exasperation. "That's it. I'm waiting outside."

It takes Jamie five minutes to eat their cereal, then another ten to dress and groom. They throw on a thin fleece jacket and turquoise gloves, while I bundle up in my navy parka and black hat and follow them outside. Mom is sitting in the car with her arms crossed and her lips pursed.

"You're late."

"Sorry, we—" I start to say but she interrupts me.

"Which means I'm late too." She turns on the car and quickly backs out of the driveway. "This goddamn weather is the worst!"

I glance at the speedometer: she's going nearly fifty on a thirty-miles-per-hour street. "You're driving like Kevin," I joke, trying to lighten the mood.

It doesn't work. Now Mom's hands are clenching the steering wheel, her knuckles as white as the snow. The last thing I want to do is exacerbate an already tense situation, so I simply turn up my heater and stare out the window at the bleak wintry landscape.

We arrive at school with one minute to spare and hurry inside. While Jamie heads to American history, I dash downstairs to the G-Wing and slip inside Voices. The floor is a mess of slush and muddy footprints. Even Miss Bacon, who always wears heels, has on a pair of brown snow boots.

Mom was right about one thing: this weather truly is the worst.

As if the morning wasn't already stressful enough, midterms are in less than two weeks. With two fewer days to prepare us, my teachers are in overdrive. Even Mr. McCarthy, who's one of the most laidback people I know, seems abnormally frazzled as he distributes thick review packets.

I flip through the eight double-sided pages, which are full of bulleted notes about the six units we've covered this semester, and sigh. Just when I thought school couldn't be more of a headache, I was sadly mistaken.

Mom picks me up at noon for lunch, and afterward, she drives back to work—but not before complaining about a disastrous staff meeting and a new coworker who keeps stealing her cranberry seltzer from the refrigerator. I can tell she's having a bad day, so I try to sympathize, all the while thinking about the staggering amount of homework I have to do before Kevin takes me to my first writing group meeting at five o'clock.

With the sound of my next-door neighbor's snowblower whirring outside the window, I close the door to my room, sit down at my desk, and open my statistics review packet.

1. Suppose the average score on a national test is 600 with a standard deviation of 50. If each score is increased by 10, what are the new mean and standard deviation?

a. 600, 50

b. 600, 60

c. 610, 50

d. 610, 60

"Dammit," I say under my breath. Why can I never remember standard deviation?

I'm somewhat confident that the answer is either *c* or *d*, so I take an educated guess and circle *c*. I make a mental note to schedule a meeting with Mrs. Hall next week. For the past few months, I've been routinely seeing her before each test to review the material. While missing my free period isn't preferable, with a current grade of eighty-eight, it's well worth it.

I finish the assigned portion of the packet around three and take a break to make a snack. With a bowl of Goldfish and chocolate chips in my hands, I return to my room and open my computer, figuring I should do some writing in preparation for the group. I browse through old files under *Documents* and select one titled *Inside My Plastic Skin*. A short story I started working on about a year ago, *Inside My Plastic Skin* follows a shy fourteen-year-old girl who feels lost and invisible in a predominately extroverted society. Kind of like how I felt at that age.

I spend thirty minutes revising the few sections I'd previously written and another forty adding to a scene where the protagonist eats lunch alone in the bathroom. I'm just getting to the climax of the story when my phone buzzes.

Kevin: headed out. be there in 15.

After sending him a thumbs up, I set aside my phone and wrap up the paragraph I was working on. Then I save the document and turn off my computer. Miss Kerr recommended in her email that I bring a notebook with me, so I find a blank journal on my bookshelf, stuff it in my bag, and head downstairs. I'm wriggling into my parka when Kevin texts me again: *here.*

Sure enough, when I walk outside, he's waiting curbside in his car. No sooner have I gotten in and buckled my seatbelt that he shifts gears and takes off down the street.

We drive in silence for a couple of minutes until Kevin breaks the ice. "So, what's this group you're going to?"

"It's for writing. My therapist recommended it. It seems kind of lame, but I figured I might as well try. It's not like I have anything better to do."

Kevin isn't listening to me; he's staring at the slow-moving car in front of us with an irritated look on his face. And when the car abruptly stops at a yellow light, he pounds the dashboard with his fist. "Dammit! I shouldn't have gone down Main Street. If this traffic doesn't let up, I'm going to be late for my meeting."

"I wish I hadn't stopped taking lessons," I say. "If I'd stuck with them for a few more months, I'd have my license now, and you wouldn't have to drive me everywhere."

"Why did you stop?" he asks.

"Winter." I laugh dryly. "I don't have the motivation to do anything when it's cold. Plus, my driving instructor was a dick. He'd yell at me for being a bad driver, and then that would make me anxious, so I'd drive even worse."

"Sounds like you need a new instructor." A pickup truck swerving out of a parking lot cuts off Kevin, and he honks. "Promise me you won't do that when you have your license."

Up ahead, the truck has just run a red light, eliciting honks from two more drivers. "I won't."

Ten minutes later, when we finally reach the library, Kevin's face is bright red with frustration. "Your mom will pick you up at six, all right?" Even his voice is sharper than usual.

"Uh-huh. Thanks for the ride."

I close the door, and he merges back onto the main road behind a school bus. I adjust my grey beanie so it fully covers both of my ears and pat my pockets to make sure I didn't leave my phone with Kevin. Then I head up a cobblestone pathway, passing an old fountain that only spouts water during the summer, and enter through a set of automatic double doors.

The library is busy at this time of the day with visitors wandering through the endless aisles of books and movies and waiting in the check-out line. In the computer lab, a tired-looking teenager sits behind the Staff desk monitoring the patrons, while on the other side, well-dressed adults file out of the Conference Room. I glance at the sign taped to the door: *Chamber of Commerce Meeting 1/6 3:30-5:00*

Next to the Conference Room, the door to the Teen Room is wide open. When I walk inside, five teenagers are sitting around a rectangular table near the back. Miss Kerr, who's at the head of the table, flashes me a kind smile.

"Come on in, Grace."

I close the door behind me and hesitantly take a seat next to a girl with purple hair and circular glasses that are too large for her narrow face. She holds a cat-patterned notebook in one hand and a candy cane pencil in the other. Her fingernails are all painted a different neon color.

"Hi," I say.

"Hi," she echoes quietly.

"Let's introduce ourselves," Miss Kerr suggests. "Kinsey, you can start."

"Oh, um, hi again," Kinsey says. "I'm Kinsey. Obviously." As she talks, she picks at the bright green polish on her left thumbnail. "I'm seventeen. I go to Riverside. I like writing. Um . . . that's about it."

"Andrew," says the boy to Kinsey's right. He's tall and lanky with unkempt red hair and clear blue eyes. "I'm sixteen. I go to Oakdale, and I also like writing, specifically dystopian. I'm working on a novel called *When the Dust Settles*. It's about two brothers who survive an apocalypse and have to work together with the other survivors to escape the zombies. One of the brothers is psychic and can predict the future—but only in his dreams."

Even though the premise sounds like a rip-off of *Supernatural* and *The Walking Dead*, I pretend that I'm intrigued. "Is it, like, a chapter book?"

Andrew nods. "I just got to forty thousand words."

Now that's impressive. "Nice."

The other two members are Tasha, a smiley junior with curly hair and sparkly cat-eye glasses, and Noel, a brooding freshman with a black fringe and piercing blue eyes. Whereas Tasha's skin is chocolate-colored, Noel is as pale as a ghost.

"Poetry is my forte," Tasha says. "I have at least ten journals at home that are filled with poems. Rhyming poems are the best in my opinion."

"Nah, free verse is obviously superior," Noel disagrees, twisting a black stud in his left earlobe. "Anyone can rhyme, but it takes real talent to write something great without rules or restrictions."

"Oh, does it?" Tasha responds sarcastically. "Does it really?"

Kinsey rolls her eyes. "Not this again."

"Kinsey is right," Miss Kerr says. "We're all entitled to our own opinions. Grace, what's your favorite genre of writing?"

"I guess realistic fiction," I say. "I haven't been writing for that long though, so I'm not entirely sure."

"That's perfectly fine," she responds. "We all start somewhere."

"I started with fanfiction," Kinsey chips in, "and now I'm writing fantasy stories with my own made-up characters. I don't have to rely on ships to inspire my creative process anymore." For the first time since I met her, she raises her head and looks me in the eyes. "You'll get there."

"Thanks," I say.

After a few more minutes of small talk, Miss Kerr announces that it's time for a "quick write." She distributes golf pencils to those of us who need them and, inspired by our conversation, asks us to describe the moment when we discovered our love for writing.

"You're not required to share, Grace," she says, as if she can read my mind. "Only if you want to. Everyone else, you know the drill. We'll regroup in ten minutes."

Other than the hum from a nearby radiator, the room is silent as we open our notebooks and start to write. I feel like I'm in Voices staring at a blank sheet of paper with a thousand thoughts racing through my mind. I can't remember when, exactly, I realized I liked writing. In treatment, it was primarily a way to pass the time; during my summer program, it was another extracurricular to add to my resume. I didn't just wake up one morning and think, *I want to be a writer*. Like most things in my life, it was a process.

So that's what I write about: my long and complicated journey to find something that I enjoyed; something that gave me hope for the future. I finish thirty seconds before Miss Kerr calls time and close my notebook.

"Would anyone like to share?" she asks.

"I would," Tasha says.

We listen to Tasha read about a research paper she wrote as a freshman about Sylvia Plath and how learning about the poet inspired her to begin writing poetry of her own. When she's finished, Noel takes his turn. His piece is darker than Tasha's, describing a time in middle school when he felt lost and hopeless.

"I thought I had nothing to live for," Noel says, "and then I discovered writing. Writing saved me. I know that sounds dramatic, but it did."

Miss Kerr smiles. "That doesn't sound dramatic, Noel. As a matter of fact, creative outlets like writing help many people overcome adversity. Thank you for sharing."

Noel goes back to twisting his stud. "Okay."

"Kinsey? Andrew? Grace? Do any of you want to share?" When we shake our heads, she says, "All right then. Before we get started on our discussion, I brought snacks." She reaches behind her and transfers a carton of apple juice and a plate of assorted cookies from a small desk to the table. "Enjoy!"

While the others eagerly grab a cookie and pour the juice into tiny Dixie cups, my hands remain folded on top of my notebook. Had I known there would be food, I would have had a lighter snack at home. But I can't turn back time, and I sincerely doubt Mom will let me eat a smaller dinner, so I decide to skip the cookies and juice altogether. I'll know better next time.

Once the excitement over the food has subsided, Miss Kerr lets us deviate from writing and instead talk about whatever we want to. For a solid thirty minutes, we share our favorite television shows and complain about school and even delve into more sensitive topics, like Noel coming out as bisexual and Tasha finding out that her parents are getting divorced.

To an extent, this open dialogue reminds me of the conversations I'd have during group therapy sessions at CHL. Although I'm pretty sure that nobody here has an eating disorder, the overall vibe is equally as, if not more, supportive. The only difference is that I'm not being forced to participate. Instead, I can sit back and listen to them offer encouragement without the added pressure of having to introduce suggestions or share my personal struggles. Just the way I like it.

Miss Kerr waits until exactly six o'clock to announce that we're out of time. "I'll see you in two weeks," she says. "Since it's the end of the month, if you want to bring something to workshop, you may."

"I'm totally bringing my vampire story," Kinsey says to Andrew.

Andrew grins. "Can't wait."

I follow Kinsey and Andrew to the front of the library. While he vanishes through the automatic doors, Kinsey remains inside and perches on a wooden bench with her elbows resting on her knees.

"Are you waiting for someone too?" I ask.

"My boyfriend," Kinsey says casually. "Oh, there he is." She zips her parka up to her chin and briskly walks towards a shabby grey sedan parked next to the curb. As she's getting in the car, my phone buzzes.

Mom: running late. be there in five.

With some time to kill, I open my contacts and click on Lou's number. I hold my phone to my ear and wait for her to respond.

"Hey, Grace. What's up?"

"I just got out of my writing group."

"Oh, yeah?" she says, and I can tell she's stifling a laugh. "On a scale of one to ten, how lame was it?"

"Pretty lame," I respond. "I think I'm gonna go back though. It could be fun."

"Whatever you say, nerd."

"And, how are you?" I ask.

"I'm all right."

"You sure?"

"Yes, Grace, I'm sure."

"Okay, well, you know you can tell me if something is up."

"The only thing that's up is my weight," she says. "I ate so much food at my gramma's house. I must have gained, like, twenty pounds in a week."

"That's impossible, Lou."

"You know what I mean. For the next five days, carbohydrates are off-limits. Cassie is coming home on the seventh, and I can't look like a fucking whale when I see her."

I'm about to respond when I notice Mom's car pull into a vacant spot. "I gotta go. My mom is here. Good luck with the carb thing, I guess."

"Thanks, girl. I'm gonna need it. Later."

"Bye." I slip my phone in my pocket and venture outside, shivering in the icy wind. "Why does it have to be so damn cold?"

"Hello to you too," Mom says. "How was the group?"

"Fine."

"And by 'fine' you mean . . ."

"Okay. Good." When she continues to stare inquisitively at me, I say, "I want to keep going if that's what you're asking."

"That's great, hon. I'm glad you gave it a chance."

"That doesn't mean I'm gonna stick with it—"

"Of course not."

"—but it's not terrible, so maybe."

Mom smiles. "I'll settle for maybe."

She turns on the radio and switches from the news to our favorite alternative station. The chorus of Coldplay's *Fix You* plays through the speakers. Mom begins to sing along.

"Lights will guide you home. And ignite your—"

"Don't," I say.

"Sorry."

I raise the volume on the radio and stare out the window, resting my forehead against the chilly glass as we drive through the busy Center. Through the front window of a pizzeria, I notice several girls on this year's Varsity soccer team sitting around a circular table. That could have been me, I realize. If it weren't for my illness, I could be at that table right now laughing with my teammates over a slice of cheese pizza. I could be normal.

In a whisper so soft that only I can hear it, I part my lips and sing, "*And I will try to fix you.*"

13

I'm dashing down the field; my cleats sinking into the muddy grass, my ponytail whacking against the back of my neck, and my knees covered with grass stains from a slide tackle I made during the first half. My skin is slick with sweat and my quads ache from the nonstop running, yet I'm smiling nevertheless.

"Go, Grace!" Mom's voice cheers.

She must raise her arm because the camera shakes violently. It briefly tilts towards the blinding sun, then refocuses on the match right as I steal the ball from a midfielder. I pass to my teammate, and a few dribbles later, she passes it back to me. Near Mom, some man is losing his mind.

"Stop the ball, Jenny! Stop the ball!"

"What are you watching?" Mom asks.

When I look up from my computer, she's standing in the kitchen doorway. "Just an old soccer video."

Mom walks behind me and peers over my shoulder at the screen. "This is old. When did I film this; ninth grade?"

"Something like that." I pause the video on a shot of me pivoting around a defender. "My hair was so long then. I wasn't as tall either."

"Five-eight isn't that tall," Mom says.

"Five-nine," I correct. "Anna measured me last week."

"So, does that mean your weight range changed too? Because when you grow, you're supposed to gain five—"

"I'm not having this conversation," I interrupt. I click out of the video player and open Chrome. "I should be studying for my midterms anyway, so if you don't mind . . ."

Mom takes the hint. "All right. Good luck with studying."

"Thanks," I say. "I'm gonna need it."

Of my five classes, I decide to start with Voices, since it's the one I've made the least amount of progress on. Before winter break, Miss Bacon had us compile a list of things, including hobbies, people, and places, that were important to us, but only last week did she specify why: we're writing an encomium. Like most of the class, I had no idea what an encomium was until she explained that it's a written piece that praises someone or something.

"Take out your lists," she instructed, "so you can choose your topic."

I found my list, which comprised of four bullet points on a green sticky note, in the front pocket of my bookbag and reread it:

- *California*
- *friends*
- *money*
- *writing*

After some consideration—and by that I mean five seconds

of determining which topic would be the easiest to write about
—I chose writing. Now, as I stare at the blinking cursor on the
screen, trying to come up with a viable introduction, second
thoughts start to creep into my mind. Then I have an idea.

*There are some things about ourselves that we know without a
doubt. Then, there are some things that we discover with time. For me,
writing was one of them. I've always been creative. As a kid, I had an
active imagination and loved to create make-believe stories in my head.
It wasn't until recently that I began to put those stories onto paper,
launching a journey of introspection and self-discovry.*

"Grace? When do you want to have snack?"

"One sec." I fix the spelling for "discovery" and title my
document *Encomium Draft*. "Now is good."

Mom walks into the kitchen and opens a Tupperware
container on the countertop. "There were chocolate chip
cookies left over from a staff meeting this morning. Do you want
to have a couple with me?"

I shrug. "I guess."

Mom takes four cookies out of the container and places two
on a napkin and the other two on a small plate. She hands me
the plate and starts to prepare a mug of tea while I stare skeptically at our snacks.

"Um, Mom? How come you gave me the biggest cookies?"

"Huh?"

"The cookies," I reiterate. "Mine are a lot bigger than yours."

"Grace, what are you talking about? They look the same
to me."

"Then you won't mind if we switch." I try to grab her napkin,
but she intercepts it before I'm able to.

"Stop it. You're being ridiculous."

"Fine. I'll just get new ones then."

I open the container and select the two smallest cookies of

the four remaining. Then I close the lid, pour myself a glass of water, and sit at the table while Mom remains at the counter with a look of disapproval on her face.

After what seems like an eternity of silence, she finally joins me. She tears off a chunk of one of the cookies and pops it in her mouth, still noticeably upset as she chews. I'm about to take a bite too when the door opens and Jamie barrels through.

"Hi, hon," Mom says. "How was school?"

In response, Jamie takes off their magenta backpack and hurls it at the wall. "Why'd you have to get me this stupid backpack?" my sibling demands angrily. "Why couldn't you have just gotten a normal color like blue or green?"

"Jamie, I—"

"I bet you had to look in the girl's section to find pink," Jamie interrupts. "Because I'm such a girl, isn't that right? You might as well have bought me a fucking dress while you were at it."

Before Mom has a chance to respond, Jamie storms out of the kitchen. A few seconds later, we hear footsteps dashing upstairs, then a door slam, then silence.

"What just happened?" I ask.

Mom takes a sip of her tea and sighs. "Jamie was ecstatic about that backpack. They couldn't wait to wear it to school." Another sigh escapes her lips. "I wish I understood why kids are so cruel to each other. What kind of failed parenting raises a child to believe that it's okay to hurt someone just because they're different than you?"

I'm not sure how to respond, so I take a bite of my cookie. It's much richer than the ones Mom makes, no doubt loaded with calories and fat. When I glance at her, her eyes are trained on Jamie's backpack. She doesn't seem sad or even upset anymore; instead, she just looks tired.

"Hey, Mom? Are you all right?"

"I'm fine," she responds. "Eat your cookies."

"I don't like them," I say. "I think I'm gonna get chips."

"So, after all that fuss about the size, you're not even going to eat them?" She shakes her head. "Whatever, Grace. Do as you please."

I feel her watching me as I open the snack cabinet and rummage through the selection of chips until I find a bag of veggie straws. As I'm shaking some into a bowl, I say, "I'm glad you raised us differently, Mom. You know, to be tolerant and open-minded and all that."

"Thank you," she responds quietly.

I return the bag to the cabinet, lean against the counter, and chomp on my veggie straws as she eats her cookies, neither of us speaking. Finally, I break the silence. "Do you want me to check on Jamie?"

Mom nods. "If you wouldn't mind."

I place the bowl in the sink and head upstairs. I'm about to knock on Jamie's door when I hear my sibling talking to someone on the phone. Unable to contain my curiosity, I press my ear against the thin wood and listen in on their conversation.

"It's such bullshit," Jamie says. "Why should I get a lunch detention when I didn't do anything wrong?" Jamie pauses. "No, the worst part was having to listen to Ms. Salvador go on and on about treating each other with respect and kindness when she's always talking shit about other teachers. Hypocritical bitch." Another pause, this one longer than the first. "I'm starting to feel like I'm in a cage, Sara. Do you remember *The Maze Runner*? Yeah, that's what it feels like at school." Sara must say something funny because Jamie chuckles. "I gotta go. My sister is standing outside my door. Bye."

Dammit. With a sigh, I enter Jamie's room and lean against

my sibling's cluttered desk. Next to their laptop, the lava lamp Mom bought them for Christmas is still in its package, unopened.

"How did you know?" I ask.

Jamie, who's sitting cross-legged on the bed, says, "I could see your feet. Next time you want to eavesdrop, don't wear bright purple socks."

"I didn't mean to eaves—" I start to say when Jamie interrupts me.

"It's fine, Grace. Just don't tell Mom about the detention, all right?"

"I wasn't going to," I assure them. "So, what happened anyway? Was it that guy again—Jack something?"

"Jack Ackerman?" Jamie nods. "I don't know what his problem is. For some reason, he really has it out for me."

"You should tell someone," I say. "Like a teacher or a guidance counselor."

Jamie shakes their head. "No way. That would only make it worse. Plus, it's not even that bad. I can handle him."

"Oh, yeah? And how's that going?" I ask sarcastically.

"Like you should talk," Jamie retorts. "I'm fine. Really."

I stare at my sibling; at the sadness and fear in their hazel eyes. "I don't know if I believe you."

Jamie averts their gaze to the floor. "Can you leave? I want to be alone right now."

I'm not in the mood to argue with them, so I merely nod. "Okay. See you at dinner."

Turning my back on Jamie, I walk into the hall and close the door behind me. As I stand at the top of the staircase, feeling more exhausted than I have in a while, I listen to the faint hum of the television downstairs and the periodic beeping of a dying smoke detector in Mom's office. Then I hear another sound; the high-pitched wail of Jamie's clarinet playing a somber tune.

I remember a time, not too long ago, when Jamie would practice the clarinet every afternoon—sometimes in the evenings as well. Now I can't recall the last time I heard its pretty sound.

I stay where I am, frozen like a statue, for a minute or two and just listen to the song. And when it's over, when the house is mostly quiet again, I turn around and head downstairs, not once looking back.

I COULD USE a day at the spa. That's the first thought that crosses my mind when Kevin gives Mom an early Valentine's Day gift at dinner: vouchers to Head, Shoulders, Knees, and Toes, a spa and ski resort in eastern Connecticut. Mom, who has just finished eating her spaghetti and sauce, places her hand on top of Kevin's.

"Thank you. You didn't have to."

Kevin smiles. "You deserve it."

"When can we go?" Jamie asks.

"Sorry, Jamie. These vouchers are just for your mom and me." When Jamie scowls, he says, "I'll tell you what; next week, I'll take you and Grace to get a manicure. There's this nail salon in the Center that my daughters love. How does that sound?"

Jamie sighs. "Fine."

"Grace?"

Even though I'm also disappointed that I won't be going to the spa, I shrug it off. "Okay. Count me in."

"I was thinking that since Valentine's Day is on Sunday, we

can go then," Kevin says to Mom. "But if that doesn't work for you, we'll find another time."

"Sunday sounds great," Mom responds. "Grace, do you think you can hold down the fort for a day?"

"As long as you don't say 'hold down the fort,' then sure."

Mom laughs. "Deal."

So, at two o'clock on Sunday afternoon, Mom and Kevin get in Kevin's car to drive to Head, Shoulders, Knees, and Toes, leaving Jamie and me home alone. No sooner have they left that Jamie announces that they're going to hang out with Sara in the Center.

"How are you getting there?" I ask.

"Mrs. Fisher is picking me up," Jamie says. "I'm gonna change my clothes."

Jamie disappears upstairs. A few minutes later, they return wearing a blue button-up shirt and black skinny jeans. The smattering of pimples on their forehead is gone, hidden behind a thick coat of Mom's concealer.

"You look nice," I say.

"Thanks." With their back against the wall, Jamie yanks on a pair of white Converse and hastily ties the laces. "That's her car. See ya."

"Have fun," I call as my sibling dashes out the door.

I watch them get in the backseat of a navy SUV; the same SUV I'd regularly ride in when Liam and I were friends. Five years later, I still remember sitting on the beige leather seats and inhaling the scents of everything bagels as Mrs. Fisher drove us around town. She'd always listen to country music on the radio, no matter how many times Liam begged her to change the station. I wonder if she still does. I wonder if Sara despises it as much as her older brother did.

Fifteen minutes later, as I'm relaxing on the couch taking random Buzzfeed quizzes, my phone buzzes.

Lou: can u come over?

I finish filling out a quiz called *Answer These Food Questions and We'll Tell You How Healthy You Really Are*. Once I've received a satisfying score of 8/10, I shut down my computer and reply: *sure. be there soon.*

Without bothering to change out of my sweats, I pull on athletic socks and sneakers and double-knot the laces. Then I open the snack cabinet and sift through it for the unopened heart-shaped box of chocolates Kevin gave Mom for their one-year anniversary in January. I doubt she'll even notice they're gone. Since it's only thirty-six degrees, I bundle up in my parka, shove a hat over my messy hair, and head outside to embark on the mile-long walk to Lou's house.

Despite the low temperature, the day is surprisingly mild with very little windchill and the sun shining brightly in the sky. I arrive at the Jackson's in fifteen minutes and ascend the icy pathway to the side door. I ring the bell, and after several seconds, Mr. Jackson lets me in. A blue dish towel is slung over his left shoulder.

"Hello, Grace," he greets me. "Did you walk all the way here?"

"Yeah, but it's not that bad out." I take off my hat and stuff it in the pocket of my jacket, which I then hang on a coatrack. The Jackson's kitchen is messier than usual with several cupboards open and dishes piled high in the sink. "Is Lou upstairs?"

"She is. My wife is sleeping, so if you wouldn't mind keeping it down . . ."

"Of course, Mr. Jackson," I say. "It'll be like I'm not even here."

While he begins loading the dishwasher, I walk into the hall and tiptoe up the staircase. Lou's door is slightly ajar, so I let myself in without knocking. She's lying on her bed, propped up by a fluffy pillow, with her computer on her lap and AirPods in her ears.

"Lou?" When she doesn't hear me, I nudge her foot, causing her to finally look away from the screen. "What are you watching?"

Lou removes one of the AirPods. "Huh?"

"Never mind. So, um, how's everything?"

Instead of answering my question, Lou points at the box. "What's that?"

"Chocolates. They're from last month, so they might be kind of stale."

"I'm sure they'll be fine." Lou puts the box on her nightstand and scoots over so I can sit next to her. "Thanks for coming. I didn't want to spend Valentine's Day alone."

"Welcome to my life," I joke. "But you're welcome. Did you talk to Cassie today?"

"We Skyped this morning, but it just wasn't the same. You know, for our first Valentine's Day together, Cassie made me a video. It was really cheesy, and the editing sucked, but it was the nicest thing anyone had ever done for me. I must have watched that video a thousand times—that's how much she meant to me." Lou smiles sadly. "I knew going into this that long-distance wouldn't be easy, but I honestly thought we'd make it work. Now I'm not so sure."

"She'll be back," I assure her. "Vermont is only four hours away."

"Sometimes, I miss her so much that four hours seems more like four hundred." Lou is quiet for a few seconds. Finally, she picks up the box and opens the lid, revealing ten assorted chocolates. "Want one?"

"Okay." I select a rectangular chocolate with a dark brown exterior and take a small bite, while she pops an entire heart-shaped milk chocolate in her mouth. "Mmm. Raspberry."

"I think mine was caramel." Lou turns over the box and examines the key. "Yep. Ooh, there's coconut too. Dibs on that." She snatches a circular chocolate with tiny white specks on top. "These are really good," she says as she's chewing. "Thank your mom for me."

"I will. How's your mom by the way?"

"Fine," she responds dismissively. "How's yours?"

"Fine too. She and Kevin are at a spa. Jamie's hanging out with Sara in the Center."

"On Valentine's Day? So, are those two, like, a couple?"

"Not sure. Jamie never tells me anything these days." I sigh. "I keep thinking about what they said on the phone about school being like a cage. That really got to me for some reason."

Lou reaches for a square-shaped chocolate with a white checkered design. "You know, I used to feel that way too. People can be really awful sometimes."

"What changed?" I ask.

"I met you," she says matter-of-factly. "You were my first real friend, and after spending years thinking that everyone was out to get me, having one person accept me made all the difference." Still chewing, Lou raises her head and smiles at me. "I love you, Grace."

I smile back at her. "Love you too, Lou."

<h1 style="text-align: center;">14</h1>

I wake up at ten o'clock on the first Saturday of March to a snowstorm. After weeks of mild, mid-forty-degree weather, this sudden shift shocks—and demoralizes—me. I pinch my arm in case I'm still asleep, but the small sting confirms that this isn't just some horrible dream; this is reality.

When I trudge downstairs, Mom is sitting at the kitchen table. "Good morning."

"No, it's not a good morning," I snap. "What the hell is happening? Can't the climate make up its mind already?" I dramatically collapse into my chair and place my head flat against the wood. "Lou was supposed to come over today. We were going to study for an important gov test."

"Oh, Lou got here thirty minutes ago," Mom responds.

"Lou is here?"

Mom nods. "She's in the TV room. Go see for yourself."

Pushing back my chair, I stand up and walk into the TV room. Sure enough, Lou, dressed in a baggy sweatshirt and jeans, is sitting on the couch with her feet propped onto the coffee table and her eyes glued to her phone. She looks up when I clear my throat.

"Hey, girl."

"What are you doing here so early?" I ask. "And how did you get here anywhere?"

"First of all, it's after ten," she responds, "and my neighbor is a snowplow driver. He gave me a ride in his truck."

"Right. Well, you know we could have rescheduled. I mean, the test isn't until Friday."

"Check the forecast."

"Okay." I unlock my phone and open the weather app. To my dismay, next to Sunday through Thursday is a tiny snowflake symbol. "You've got to be kidding me."

"See what I mean? Anyway, I have something I need to tell you. You coming?"

"Can I have breakfast first?" I ask.

"Bring it with you. I'll meet you upstairs."

I wait until Lou has left the room to return to the kitchen. "She's crazy," I say to Mom.

"She's determined, I'll give her that," Mom says. "Now go before she gets impatient."

"So, you're cool if I eat my breakfast in my room?"

"Sure. Is there any reason I shouldn't be?"

"Of course not," I say. "Just checking."

I shake some Cheerios and granola into a bowl and add a splash of milk. Then I grab a napkin and head upstairs, where Lou is lounging on my bed. I unplug my computer from its charger and sit next to her. With the cereal in my right hand, I use my left hand to enter my password and open Chrome.

"So, what is it you wanted to tell me?" I ask as I'm waiting for Quizlet to load.

"I think I have a stalker," she says.

I glance up from the screen and shoot her a confused look. "What?"

"Do you know Danielle Dicks?"

"Um . . . no, I don't think so. Who is she?"

"This British girl who sits behind me in world history. She basically showed up out of the blue a month ago, and the other day, she liked every picture I'd posted on Instagram—all seventy-three of them. Then she went on my Finsta and liked all of those pictures too."

"Oh my god," I say. "Why did you give her access to your Finsta?"

"I didn't at first, but she kept sending me follower requests, and I figured if she saw my bedhead and double chin, she'd lay off. She didn't."

"What a creep."

Lou shrugs. "I think it's endearing. I mean, no one has ever seen her before. Maybe this is her bizarre way of making friends."

"Is it working?"

"Hell no. But I appreciate the effort. Next thing I know, she'll be stalking my Twitter too." As if by coincidence, Lou's phone lights up with a Twitter notification, and then another one, and then several more after that. "No fucking way. Think I need a restraining order?"

I finish chewing a spoonful of cereal and shake my head. "Nah, that seems a bit extreme. Now can we study for the test or are you strictly into Dicks?"

Lou rolls her eyes. "Haha. You're a total comedian. Yes, we can study. Quiz me."

"You haven't even looked at the flashcards."

"So? I watch CNN. I'm sure this will be a breeze." *Ding!* Lou checks the latest notification on her lock screen. "Oh my god! Now she's commenting on my tweets too!"

"Lou!" I exclaim. "Turn that thing off. You have to focus."

With a sigh, Lou silences her phone. "Go on then."

"Tinker vs. Des Moines," I read from the screen.

"Huh? We didn't learn about that."

"Yes, we did. Last week. Don't tell me you weren't paying attention again." When she doesn't respond, I say, "Lou, if something is going on—"

"Nothing is going on," she interrupts. "I just have a lot on my mind. I'm supposed to hear from Weston any day, and if I don't get in . . ." She sighs. "I've dreamed of getting out of here for years, but by the way things are looking, I'm gonna have to commute to community college, which means I'll still live with Ma and Pa. And I don't know how much more of them I can handle." Another sigh escapes her lips. "If I'm being honest, that's the real reason I wanted to come over so bad."

"To get away from your parents?"

"Yeah. Ma is on the warpath, and I can't be around her when she's like that. I needed an out."

"So . . . something is going on then?"

"I guess you could say that," Lou admits. "She's upset that the meds aren't working, so she's been taking it out on me. That's why I have to get into Weston. I've spent most of my adolescence being her punching bag—metaphorically speaking, of course. I don't want to spend my adult life putting up with her shit too."

"You'll get in," I assure. "Just relax."

"Easy for you to say," Lou retorts. "In six months, you'll be in Boston having the time of your life with your new artsy friends who wear cooler clothes than me and have better hair—"

"I like your hair," I say, "and even if I do make new friends—

which is a big if—you'll always be my number one. You know that, right?"

Lou is quiet for a moment or two. "It was a court case in the sixties," she says finally. "Students wore black armbands to protest the Vietnam War."

"What are you—oh, right." I tap a random key on my computer, as the screen had gone black while we were talking. When the webpage reloads, I double-check Lou's answer even though I'm mostly certain that she's right. "Yes. It cemented the students' right to free speech."

"Glad that stuck," she responds sarcastically. "What's next?"

"Are you sure you don't want to talk—"

"I'm done talking. It's out of my control. But you know what isn't?" She adjusts her position on her bed so she's facing me. "This test. And the last thing I need is another shitty grade. So let's keep going, okay?"

"Brown vs. Board of—"

Ding!

"Lou!" I exclaim.

"Shut up. It's from Weston."

I watch as she unlocks her phone with shaky hands and opens the email. I'm reminded of how tense I felt when I received the notification from SBU, as if time had completely stopped. I try to gauge Lou's reaction, but her neutral expression gives little away.

Finally, she looks up from the screen. "I got in," she whispers.

"For real?"

"I got in," she echoes, only now her voice is louder, full of excitement. "Holy shit, I got in. I'm going to California!"

"I told you you would," I say even though I'd secretly had my doubts. "Lou, I'm so happy for you."

Lou beams. I realize that it's been a while since I've seen her smile so genuinely. "You know what? I think I'm happy too."

DRIP . . . drip . . . drip . . .

"Please make sure that when you submit your encomium draft, it's in MLA format. That means the font must be size twelve. Not fourteen. Not thirteen. Twelve. And as for the line spacing . . ."

Drip . . . drip . . . drip . . .

With Miss Bacon's voice a mere murmur in the background, I rest my chin on my folded hands and stare out the window at the drops of slush dripping off the gutters. Light grey clouds dominate the sky, while the trees surrounding the courtyard are depressingly bare. It's been one week since spring officially began, and I'm still waiting for the first robin sighting. They usually appear around this time of the year to explore the lingonberry bushes in my front yard or scavenge for worms in the grass.

I turn away from the window when I hear the sound of footsteps padding against the floor. My classmates hurry towards the Chromebook cabinet in the front of the room, like a swarm of bees surrounding a hive.

"Get one for me?" I call to Liam.

"Sure thing," he responds.

He returns with two Chromebooks a minute later and hands me #23. "Thanks. So, what exactly are we doing?"

"Working on our encomiums. Did you not hear anything Miss Bacon said?"

Now I know how Lou feels. "No, I wasn't paying attention. We're just editing them?"

He nods. "Pretty much."

Since I'm already ahead of schedule with my encomium, I decide to clean my cluttered inbox instead. I log onto my school account and scroll through endless Classroom announcements, event and extracurricular reminders, and student surveys.

Should school start later?

Are the bathrooms a safe space?

How are you managing your stress?

Every so often, I'll come across an email from SBU. Most are either about financial aid, which I already applied for, or Student Accessibility Services, but they make me smile nevertheless. In four months and twenty-five days (not that I'm counting), I'll have moved into my dorm and begun Orientation. And if there's one thing motivating me to get through the rest of this school year, it's the thought of a fresh start.

I've reduced the number of emails in my inbox from eighty-two to fifteen by the time the bell rings. While I wait in line to return my Chromebook, I look out the window once more. The clouds have begun to part and tiny rays of sunlight now cast a golden glow onto the dismal landscape. On the withered branch of an oak tree, a single robin flaps its grey wings.

I grin. Maybe spring is finally coming after all.

I'm in a relatively good mood when Mom picks me up around noon. At home, I melt provolone cheese on a medium-sized bagel and slice a red apple into thin slivers. Mom, whose lunch consists of miso soup and yogurt, waits until I'm sitting at the table to start eating.

"You're unusually upbeat," she observes. "Good day?"

"School was boring," I say, "but for the first time in a while, I feel like I have things in my life to look forward to. Like college and graduation and even my writing group."

Mom smiles. "I'm glad to hear it. Just make sure you feed yourself enough. Your lunch seems on the smaller side today."

I roll my eyes. "It's not. I used two slices of cheese."

"All right," she responds, not sounding convinced. "As long you're staying on top of it—"

"I am," I assure her. "Believe me, Mom. Why would I slip now when everything is just starting to fall in place?"

"You're right. I trust that you know what you're doing. This is your recovery after all."

"Yeah." After a brief pause, I add, "I do know what I'm doing by the way. I promise."

She nods. "Good. I'm glad to hear it."

Once we've finished our lunches, Mom carries her dishes to the sink and neatly stacks them in the crowded dishwasher. I wait until she's left the room to follow suit. I've just crammed my plate between two bowls when my phone dings. To my surprise, Katie Brinkley's name appears on my lock screen.

Katie: hi grace. i saw on fb that ur going to sbu. congrats!!! u might know that im there this year. im on spring break now but if u want u can come stay with me and my roommate sometime in april to get an idea of what college is like. totally up to u but i did that last year and it helped a lot with my nerves. lmk!

She ends the text with three smiley face emojis. As I'm rereading it, I realize that I'm smiling too.

"Hey, Mom!" No response. "MOM!"

Mom pokes her head into the kitchen. "Grace, what have I told you about yelling?"

"That if I need something, I should find you," I respond.

"Exactly. I'm on hold with our insurance. Can this wait?"

"It'll only take a second. Remember Katie Brinkley?" When Mom nods, I say, "She just texted me. She heard I'm going to SBU, and she says if I want to stay with her for a day or two, you know to experience college and all that, I could. Is that okay with you?"

"When were you thinking of going?"

"Spring break?" I suggest.

Mom checks the calendar taped to the pantry door. "I'm on call at the beginning of the week, but I can drive you down on Wednesday."

"Wednesday is my writing group. How about Thursday?"

"Thursday is fine as long as you don't mind taking the bus home on Friday. Jamie's jazz band performance is that afternoon, so I won't be able to pick you up."

"Oh, crap. I totally forgot about the performance. You don't think Jamie will mind if I miss it, do you?"

"I doubt it. Jamie didn't even want me to come, but they need a ride and refuse to carpool with anyone else."

"Well, in that case, I'll take the bus. Let me just make sure Thursday works for Katie." I send Katie a text saying: *thanks id love to! how about thursday the 15th?*

Katie: perfect!

"She says yes," I inform Mom.

Mom jots down *grace boston* on the calendar. "Did Katie say how she liked the school?"

I reread Katie's first text. "No, but I'm sure she does. It's college after all. Like I said, I honestly can't wait for next year."

"I remember how excited I was when I got into UCLA," Mom says. "I felt like I'd finally been given the chance to leave my town and everyone I'd grown up with behind and start over."

"I know what you mean. Maybe I'm being too optimistic—"

"No such thing," she interjects.

I smile. "Either way, I have a really good feeling about this."

15

"And then the Vampire Girl sunk her teeth into Lord Adriel's neck, savoring the sweet taste of his royal blood as it trickled down her pale skin, the crimson droplets staining her ivory blouse. Lord Adriel's body tumbled onto the dungeon floor, where he lay, as limp as a ragdoll, at Vampire Girl's feet. She turned to the Vampire Prince and untied the ropes binding his hands together. His wrists were marred with burns, and his face was gashed and bruised, and yet his strength was unwavering. He took her in his arms, pressed her against the wall, and kissed her passionately, raking his fingers through her hair as she grabbed his eight-inch co—"

"All right, Kinsey, I think we've heard enough," Miss Kerr interrupts. "Thank you for sharing that, um, creative story with us. What did you say it was called?"

Kinsey closes her dragon-patterned notebook. "*The Dawn of the Odenkirk Empire.*"

"Right. Does anyone have feedback for Kinsey?"

"I have a question," Andrew says. "So, I love the dynamic

between Vampire Girl and Vampire Prince, but what about Tentacle Boy and Prince Torian? They clearly have chemistry, but are they endgame? Because that's a ship I could totally get behind."

Kinsey grins mischievously. "You'll have to wait and see."

"So . . . you don't know?"

"Oh, I know. I just haven't gotten to it yet. I've been busy."

"Me too," Tasha gripes. "My mom made me join an SAT prep group, and it's taking up all my time and energy. I've been so tired that I haven't written anything in days!"

"It's okay to take breaks," Miss Kerr says calmly. "Your writing isn't going anywhere. It will be there when you're ready. Speaking of which, how are you getting along, Grace? You mentioned last time that you were having writer's block."

She's right; it's been over a month since I've written anything other than an expository essay and several Voice's prompts. "It's not a big deal," I say. "I'm not like everyone else. I don't have a forty-thousand-word dystopian novel or smutty Wattpad story I'm working on. I have some ideas for a book, but that's as far as I've gotten."

"Would you be open to sharing your ideas?" Miss Kerr asks. "Perhaps we can help."

"I guess so," I agree hesitantly. "Um, as you know, I like realistic fiction, so it would probably be a story about a girl in high school dealing with, you know, teen stuff."

"Like relationships?" Kinsey asks. "'Cause I could help with that."

I shake my head. "Not relationships. Maybe there'd be some romance, but that wouldn't be the main storyline. I was thinking more like mental illness."

"That's a good idea," Andrew says. "I have depression. So

does my brother. I think a book like that could help a lot of people."

"I have depression too," Kinsey adds. "There aren't enough books that get mental illness right. When I was in a bad place, I was always looking for something that I could relate to or that made me feel less alone. But most of the time, the books I read and the movies I watched only made me more confused than I was before. You know what I mean?"

I nod. "I do. The thing is, for the past year, I've been dealing with some mental health struggles of my own. It can be really hard to talk about, but when I write about it, it's like a weight has been lifted off my chest if that makes sense."

"I used to be too scared to tell people that I'm bipolar," Noel says. "I thought they would judge me or think I was a freak. I'd spend entire afternoons alone in my room listening to My Chemical Romance and wishing I wasn't alive. And then I discovered writing. It didn't cure me, but it helped me cope. I know I've said this before, but writing honestly saved my life."

"Same here," Andrew says, while the rest of us nod in agreement.

"This club is literally turning into group therapy," Kinsey jokes.

"And I thought your vampire porn would be the weirdest part of my day," Tasha says. "In all seriousness, though, I'm glad I can be open with you guys. Things haven't been easy lately, so this just feels like a safe space for me."

Across the table from Tasha, Miss Kerr is smiling. "I feel like a proud parent," she says. "I was going to give you an assignment on slam poetry, but instead, I want you to write about the ways that writing has impacted your life. We can share at our next meeting. I'm afraid our time is up."

While Miss Kerr brushes crumbs from our snack—miniature

blueberry muffins—off the table, I stuff my notebook in my bookbag and follow the others out of the Teen Room and through the quiet library. We disperse in the parking lot: Kinsey, Tasha, and Noel heading towards their cars; Andrew and I waiting on the sidewalk for our rides to arrive.

While he stares at his sneakers, I take out my phone to text Mom. Before I can even enter my password, however, she pulls up to the curb.

"Bye, Andrew," I say. "I'll see you."

Andrew waves. "Later, Grace."

"Is that a smile I see?" Mom teases as I buckle my seatbelt. "I take it you had a good time."

I roll my eyes. "You're annoying. And, yeah, I guess it was all right."

"So, nothing interesting to report?"

"Unless you count the vampire porn, not really."

"Vampire porn?" Mom shakes her head. "No, I don't want to know." She turns onto the main road behind Kinsey's car: a silver sedan with a *Stay Weird* bumper sticker above the license plate. "Although I have to say that I'm glad you gave it a chance. It's nice to see you socializing again."

"I know, Mom," I respond. "I'm glad too."

THE FIRST THING I notice when I walk into Lou's bedroom is the excessive amount of Weston merch. From the massive red pennant on her wall to the crumpled sweatshirt on her floor to the mug and lanyard on her dresser, she's gone completely over-board. She even has a plush whale—Weston's mascot—at the foot of her bed.

"Oh my god," I say. "Jeez, Lou, how much did all of this cost?"

Lou, who's sitting on her bed with her eyes glued to her phone, shrugs. "Dunno. A lot."

"No kidding." I pick up a beanie on her nightstand and flip over the price tag that's attached to the cuff. Twenty-five dollars. "Um, I don't think you'll be needing this in California."

"Huh?"

"The hat. SoCal is, like, really warm most of the year." I place the beanie back down and sigh dramatically. "I still can't believe you're going to California, and I'm stuck in New England. You'd better let me visit you."

No response.

"Lou? Did you hear what I just said?" I sit next to her and nudge her knee. "What's going on? Are you all right?"

Lou finally raises her head. Her brown eyes are full of sadness, as if all the joy has been sucked right out of them. She mumbles something under her breath that I'm unable to make out.

"I can't hear you."

"My mom is dying," she whispers.

It takes me a moment to process what she's said, and when I do, my stomach sinks. "What do you mean?"

"We've known she's been sick for a while, but lately, she's gotten so much worse." Lou takes a shaky breath. "She was admitted to the hospital on Thursday. Her doctor told us that the cancer is spreading, and there's nothing he can do to stop it. Then he started talking about Hospice, and I couldn't listen anymore so I left. I haven't been back yet. I just can't stand seeing her so . . . so . . ."

I scoot closer to Lou and wrap my arms around her trembling body. "I'm sorry, Lou. I had no idea."

Lou is quiet for a few seconds. When I look at her, tears are silently streaming down her cheeks. She wipes her damp eyes with the sleeve of her Weston shirt and reclines into the mattress, staring blankly at the ceiling. I lie beside her and rest my head against her shoulder.

"Can we just stay here forever?" she asks.

In response, I reach for her hand and hold on tightly. "We can."

I'M jerked awake by the sound of my phone buzzing. Rubbing my eyes, I squint at the digital clock on Lou's nightstand: six thirty-seven. I hadn't even realized I'd been asleep—much less for almost two hours.

I slowly retract my hand from Lou's and reach across her limp body for my phone. "Hi, Mom."

"Grace, where are you?" She sounds annoyed—angry even. "You promised you'd be home an hour ago to help with dinner."

"I'm sorry. I fell asleep."

"You what?"

"I fell asleep," I echo. "At Lou's. We were talking, and, well, I guess I just dozed off. I promise I'm leaving right now."

"You'd better. Dinner is getting cold."

"Start without me. I'll be home in fifteen."

"Uh-huh," she mumbles and ends the call.

Careful not to disturb Lou, I climb off her bed and pull on my sneakers. Before I walk away, I bend down and kiss her cheek. "You'll be okay," I whisper in her ear.

I tiptoe out of her room and close the door behind me. At the top of the staircase, I hear a small clatter and turn around. The rectangular Western placard Lou had taped to her door is on the floor, face-down. I pick up the placard and try to stick it back on the door, but the tape isn't holding.

"Oh, for God's sake," I mumble as I take off the tape and refold it into a messy rectangle to try again. No such luck.

Defeated, I leave the placard on the floor and quietly descend the staircase. Although this time, I don't look back.

16

The last time Mom and I visited Boston was only one year ago, and yet so much has changed since then. The idea of moving to a brand-new city, which once seemed foreign and daunting, now fills me with excitement and anticipation. Maybe it's the senioritis kicking in. Maybe it's the fact that I've stayed in my weight range for over a month. Maybe it's because I can't wait to get away from Mom and her antics. Whatever the reason is, I've never felt more ready.

Cruising down the highway, watching the other drivers speed by, I catch myself smiling in the reflection of the window. Mom must notice too, because she says, "You seem excited."

"Oh, I am," I respond. "How much longer until we're there?"

"Not long. Twenty minutes at most. I'll have you turn on Siri when I get off the highway. Did Katie say where she'll meet you?"

"Outside the dorms, I think."

"Crap, there's the exit." Mom quickly cuts across two lanes, eliciting a honk from another car, and takes Exit 22 onto Huntington Avenue. "You can turn her on now."

"Okay." I reach for her phone and press the green GO on Maps.

"Starting route to Southern Boston University," Siri's robotic voice says. "In half a mile, keep right towards Copley Square."

Following Siri's directions, Mom zips through a dark tunnel and turns onto the Square, passing a statue of a famous painter that I recognize from our last visit. After two lefts and one more right, she parks in a loading zone next to SBU's Visitor's Center, and we both get out of the car. While she stretches her legs, I cup my hand over my eyes and squint into the bright sunlight at the three tall buildings that make up the school. Vertical flags with *Southern Boston University* printed in purple capital letters flap in the wind. Students mill around the vicinity: some carrying bookbags and textbooks; others Starbuck's coffees and pastries from the dining hall. Three Asian girls hurry past me speaking Mandarin. Another girl with skin as white as snow stands outside the dormitories smoking an e-cigarette.

"So, I'll see you tomorrow afternoon," Mom says. "You sure you'll be okay riding the bus on your own?"

"Mom, I'm almost eighteen," I respond. "I'll be fine."

She nods. "Of course you will. Text me if you need anything."

"All right."

She leans forward as if she's going to hug me, but she must change her mind at the last second, because she pats my shoulder instead. "Have fun." Then she steps into the car, closes the door, and merges back onto the busy street.

I take out my phone to text Katie that I'm here. She responds a few seconds later saying she'll be down in a minute. While I wait for her, I continue to glance around me in intrigue. On the corner of the street, the new freshmen dormitory—

which was a mess of bricks and caution tape last year—is now nearing completion. I'm going to live there soon, I realize. In just a few short months, that building will be my second home.

"Hi, Grace." Katie stands in the doorway of the current dormitory wearing a purple hoodie and baggy black jeans. "Come on, I'll check you in."

I follow her to a desk, and she hands her Student ID to the grumpy-looking man sitting behind it. "She's with me," Katie says.

The man hands me a clipboard with a guest sign-in sheet and pen attached. I scribble my name and the time in the next available column and return it to him. He scans Katie's ID, and when the scanner flashes green, we head upstairs to the elevators.

While we wait, I say, "Thanks again for inviting me."

She smiles kindly. "No problem. I'm glad you came."

The third elevator from the right dings, and a dozen or so students bustle out. Katie and I wait for the crowd to clear to follow a purple-haired girl inside. Katie presses 4, and just like that, we're on our way up.

When the elevator arrives at her floor, Katie leads me down a long hall to Room 413. On the door, two white name tags—Katie and Melanie—are taped to the purple wood. Katie uses a silver key to unlock the door and beckons me inside.

"You can put your bag wherever," she says.

I place my duffel bag on the floor next to a laundry basket and glance around curiously. Katie's room is smaller than I'd expected and packed with two twin beds, two armoires, two desks—one organized; the other covered with papers and textbooks—a mini-refrigerator, and countless plastic storage bins. A large cardboard box overflowing with packaged snacks is crammed in the corner with what appears to be a . . .

"Is that a popcorn machine?" I ask.

Katie nods. "It's Melanie's. Technically, they're not allowed, but no one has busted us yet. Do you want some? I think she keeps extra bags in her desk."

"Now?" I shake my head. "I had a muffin in the car."

"Yum." Katie takes off her hoodie, tosses it onto the neater bed, and adjusts her grey t-shirt. Her arms are thinner than I remember, and her collarbones are shockingly prominent. "If you like muffins, you should try Georgetown Cupcake sometime. It's only, like, half a mile down the road. The Lemon Blossom is my favorite."

"I'll keep that in mind," I say. "So, where's your roommate?"

"In class, I think. She's rarely around during the day. Speaking of which, I have my media arts history seminar at four if you want to come with me. I mean, you could stay here, but you might get kind of bored."

"Yeah, I'll come. Will your teacher be okay with it?"

"Professor Sharfman won't care. There are, like, a hundred kids in that class anyway."

"A hundred?" I repeat in disbelief. "Jeez. My Women's Lit class has twenty-five, and I thought that was a lot."

"I thought the same thing at first," Katie says, "but you get used to it. Plus, all my other classes max out at thirty, so it's not that bad."

"Do you like your other classes?"

Katie opens the mini-refrigerator and takes out a blue Tupperware container. She removes the lid and pops a cube of cantaloupe in her mouth. "As far as gen eds go, they're all right. I'm looking forward to taking courses that are relevant to my major next year."

"What are you studying again?"

"Screenwriting," she says with a smile. "It's been a dream of mine to write movies since eighth grade. What about you? You're doing Creative Writing, right?"

I nod. "I've always liked writing, but it wasn't until last year that I really got into it. I have all these ideas for a book. Now it's just a matter of putting them to paper."

"You've got time." Katie places the container next to an unsweetened vanilla almond milk and closes the refrigerator. "We should probably get going. We'll take the stairs since the elevators are super crowded between classes." She ushers me back into the hall and leads me to a door across from the elevators. Right as she's opening it, two large boys barrel through. Whereas I dart out of the way, Katie boldly calls after them, "Watch where you're going!"

"Do you know them?" I ask.

"Not personally, but Jake and Tim are notorious for being colossal douchebags. I'm honestly surprised they haven't been expelled. Just last week, a girl had to be wheeled out of their room on a stretcher from alcohol poisoning. And do you know what their punishment was?"

I shake my head. "What?"

"A two-hour class on safe drinking. That's it." Katie rolls her eyes. "Assholes."

"Was the girl okay?" I ask as Katie and I walk past the security desk on the first floor.

"I'm sure she's fine. People here get taken to the hospital all the time for that stuff." When she sees the alarmed look on my face, Katie says, "I know it sounds bad, but as long as you avoid the whole party scene, you won't have to worry about any of that —I promise. Go left."

I turn onto the busy sidewalk and walk with Katie past the mailroom, the Visitor's Center, and the SBU police headquarters. She stops next to a narrow doorway that students are pouring out of and waits for an opening to step inside. After flashing her ID at another security desk, we squeeze past more students clustered around the elevators and begin to ascend a winding staircase.

"You do a lot of walking here," I observe, struggling to catch my breath. Even when I was in the best shape of my life, stairs were always my weakness.

Katie nods. "It's a good workout."

"No kidding," I huff.

When we reach the third floor, Katie takes off down a long hall, and I hurry after her. I'm about to ask why she's in such a rush when I check my phone and realize that it's two minutes until four. Katie navigates around a girl wearing headphones and enters Room 328 with me right behind her.

The second I see the overabundance of students loudly conversing over the Italian opera music that's blasting through the speakers, I'm overcome with anxiety. My brain urges me to walk away, but my feet obediently follow Katie to a row in the back. She claims the second seat from the aisle and starts chatting with a small blonde girl with circular glasses, while I sit next to her and tap my fingernails against the armrest. The shortness of breath I felt when I walked up the stairs is nothing compared to the current tightness in my chest. I close my eyes and force myself to breathe deeply.

In . . . out . . . in . . . out . . .

Then someone behind me roughly knees my seat, and I'm jerked back to reality. Katie is still chatting with the girl, who's griping about a twelve-page sociology essay.

"I don't know how they expect us to keep up with everything. I'm so far behind that I've barely left my room all week."

"I know the feeling, Haley," Katie responds. "I haven't slept since Sunday. I'm starting to feel like a zombie."

"Good morning, students," Professor Sharfman—a short man with a bald head as shiny as a bowling ball—says. He stands at the front of the room with a clicker in one hand and a can of Diet Coke in the other. "Take out your notebooks. We're picking up where we left off on Monday." He turns on the projector, and a portrait of a man with a handlebar mustache appears on the screen. "George Méliès was one of the first people to introduce screen editing. Today, we'll be watching a popular film of his called *The Impossible Voyage*. Pay attention to the different styles of editing Méliès uses. We'll discuss afterward."

Professor Sharfman switches tabs to YouTube, where the twenty-four-minute video is queued up. He presses play and dims the overhead lights as the opening credits roll. There's no sound, so I assume he forgot to turn on the volume. But as the video progresses, and he doesn't budge from his stool, I realize that *The Impossible Voyage* is a silent film.

The sounds of whispering and chewing seem to get increasingly louder as the film progresses. Every couple of minutes, I glance at Katie, who's doodling in a lined notebook. Next to her, Haley is constructing an elaborate sketch of a girl's face in her notebook. As I'm watching her add lashes to the girl's anime eyes, I start to wish I'd brought a notebook too to keep myself occupied. Had Katie warned me that this class would be a snoozefest, I would have come better prepared.

When *The Impossible Voyage* ends, Professor Sharfman turns the lights back on and reopens his PowerPoint presentation. He then proceeds to give an hour-long lecture on twentieth-century film editing accompanied by several bulleted slides. Afterward, he answers questions, and when he's finished clarifying his convoluted lesson, we're finally allowed to leave.

"Sorry about that," Katie says as she stuffs her notebook in her backpack. "Sharfman can be really boring sometimes. It's his last semester here, so I think he's run out of fucks to give. You'd probably have been better off staying in my room after all."

"No, it wasn't boring," I lie. "It was, um, interesting."

Katie snorts. "Try sitting through it twice a week. It won't seem so interesting then." She tugs the zipper of her sweatshirt up to her chin. "That, and this classroom is always freezing cold. Come on, let's get out of here."

"Where are we going now?"

"The dining hall." To Haley, she says, "Grace and I are headed to dinner. Do you want to come with us?"

Haley shakes her head. "Thanks, but I'm meeting with someone from *The SBU Scoop*. I'll see you around."

"See ya," Katie echoes.

"*The SBU Scoop?*" I ask as Katie and I descend the winding staircase.

"SBU's magazine," she explains. "I tried out for a position, but I didn't get in. Probably 'cause I only started school this semester."

"Oh. Are you part of any clubs?"

"They're called orgs, and no." Despite the wry smile on her face, her disappointment is evident. "But it's okay. I'm sure I'll have better luck next year."

She holds open the heavy dining hall door for me, and I enter a large, well-lit seating area. She hands her ID to a Hispanic woman sitting behind a register and explains that I'm a guest.

"You have five guest passes left," the woman informs her. "Next!"

While she continues swiping IDs, I follow Katie down a narrow staircase to the crowded lower level, where the food stations are located. "Help yourself," she says. "I'll meet you back upstairs, okay?"

"Is there a vegetarian station?" I ask.

"Over there." Katie points to the corner of the room. Next to the salad bar, a digital sign, kind of like a television, is hanging from the ceiling.

THE VEG
Jerk tofu
Black-eyed peas and rice
Roasted broccoli
Roasted beets

I grab a plate and make my way over to the station. Although I have no idea what jerk tofu is, I serve myself three cubes along with some roasted broccoli and sweet potato fries from an adjacent station called The Grill. I fill a small bowl with lettuce, cucumbers, tomatoes, and black olives and drizzle an Italian vinaigrette over top. I would have preferred balsamic, but the only options were Italian, ranch, and an unidentifiable reddish dressing.

When I return upstairs, Katie is seated in a booth talking to a boy. His black hair is shoulder-length, and two silver hoops pierce his left earlobe. The bottom half of a star tattoo pokes out from the sleeve of his skintight black shirt. While his tray is piled high with a cheeseburger, waffle fries, and broccoli, Katie's dinner consists of an undressed salad and two halves of a hard-boiled egg.

"Hey." I place my tray on the table and slide in next to Katie, nearly knocking over her glass of water in the process. "Sorry."

Katie mops up a few drops with her napkin. "Don't sweat it. This is Spark by the way. He's in my visual arts class."

Spark flashes me a kind smile. His teeth are so white that they practically sparkle in the bright overhead lighting. "So, what do you think of SBU?" he asks.

"It's a lot different than I expected," I respond truthfully.

"It certainly is an adjustment," Spark says. "I was really nervous at first, but now that I've met people and know my professors, college is great. It honestly feels like my second home here."

"What's your major?"

"Musical theater."

"Spark is really good," Katie says. She stabs a cucumber with her fork and pops it in her mouth. "He's gotten roles in every major production this year."

"Small roles, but that's usually the case with freshmen," Spark says. "I'm lucky I even got in."

I remember reading something about theater productions on SBU's website. They put on quite a few—way more than the other colleges I looked at. "I could never do theater. I get panic attacks just giving PowerPoint presentations at school."

"If it's any consolation, I still take an Ativan before every opening night," he responds.

"I could use some Ativan right now," Katie says. "I have a psychology test tomorrow, and I'm so underprepared. I've been too busy working on an essay for Intro to Writing to focus on anything else." She uses her fork to scoop the yolks out of the eggs, then grabs the salt shaker and sprinkles salt over the whites. "How about you, Grace? Are things slowing down yet?"

"I guess a little. But I'm sure they'll pick up again in a week or two, what with AP exams and finals and all that." I glance at Spark, who's polishing off his cheeseburger. "If you happen to have any Ativan I can borrow . . ."

Spark laughs. "Nice try. I'm gonna get dessert. You girls want anything?"

"No, thanks," I respond at the same time Katie says, "I'm good."

"Lightweights," Spark jokes. "I'll be right back."

I watch as he disappears into the crowd of students, which seems to have doubled since we sat down. "Is it this busy every night?"

"You mean the dining hall?" Katie nods. "Pretty much. It's a little quieter over the weekend when people go out to party."

"Do you?"

"No, I never have enough energy. I usually just stay in my room and watch Netflix and try not to think about how far behind I am on everything." Katie sighs. "I wish someone had told me how hard college is. I mean, I knew it wouldn't be easy, but it's just so . . . I dunno. Sorry, I'm probably freaking you out. It's really not that bad. You'll be fine."

"Are you fine, Katie?"

Katie stares down at her plate, where one pruney tomato and the greyish yolks remain. "Never been better."

I've never ridden a bus on my own, but like Mom always says, you have to start somewhere. And for me, that somewhere is South Station. After missing the entrance and aimlessly walking around a shopping center for a while, I finally find the station and ride a crowded escalator to the platform. Only when I locate my loading area am I able to relax. With ten minutes until boarding, I sit on a metal bench and rummage through my backpack for my earbuds to listen to music. But they're not there.

"What the hell?" I mumble. I message Katie, asking if I left them in her room, and two minutes later, she responds: I have. Dammit.

Katie: want me to mail them to u?

Grace: yes plz. thnx.

Leaving iMessage, I open Instagram and listlessly scroll

through my explore page until the bus is ready to board. With my battery at six percent, I pull up my ticket on the app and hand my phone to the driver so she can scan it. Once it's processed, I walk through the aisle to the back of the bus and sit next to a large woman with a computer on her lap. I slide my backpack under the seat and exhale deeply. I made it.

Passengers slowly file onto the bus. While most are adults in professional-looking clothing, I notice a few other teenagers as well. I wonder if they're also visiting colleges. It is that time of the year after all.

Once everyone has boarded, the driver starts the engine and leaves the station, maneuvering through the busy streets of Boston before picking up speed on the highway. I press my hand against the glass and watch the road signs and trees whiz by. Once withered and bare, their vibrant green leaves have finally started growing back. I remember when I was younger, maybe eleven or twelve, and I'd visit our local park in the spring to scale the large maple tree near the duck pond. I'd climb so high that I could see the rooftops of the surrounding houses and the doll-sized people who lived in them going about their days. On some afternoons, I'd stay in the tree for hours, the cool breeze rustling my hair and my knees scraped and bloodied from rubbing against the bark. It was the only place where I truly felt at peace.

The town decided to cut down the tree over the summer before I started high school. I hadn't gone climbing in years, but it still saddened me to see something that was once so beautiful and alive in mutilated pieces on the ground. By that spring, a new housing complex was taking shape where the tree used to be. To this day, I still get a sick feeling in my stomach whenever Mom and I drive past it.

Outside my window, we've just passed the *Welcome to Connecticut* sign. The bus is moving a lot slower now that it's rush hour. I impatiently tap my fingernails against the sill and wish I hadn't forgotten my earbuds in Katie's dorm room. Hopefully Jamie will let me borrow theirs while mine are in transit.

No matter how hard I try to redirect my thoughts, I can't stop thinking about Katie. She looked so thin and tired compared to the last time I saw her, scarily similar to how I looked when I was at my worst. I desperately want to believe that won't happen to me next year; that I'll be able to stay in recovery in spite of my triggers. But if Katie, who always seemed strong and put-together, could fall apart so easily, who's to say I won't fail too?

By the time the bus arrives at the station, I'm no longer feeling the same optimism I had at the beginning of my visit. With my backpack clutched to my chest like a shield and my phone's battery as low as my confidence, I follow the other passengers off the bus and scan the crowd for Mom. I find her waiting outside in her car. When she sees me, she unlocks the door, and I get in, wrinkling my nose at the pungent eggy stench polluting the interior.

"Sorry about the smell," Mom apologizes. "Jamie had a hard-boiled egg on the drive home from their performance. So, how was your trip?"

I open my mouth to respond, but before I can squeak out a "fine" or "okay," I burst into tears. "Can we get out of here?" I ask between sobs, my voice trembling. "Please?"

I don't have to look at Mom to know that her face is full of concern. "Okay." She hands me a tissue from the console, which I dab my mascara-stained cheeks with. "Let's go home."

17

"You're quiet today," Anna observes. "What's on your mind, Grace?"

I cross my legs, then uncross them, then cross them again. "A lot."

Anna leans forward and rests her elbows on her knees. "Like what?"

"Well, uh, you know how I went to SBU to visit a friend over break?"

"Oh, yes. How was that?"

"It was . . ." I clear my throat. "Different, I guess. I don't know what I'd expected, but I didn't think it would be so overwhelming." I close my eyes and envision myself in the lecture room; how nervous I felt simply standing there surrounded by all that noise and commotion. "The classes, the dining hall, the dorms—even Katie's dumb roommate, who stayed up until three AM Skyping her boyfriend. Between that and the car horns, I slept for, like, an hour tops."

"You could apply for a single," Anna suggests. "That way,

you'll have a space all to yourself to decompress."

"I already spoke to Mom about it. I doubt I could function if I had to share a room with someone like that."

"Since you're on a 504 Plan, you shouldn't have a problem getting one. You should reach out to Student Accessibility Services. I'm sure they'd be happy to help."

"I guess . . ."

Anna's eyes narrow slightly. "Something else is bothering you, isn't it?"

I sigh. "It's Katie—the girl I stayed with. I think she's sick."

"Sick how?"

"Sick like I was last year. She's very thin, and at dinner, all she had was a salad and a hardboiled egg. She didn't even eat the yolk. Plus, my mom knows her mom from an eating disorder support group, so it's obvious that she relapsed. And I just thought . . ."

"You thought that might happen to you," Anna finishes.

"Basically, yeah."

"It's always a possibility," she says, "which is why we're taking all these precautions to make sure you transition successfully. For instance, sometime in the next few months, it's important that you find a therapist in the area. Your mom mentioned that SBU has an on-campus nutritionist; you should meet with her before the school year begins as well."

"And the dining hall?"

"What about the dining hall?"

"It's a lot to deal with. It's loud and crowded, and there's, like, nowhere to sit."

"Perhaps you can go during off-hours," Anna suggests. "If you find someone to eat with, that might also make the experience less overwhelming."

"You think so?"

"I do. I know it's an adjustment, Grace, however I trust that you'll adapt. Of all my clients who are leaving for college next year, you're the one I'm the least worried about. You've come so far. If anyone can succeed, it's you."

I'm not sure if her confidence makes me feel better or worse. "It's two thirty," I say.

Anna glances at the clock on her desk. "Well, that went by quickly. Thank you for being honest with me. I think this went well."

"Uh-huh." I slide on my untied sneakers, which I'd removed when she weighed me, and stand up. "I'll see you in two weeks. Same time, right?"

"Yes. I'll see you then."

As Mom and I drive home, listening to alternative songs on the radio, my phone lights up with a text from Lou: *can u talk?*

I respond: *sure. u home now?*

Lou: *no call me.*

"Mind if I make a call?" I ask Mom.

"Go ahead," she responds.

Lowering the volume on the radio, I dial Lou's number and hold my phone to my ear as I wait for her to pick up. When she does, I hear muffled voices and machines beeping in the background; she must be at the hospital. "Hey, are you all right? What's going on?"

"It's Ma," Lou whispers, and I know even before the words have left her lips what she's going to say. "She's gone."

THE FUNERAL WAS ARRANGED for April 17th, but because Grandma and Grandpa Jackson's flight from New Orleans got canceled, it's moved to the following morning. Mom parks behind a long lineup of rental cars, and we walk across the street to the funeral home. Inside, people mill around the dimly-lit room talking with one another in somber voices. I scan the crowd for Lou and spot her standing by herself next to the mantle. She's wearing a knee-length dress, opaque tights, and flats with velvet bows. I can't remember the last time I saw her in all black.

Taking a deep breath, I cautiously approach Lou and tap her arm. "Hi, Lou."

"Hi." Her eyes are dry, but her voice trembles slightly.

"How are you holding up?" I ask.

"How do you think?"

"Sorry. That was a stupid question."

"I just can't believe that this is real," she says. "We all knew it was coming, but until it actually happens, you don't realize how much it's gonna hurt."

"Right. Um . . ." I hesitate, trying to think of something to say to her. "A lot of people came."

Lou nods. "You know how close my family is. I think some of them are surprised she chose to be buried here and not in New Orleans, but she always said that Connecticut was her home. Don't ask me why."

"Maybe because you were born here?"

"I dunno," she mumbles, not sounding convinced. "Maybe."

"Folks, if you can hear me." The minister—a middle-aged man with a silver cross around his neck—taps the microphone. "Please be seated. We're about to start the service."

Lou and I follow the crowd to the six rows of beige folding chairs surrounding Mrs. Jackson's mahogany casket. Behind the casket is a colorful array of flowers, an enormous wooden cross, and a framed photograph of Mrs. Jackson. In the photo, she looks like the strong-willed, tough-loving woman who Lou introduced me to the first time I came over to her house in fifth grade. She looks healthy. She looks alive.

Lou sits in the front row with her father and grandparents. I start to head towards the middle, where Mom is seated, but Lou grabs my arm and gestures to the empty chair between her and her grandmother.

"Stay. Please."

So, I take a seat on the stiff chair and cross my legs. The minister waits until everyone is settled to proceed with the service. He begins by thanking us for coming, then asks us to put our hands together for the Serenity Prayer.

"God grant me the serenity to accept the things I cannot change, courage to change the things I can, and wisdom to know the difference. Living one day at a time. Accepting hardships as the pathway to peace. Taking, as He did, this sinful world as it is . . ."

To my right, Grandma Laila's eyes are closed, her hands clutching a pink pocketbook. To my left, Lou fidgets in her chair. I can hear her fingernails tapping against the metal armrest, and when I peek at her, her eyes are fixed on her mother's casket.

"So I may be reasonably happy in this life and supremely happy with You forever in the next," the minister concludes. "Amen."

"Amen," the audience echoes.

Next, the minister reads several verses from the Bible. I try to pay attention, but my mind is in a thousand different places. Judging by the glazed-over look on Lou's face, I imagine I'm not the only one. When the minister finishes the final verse—something about the lord being a shepherd—he closes the Bible and announces that it's time for Mrs. Jackson's family members to give their eulogies.

Lou goes first. Taking a deep breath, she walks up to the alter and stands behind the podium. I notice that her hands are shaking as she unfolds a piece of paper.

"Thank you all for being here today. I think Ma would be happy to see so many familiar faces." She briefly looks up and scans the rows of people, then reverts her gaze to her eulogy. "Um, when I found out I had to speak, I honestly had no idea what to say. The truth is, my ma and I didn't get along so well. For as long as I can remember, we've been at war with each other. I know I wasn't the daughter she'd dreamed of having. I know I did things that went against her beliefs. I know I said things that upset her. I know there were parts of me that she wished she could change. But I also know that no matter how many times I sinned in her eyes, she never stopped loving me."

"When I was younger, she'd tell me every night before I went to bed that angels were watching over me; that they were protecting me from evil and leading me down the Path of Right-eousness. I now know that she is one of those angels. She is my Archangel, and she will watch over me until the day I die. Nobody knows for sure if there is a heaven or a hell, but I do know that if I'm ever reunited with her, I will tell her every day that I love her. Because I sure didn't say it enough down here." Tears pool in Lou's eyes, but she quickly wipes them away. She turns to the photo of Mrs. Jackson and quietly says, "Wherever you are, Ma, I hope you're in a better place. I love you."

There isn't a dry eye in the room as Lou returns to her seat. Mr. Jackson wraps his arms around her shoulders and holds her head to his chest. "She would be so proud of you," I hear him whisper.

I place my hand on Lou's thigh, feeling the silkiness of her dress beneath my fingertips. "She really would."

When the service ends, Mr. Jackson and five of Lou's male

relatives gather around the coffin to prepare for the procession. Outside, the clouds have parted and the sun is shining brightly in the clear blue sky; a perfect day for a burial.

"I'll be right back," Lou says to me.

I watch her walk to the corner of the room, where Cassie, who I hadn't noticed before now, is standing. Like everyone else, she's wearing all black from her blouse to her velvety dress pants to the headband holding her wavy hair in place. When she sees Lou, she steps forward and embraces her. Lou nestles her face in Cassie's neck, while Cassie gently rubs her back. They're still holding each other when Mom approaches me.

"How are you feeling?"

I shake my head. "Sad mostly. You?"

"I'm sad too. She was a good woman."

"So, um, what now?"

"We'll drive to the cemetery for the burial," Mom says. "I'm not sure what happens after that. I've only been to one funeral before, and it was years ago."

"Whose funeral?"

"My aunt. She had cancer too."

"Oh, wow. I never knew that."

"I never told you. She was actually the reason I decided to study oncology." Mom stares out a nearby window with tears in her eyes. Through the glass, we watch as the guests file to their cars. "We should probably get going," she says, but she doesn't budge.

"Mom?" I touch her shoulder, and she flinches slightly. "Mom, are you ready?"

Mom turns away from the window and pats her damp cheeks with the sleeve of her dress. Then she takes a deep breath and nods. "Yes. I'm ready."

18

"Grace! Come on, Grace! You're going to be late!"

"Okay, okay. You don't have to yell." I walk into the kitchen and open the closet, rummaging through our collection of jackets for my raincoat. "Can't we wait for the rain to let up? I'm gonna get soaked."

"Oh, stop being so dramatic. A little rain won't kill you." Mom hands me a pair of ugly black rain boots. "Here. Wear these."

"I'm *not* wearing those."

"I'll wear them." Jamie takes the boots from Mom and shoves them over their polka dot socks. My sibling then crams a pair of red Converse into their backpack and joins Mom at the door. "I'm ready."

I feel Mom and Jamie impatiently staring at me as I pull on the coat and adjust the hood so it fully covers my ponytail. Slinging my bookbag over my shoulder, I roll my eyes and follow them outside into the downpour.

The weather is even worse than I'd expected. Huge droplets

pound against the pavement while threatening black clouds loom overhead. Thunder rumbles and lightning illuminates the grey sky as Mom cautiously drives us to school. Even with the windshield wipers moving at full speed, the visibility is horrible.

When Mom pulls up to the entrance, Jamie and I say a quick goodbye and break into a sprint, not slowing down until we're through the door. Inside, the floor is covered in muddy foot-prints and puddles of water. I navigate around them to Voices and sit next to Liam, whose shirt is soaking wet.

"What happened to you?" I ask.

"Look, until you have a car and have to park in the back of the student lot because some asshole stole your spot, don't come at me," Liam grumbles. After a brief pause, he adds, "I also forgot my rain jacket."

"Ah."

"The worst part is that I'm supposed to have a lacrosse game today. This is the third one we've had to reschedule since the season started. I hate April!"

"I know the feeling. I used to play spring sports too."

"Do you think you'll ever play again?"

I consider this. "I hope so. It'd be nice to get back on the field someday."

"Well, there shouldn't be much competition at that artsy school you're going to," he jokes.

"You know, SBU has one of the best squash teams in the country," I respond. "Apparently, we placed second in the College Squash Association's National Championships last year."

Liam laughs. "That's the best thing I've heard all week. 'College Squash Association.' Fucking hilarious."

"Happy rainy Monday," Miss Bacon says chipperly. She hangs her bright blue raincoat on the back of her chair and adjusts her violet blouse to cover her bra straps. "I hope you all had a relaxing weekend because we have a very busy week ahead of us. We're wrapping up our poetry unit, so hopefully by Friday, we'll be able to start working on our final projects. I know you guys are ready for graduation, but let's make these last two months as excellent as we can. After all the hard work and dedication you've applied to this course, you deserve to go out on a high note."

"Can we have a pizza party?" Tommy calls from the back of the room.

"Ew, Tommy," Becky says. "Who eats pizza at eight in the morning?"

"Fine, bagels then," Tommy says. "How about it, Miss Bacon?"

Whereas most teachers would take offense to Tommy's interruption, Miss Bacon smiles. "I'll see what I can do."

Tommy fist-pumps the air. "Awesome."

Just like Miss Bacon, Miss Kiley spends most of Women's Literature mapping out assignments for the rest of the semester, including our last novel, *The Secret Life of Bees*, and some big project about picture books. Then she begins discussing the final —but not before mentioning that anyone with a B or higher is exempt from taking it.

Under my desk, I subtly take out my phone, open Power-School, and select *Women's Literature* on the dashboard. With every assignment except one chart entry in, my grade is a satis-fying ninety-five. Given that Women's Lit is by far my easiest class, maintaining an A for the next two months shouldn't be a problem.

Psychology is a different story. Not only is my grade ten points lower; Dr. Green, who's always high-strung, has been exceptionally neurotic lately, making psych my most dreaded period. But when I enter the classroom and see Lou, that dread vanishes. She's sitting at our shared desk in the back with her chin resting on her folded hands. Her eyes are puffy, and she's wearing an oversized navy sweatshirt and grey leggings—a stark contrast to her usual chic attire.

"I thought you weren't coming back until next week," I say.

"I thought so too," she responds, "but I had to get out of that house. I needed something to take my mind off . . . you know. It turns out school is a pretty good distraction."

"What are you doing after school?" I ask. "Because if you need another distraction, you should come over to my house. My home life is literally turning into a soap opera."

"I can't. My grandparents are still staying with us, so I have to keep them entertained while Pa is at work." She rolls her eyes. "Lucky me."

"Maybe another time then."

Lou nods. "Definitely."

"All right, scholars," Dr. Green says. "It's that time of the year. AP exams are just around the corner, and we have a lot of preparation to do. I know that many of my colleagues let you opt out of the exam, and by law, so must I. However, if you choose not to take it, you'll have to come to school on June 18th and take the final instead, which will count towards your GPA. It's up to you."

"Is she allowed to do that?" Lou asks quietly.

I shrug. "No idea. It doesn't seem right though."

When I look around the room, I can tell that aside from a few overachievers who were planning to take the exam anyway, my peers share our frustration. And, as Dr. Green passes out thick review packets, the grumbling begins. Dr. Green must be used to this because she ignores our complaints and starts to go over important dates without batting an eye.

"And don't forget that your essays are due by the end of the month. For every day they're late, you'll lose ten points."

"I can't wait for this fucking year to be over," Lou mumbles to me.

I nod in agreement. "Me too."

I'm feeling crankier than usual when the school day finally ends. As Mom and I drive home, I stare out the window and viciously pick at my cuticles. By the time we pull into the driveway, both my index and middle finger are bleeding.

"Bad day?" Mom asks.

"I thought the end of senior year was supposed to be easy," I say. "Things seemed to be slowing down a month ago, and suddenly we're going full-throttle again. What's up with that?"

"I know it's a lot, but you're so close. Just think that in less than two months, you'll never have to step foot in Everett again."

"That's a nice thought."

"It's a reality," she says. "Not to rush you, but can we get going on lunch? I have a meeting at one o'clock."

"All right." I retrieve soy bacon, light mayonnaise, lettuce, and a tomato from the refrigerator and pile them on the counter with two slices of white bread. Once I've assembled my BLT, I dump a single-serving carton of banana yogurt into a small bowl and sit next to Mom at the table. "You'll never believe what my psych teacher did," I start to say when her phone buzzes with a text.

"Who's that?"

"Kevin. He wants to know if he can bring home cookies. Staff meeting leftovers, I assume."

"What kind of cookies?"

"I'll ask." But before she has a chance to do so, her phone

buzzes again. "He said he'll bring them anyway. If we don't eat them, the twins will."

"Crap. I forgot they're coming over this weekend."

"Oh, come on. They're not so bad. I've actually been enjoying getting to know them."

"I don't want to know them," I say. "They're annoying, and they take too long in the bathroom. Plus, they eat my cereal."

"It's not *your* cereal. Unless you want to buy your own food, you'd better get used to sharing." Mom glances at her watch. "I should go. I'll see you for dinner. How do burgers sound?"

"Burgers are fine."

Mom rinses off her plate and coffee mug, then squeezes them into the loaded dishwasher. "Can you start the dishwasher?"

"Yeah, okay."

"Thanks." Mom grabs her keys and raincoat—even though it stopped raining hours ago—and hurries out the door. A few seconds later, I hear her car's noisy engine roar to life.

Once I've added my plate and bowl to the dishwasher, I find detergent under the sink and shake some into the soap container. Then I shut the door and select Express. I wait until the dishwasher has started to amble into the TV room and collapse onto the couch with my computer. I spend the next hour catching up on my YouTube subscriptions, then twenty more minutes browsing social media. Around two o'clock, I figure I should probably get started on my homework. After briefly debating between a statistics worksheet on quantitative data or my psychology essay, I choose the latter. I pick up my computer and phone and take a seat at the table, where there's better lighting.

I'm partway through the second body paragraph when the door opens and Jamie walks into the kitchen. Like me, my sibling seems more irritated than usual. I notice that both of their knees are red and one of their elbows is all scraped up.

"Yikes," I remark. "What happened to you?"

"I tripped." Jamie drops their backpack on the floor and opens the refrigerator. "Where are all the banana yogurts?"

"Oh, I ate the last one at lunch. There should be a few blueberries left."

"I don't like blueberry," Jamie says, forcefully closing the refrigerator. "I've told you that, like, ten times."

"Look, I'll text Mom and ask her if she can pick some up on her way home. Okay?"

"Whatever." Jamie sits down at the table and stares at the wall, tapping their fingernails against the wooden surface.

After a minute or so, the tapping begins to get on my nerves. "Jamie, can you stop? I'm trying to work."

Without saying a word, Jamie stands up and storms out of the kitchen. A few seconds later, I hear their footsteps running upstairs, then a door slam shut, then nothing.

I unlock my phone and text Mom: *out of banana yogurt. can u get more?*

Mom: maybe tomorrow. wont have time tonight.

With a sigh, I put down my phone and return my attention to my essay. I've just started writing the conclusion when angsty punk music blasts through the entire house.

"Jamie! Turn that down!"

No response.

"Oh, for God's sake," I mumble. Pushing back my chair, I march upstairs and barge into my sibling's room without knocking. "Jamie, what the fu—" I trail off when I see Jamie sitting on the bed with tears streaming down their cheeks. "Oh my god. Are you okay?"

Jamie quickly wipes their eyes. "Leave."

"But—"

"Leave!"

"All right, all right. I'm leaving."

I feel Jamie's eyes watching me as I walk back into the hall and close the door. I stay where I am for a minute, listening to the sound of my sibling's sniffles, and when I blink my eyes, I realize that they're slightly damp too.

Something is wrong with Jamie. I've known that for a while —we all have. I wish there was a way that I could help them, but then again, it's hard to help someone else when you're still figuring out how to help yourself.

AFTER MY EIGHT-MONTH hiatus from driving, I'd forgotten how daunting being behind the wheel is. The vacant parking lot at the end of the block that Mom and I have been practicing in for the last few weeks hasn't prepared me for the challenges of driving through town. Even with school still in session, the main roads—and some of the side ones as well—are busier than I'd expected. From construction workers to pedestrians to other drivers, most of whom are exceeding the speed limit by at least ten miles per hour, I feel like I'm back in Liam's bedroom playing Mario Kart with him and Lou. Except unlike in the game, I don't have unlimited chances to get this right.

"Grace, you're too close to my side. Please center yourself." Mom places her palm against her window, her expression strained. "Grace! Center yourself!"

"Don't yell at me," I snap as I tilt the steering wheel slightly to the left. "I'm doing my best."

"I know that." Mom sighs. "I just want you to be sa—where's your signal? You need to signal if you're turning."

"Sorry," I mumble. "I forgot."

"Well, you can't forget things like that. You have to stay alert or else you'll cause an accident. Take that car." She points at a grey sedan that's backing out of a nearby driveway. "Did you notice it?"

Even though I hadn't, I nod.

"If you were any closer, you'd have had to slow down so you wouldn't hit it."

"Uh-huh." I turn onto Summer Road, remembering to signal this time. I'm halfway down the street, keeping my eyes peeled for other cars, when I accidentally run a stop sign. I glance at Mom, and her hand is against her forehead. "Sorry."

"Just drive," she responds flatly.

I coast through the surrounding neighborhoods, not once raising my speed above twenty miles per hour, for fifteen more minutes until I've decided that I've had enough for today. Only when I crookedly pull into the driveway are Mom and I able to relax.

"We'll try again tomorrow," Mom says. "I'm working all day on Saturday, so if you'd like to practice then, Kevin can take you."

"I think I'll pass," I respond. "I don't want to deal with his road rage just yet."

"I understand." Mom chuckles. "He does get awfully impatient, doesn't he?"

"That's an understatement. One red light, and he loses his mind."

"You won't say anything, will you?"

I shake my head. "He gave me a car, remember?" I use our house key, which is linked between her car key and an expired gym pass on a silver keychain, to open the door. "I'm not gonna make him regret it."

Inside, Mom kicks off her shoes and collapses onto the couch in the TV room. I sit next to her and prop my feet atop the coffee table. When she nudges my leg with her knee, I reluctantly remove them and cross my legs instead. We're quiet for a minute, gazing out the window at the light pink flowers on our dogwood tree. Looking at them, I'm reminded of a distant childhood memory, one I haven't thought about in years. I was in sixth grade, and it was Mother's Day, but I'd forgotten to buy Mom a gift. So, while she was out running errands, I found a ball of string in the basement, picked a dozen or so flowers off the tree, and with determination and a lot of Super Glue, assembled a necklace. Even though the flowers shriveled up and died within a few days, I'll always remember the smile on Mom's face when I gave her my gift. It was the first time I'd seen her smile like that since Dad left.

Mom isn't smiling now; instead, she looks pensive, as if she's deep in thought. I'm tempted to ask her what's on her mind, but she beats me to it.

"I've been thinking a lot about Lou lately," she says. "How is she?"

"I'm not really sure," I respond honestly. "She doesn't talk much about her mom, but I guess that's understandable. I wouldn't want to talk about it either. I mean, can you imagine how horrible that would be? Losing someone like that?"

"I try not to. I find I'm better off focusing on the positive moments in life, like spending time with my beautiful daughter."

In my periphery, I notice Mom move her hand closer to mine. After a brief hesitation, I extend my hand as well. Her skin is dry and coarse, vaguely resembling the texture of sandpaper.

"I've been thinking too," I say.

"What about?"

"Dad." I steal a glance at her, hoping to gauge her reaction, but her face gives away nothing. "I used to be really angry about the whole thing. I mean, what you did with that man . . ." I realize that even after all these years, I still can't say his name without feeling sick to my stomach. "It was awful. I thought I'd never be able to forgive you."

I feel Mom's grip tighten. "Grace, I'm sorry."

"I know that. I know if you were to go back in time, you'd do things differently. If I went back, I'd do a lot differently too. But I can't change the past. All I can do is make the best of what I have now, and if that means letting go of this anger and resentment that I've been carrying around for years, then I'll find some way to do that."

Mom runs her thumb over my skin. When I look at her, her eyes are suspiciously wet. "You'd do that? For me?"

"Well, for me mostly, but yeah, I would. I'm gonna need time though."

Mom nods. "Take as much time as you need. I'm not going anywhere."

"Thanks, Mom," I say.

Mom retracts her hand from mine and touches my cheek. Her eyes, while still damp, glisten in the late-afternoon sunlight. "You're welcome, Grace."

19

As an experienced eating disorder therapist and someone who has been recovered from anorexia nervosa for over twenty years, I'm able to help young adults navigate the challenges of recovery and identify underlying issues that are being repressed by maladaptive eating disorder behaviors. I'm committed to supporting clients and their families throughout their battle and believe that full recovery is possible with awareness, support, and courage.

I finish reading Kari Leon's—a Boston-based eating disorder therapist—profile on *Psychology Today* and save the page to my bookmarks bar. Of the dozen or so therapists I've checked out this afternoon, she, along with two others who are walking distance from SBU, seem like potential fits. Once I've renamed the bookmark *Kari L*, I unlock my phone and text Mom.

Grace: found a few therapists that might work. can u call them later?

Mom: how about u call them?

Grace: id rather u do it instead.

Mom: give it a try. i believe in u.

Rolling my eyes, I scroll down the page until I find Kari's

contact information and reluctantly dial her number. Just as I'm about to call her, my phone goes off, causing me to flinch in surprise. What's even more surprising, however, is the name of the caller: Liam Fisher.

"Hey, Liam," I answer. "What's up?"

"It's Jamie," Liam says. "He's at my house, and he doesn't look so good."

I don't bother to correct Liam's pronouns. "What do you mean? What's wrong?"

"I'm not sure. He showed up here ten minutes ago looking for Sara, but she's with my mom at some fundraising thing. I let him in anyway, and he started to cry. He wouldn't tell me why, and I don't know what to do."

"Hang on. I'll be there as soon as I can."

I end the call and slip my phone in my pocket. Then I dash upstairs to Mom's room and search through her drawers for the key to my Kia. I eventually find it in her nightstand and hurry back to the kitchen, nearly tripping on the second-to-last stair in my haste. I slip a pair of sandals over my grey ankle socks and head outside to the car. I'm fully aware that I could get in a lot of trouble for driving on my own with just a permit, but I'm willing to take that chance for Jamie. I don't know what's going on, but one thing is clear: they need me.

I cautiously navigate through the neighborhood, clutching the wheel so tightly that my fingers start to ache. Thankfully, Liam only lives a couple of miles away. The Fishers must have recently redone their driveway because smooth asphalt has replaced the cracked concrete where Liam and I used to play basketball. We'd spend entire afternoons launching balls at the wobbly hoop attached to the garage roof or simply passing one around while we chatted. We could talk for hours without running out of things to say.

I pull into the driveway and park my car under the hoop. The backboard is smudged and faded, and the net has started to fray. The sight of it makes me feel kind of sad—no, not sad: nostalgic.

I ring the doorbell, and a few seconds later, Liam lets me in. Behind him, Jamie is sitting at the kitchen table eating a bag of Nacho Cheese Doritos. Jamie's cheeks are tear-stained, and their eyes are red and puffy.

"Hey." I stand behind Jamie and place my hand on their shoulder. "Want to go for a drive?"

Jamie nods. "Okay. But I'm gonna wash my hands first."

"Good idea. I don't want your orange fingerprints all over my white seats." While Jamie is at the sink, I turn to Liam. "Thanks for looking after Jamie."

"No problem," Liam responds. "Can I call you later? You know, to make sure everything is all right?"

"Of course."

Offering him a parting smile, I hold open the door for Jamie, and the two of us walk to my car. Once we're buckled in, I start the engine and back out of the Fisher's driveway. We drive in silence for a few minutes: Jamie staring out the window; me making sure I stay centered in my lane.

When I reach the local park, the one where I used to climb the now-nonexistent maple tree, I pull into the parking lot and stop next to a bike rack. With the sounds of children playing and dogs barking in the background, I turn to my sibling, who's still facing the window.

"What's going on?"

Jamie doesn't respond.

"Come on," I urge. "Talk to me."

Finally, Jamie looks away from the window. "Why do people say such mean things?"

"I'm not sure," I respond. "I think there are a lot of reasons. Why are you asking?"

"You know why."

"You're getting bullied again, aren't you?" When they nod, I ask, "What happened this time?"

"It's not just one thing. Or one time, for that matter. It's every day." Jamie stares at the yellow wristband around their wrist. The word *STRENGTH* is engraved into the flimsy elastic. "And the worst part is, I have no idea how to stop it. No matter who I hang out with or what clothing I wear or how I identify, nothing changes. I'm still a freak."

"That's bullshit," I say. "Jamie, you're not a freak."

"That's not what everyone else says," Jamie responds, their voice trembling. "You should hear the things they call me, Grace. Freak, loser, queer—and those aren't even the worst ones. People yell things at me when I walk through the hall and pass notes about me during class and write stuff on my locker. Last week in gym, we were playing basketball, and this guy tripped me and called me a fag, and no one did anything. They just stood there and stared. Even Coach Berger pretended like nothing had happened."

"Jamie, I—" I realize I'm at a loss for words. To imagine my sibling, who's one of the sweetest people I know, having to deal with that kind of hatred and bigotry makes me furious. I wish there was some way I could fix it, but I know that at this moment, the best thing I can do is be there for them.

Without saying a word, I lean across the console and wrap my arms around Jamie. They bury their face in my shoulder, while I gently stroke their hair.

"What am I gonna do?" Jamie mumbles into my shirt.

I continue to hold Jamie, running my hand up and down

their back. "You're gonna get through this," I say and kiss the top of their head. "It'll be okay, Jamie. You'll be okay."

———————

MOM WAS VERY upset when she found out I broke the rules of my permit. Even after I'd explained what happened with Jamie, she still proceeded to lecture me for thirty minutes and then threatened to cancel my upcoming road test. But, with a lot of pleading and apologizing on my end, she came around. She even seemed genuinely excited for me as we drove to AAA on Thursday afternoon.

Now, as we sit in the AAA waiting room at one minute past two o'clock, I can feel the nerves setting in. I wipe my sweaty palms on my jean shorts and stare at a poster on the dangers of drinking and driving that's taped to the wall. The distraught-looking cartoon girl in the top-right corner sort of reminds me of Jess. I wonder how she is. Unlike last year, when we were in biology together, I rarely see her anymore.

I remember how shocked my peaceful town was when they found out about the car accident. From coverage on local television stations to online articles to Facebook posts, everybody knew in no time at all. It wasn't long until that shock became speculation, and as rumors spread, people tried to make sense of the blurry details and convoluted cover-up stories to figure out what really happened that night.

After Bianca told me her version of the story, I tried to keep in touch with her over the summer. I'd text her now and then asking if she had updates, but she always said she didn't. Whether or not she was being truthful, I don't know. But for whatever reason, I couldn't—and still can't—shake this gut feeling I have that there's more to that night than a few bottles of beer and a winding road.

"You're up, Grace."

A man's gravelly voice jerks me back to reality. When I turn around, my old driving instructor Mr. Ren stands in the doorway of the room. "O—okay," I stutter.

"Good luck," Mom says, patting my arm reassuringly.

"Thanks."

With my heart pounding like a drum in my chest, I follow Mr. Ren upstairs and into the AAA lot, where a white sedan is parked next to the curb. I watch as a boy with curly hair emerges from it with a satisfied grin on his face.

Mr. Ren hands me a pink sheet of paper. "Give this to Frankie. He'll be your instructor."

Nodding my head, I take the paper from him and get in the driver's seat beside Frankie. He's an older man dressed in khaki shorts and an olive shirt that stretches tightly over his large stomach. Below his handlebar mustache, his lips are set in a frown.

"Hi," I say.

Frankie clips the paper to the clipboard on his lap. "Welcome to your road test," he says flatly. "We'll start with back-in parking. When you're ready, drive to the corner of the lot near that tree." He points out the windshield at an oak tree on the small strip of grass between the lot and the street. "Okay?"

"Okay," I echo.

Taking a deep breath, I check my mirrors and inch my seat forward with the switch on the left side. Then I wedge the key into the ignition and twist until the engine hums to life. I feel beads of sweat forming on the back of my neck as I shift into Drive, although I can't tell if they're from the stifling heat, my anxiety, or both.

With my hands clenching the wheel, I pull away from the curb and coast through the crowded lot. I alternate between using the rearview camera and glancing over my shoulder to back into the spot. Once I've successfully parked, I look at Frankie and try to gauge his reaction, but his face is a blank slate.

"Now you're going to leave the lot," he says. "Go out the back exit."   •

Following Frankie's instructions, I drive past the AAA building and turn left onto a side street. I come to an abrupt stop at a stop sign, making sure my foot is fully on the brake before I continue through. As I'm glancing at the speedometer to check that I'm not exceeding the thirty-mile-per-hour speed limit, a pick-up truck suddenly whips out of a driveway. I jam on the brake again, this time causing the car to jolt forward.

"Sorry," I apologize meekly.

"Keep your eyes on the road," Frankie says. "Turn right at the light and take the first left onto Main Street. Then we'll head back to AAA."

"Already?" I've been driving for barely five minutes, so that can't be good. "Did I fail?"

"Not yet," he responds to my relief.

Main Street is busier than I'd expected with cars lined up at lights, pedestrians jogging on the roadsides, and school buses every direction I look. Thankfully, the front entrance to AAA isn't too far. Frankie has me loop around the lot once more before I pull up next to the curb and turn off the car.

"Congrats," Frankie says. He has yet to display any emotion. "You passed. Give this to Kathy, and she'll tell you what to do next." He scribbles his signature onto the pink paper, unclips it, and holds it out to me.

Taking the paper from him, I unbuckle my seat belt and

leave the car. My entire body is shaking as I reenter the building and descend the staircase. I find Mom exactly where I left her; sitting in the waiting room with her eyes glued to her phone. She looks up when she hears me approaching.

"How did it go?"

"I passed. I thought I didn't, but look!" I show her the sheet of paper. "Frankie told me to give this to Kathy. Then I can get my license!"

Mom smiles faintly. "Well done, hon."

"Are you all right?" I ask. "I thought you'd be happier for me."

"I am happy," she says. "I promise. There's just a lot on my mind—that's all. But I don't want you to worry about it. Let's go see Kathy, okay? I have to get you to Anna in . . ." She glances at her watch. "Seven minutes."

I follow Mom to a cubicle adjacent to the waiting room, where the receptionist Kathy is talking on the phone behind a desk. Mom waits until she's hung up to hand her the paper.

"Congratulations on passing," Kathy says. She inputs my information into the computer, then gives me a form with instructions for obtaining my driver's license. "Our number is on the bottom if you have any questions. Have a good day."

I'm still a little shaky as Mom and I drive to Anna's. Not too long ago, having my license was one of the last things on my mind. Now that I'm gaining more independence, however, the timing couldn't be better.

"I guess I won't be needing your services anymore," I joke.

"I guess not," Mom says as she pulls into the parking lot. "I really am proud of you. You know that, right?"

"Yeah, Mom, I know. I have to go, okay?"

Mom nods. "I'll see you in thirty minutes."

"See ya."

I get out of the car and speed walk into the building, navigating around a woman with a stroller to reach the staircase. I arrive at Anna's suite two minutes late and stand in her doorway while she rearranges a stack of papers on her desk. After several seconds of waiting, I clear my throat.

"Can I come in?"

"Grace! I didn't see you there. Yes, please come in."

Anna leaves the papers as they are and follows me to the scale. Once she's recorded my weight, we settled into our respective seats. I watch her smooth out a crease in her floral capris.

"So, how was your driver's test?" she asks.

I smile. "I passed. Mom and I are going to the DMV this weekend to get my license."

Anna leans forward in her chair and gives me a high five. "Congratulations. You must be very relieved. I know you were worried about failing."

"I actually thought I'd failed," I say. "The website said tests take fifteen minutes, but the man who proctored mine made me come back in less than ten. He was weirdly chill though. I think he might have been on something."

"Either way, it's behind you. And now you can finally put Kevin's car to good use."

"It's my car now," I say with a grin. "I can't wait to start driving all on my own. Lou has a flat tire, so I promised I'd drive her to school until she gets it fixed."

"That's nice of you," Anna says. "How is Lou?"

"Lou is . . ." I shrug. "I dunno. Ever since the funeral, she's been super withdrawn. She doesn't talk about her mom or her feelings or whatever. It's just so weird, you know?"

"What's weird?"

"That things are finally coming together for me, while at the same time, the people I care the most about are falling apart.

Lou losing her mom, Jamie getting bullied at school. It almost feels wrong for me to be happy when they're in so much pain."

"I understand that's how you feel," Anna responds. "That said, you being in a better place means that now you can be there for them. Your experiences have taught you skills and given you insights that you can use to help them overcome their struggles. So, if anything, your happiness and wellbeing is something you should embrace—not feel guilty about. Does that make sense?"

"I guess. The problem is that both of them are so closed off. Hell, I can't even ask Jamie how their day was without them getting all defensive."

"When I met you, you were very closed off as well. Now look at how much you've changed."

"So, you're saying I should just give it time?"

"Exactly. And in the meantime, make sure they know that you're there for them. Knowing that you're not alone and that someone has your back can make all the difference. You understand that, don't you?"

I nod. "I do."

By the end of my session with Anna, that shameful feeling I had at the start is gone. I leave her suite motivated and determined to do what I can to make things right. Outside the building, I scan the crowded parking lot for Mom's car. I spot it in the back near a dumpster and walk over. When I get in, Mom is talking to someone on speakerphone.

"So, how soon can I schedule an appointment?"

"Dr. Zimmerman has an opening on the 14th at four thirty," a woman responds. "Appointments are usually fifty minutes but consults sometimes take longer. Would you like me to put Jamie down for then?"

"Yes, please. Thank you, Wendall."

"You're welcome, Ms. Sinclair. Have a nice day."

"You too," Mom says and ends the call.

"What was that about?" I ask.

"I'm looking for a therapist for Jamie," she explains. "I think it'd be good if they had someone to talk to."

"No kidding. Have you spoken with Principal Meyers yet?"

"Yes. Jamie and I are meeting with him on Friday. Between you and me, I'm not sure that they should stay at Everett—not after everything that's happened. Obviously I have to talk about it with Jamie, but we might have to look for a new school over the summer."

"Like a private school?"

Mom nods. "I know they're expensive around here, but if it's what's best for Jamie, we'll find a way to make it work. Just like we did for you."

"Let's hope it's not anything like it was for me," I say.

"I'll second that." Mom unbuckles her seatbelt and hands me the keys from the ignition. "How about you drive us home? The more confident you are on the road, the better."

"You know I just passed my road test, right?" I ask, but I take the keys from her nevertheless. Once I'm behind the wheel, I adjust the seat and rearview mirror and start the car. "Does this mean you're not still upset that I drove without you?"

"Not anymore," she responds. "If I'm being honest, I was never that upset to begin with. I was mostly just relieved that you were okay. The last thing I need is for you to get in an accident, like that girl did last year."

I think about the poster in the waiting room. "Jess was drunk. I would never do that."

"I believe you. That said, mistakes happen. When I was in college, my roommate hit another car. She was sober, well-rested, and one of the most responsible people I knew. But she took her eyes off the road for a split-second, and it cost her badly. She broke her nose and had to get facial reconstructive surgery. And that was a week before we were supposed to travel to Miami for spring break."

I wince. "I'll be safe, Mom. I promise."

Mom pats my thigh. "I sure hope so."

When we get home, Mom shoos me from the kitchen so she can prepare a "surprise treat" for my eighteenth birthday tomorrow. Although I told her two days ago that I wanted angel food cake, I simply shrug and head upstairs to start my homework while she preheats the oven. I log onto my computer and open Classroom, where Miss Bacon has posted the rubric for our final project. I read through it with my stomach in knots, trying not to overthink the fact that in one month, I'll have to memorize and present my narrative to an actual audience.

We spent all of the third quarter writing poetry. Our project —a slam poem that tackled a social issue we were passionate about—was the first major assignment we had to recite from memory. Standing at the front of the classroom, delivering my thirty-line poem on society's warped beauty standards, was both very nerve-wracking and surprisingly liberating.

But thirty lines is nothing compared to the approximate seven-to-ten minutes of speaking time I'll need to earn a "proficient" on the rubric for the final. A deep sigh escapes my lips. What have I gotten myself into?

Desperate for a distraction, I leave Classroom and dig my psychology review packet out of my homework folder to study for next week's AP exam. I flip to a practice test on page three and peer at the first question:

1. Psychology is defined as

a. the humanistic study of emotions and feelings

b. the sociological study of individual and group dynamics c. the scientific study of behavior and mental processes

d. the study of supernatural phenomena

I'm circling *c. the scientific study of behavior and mental processes* when the tip of my pencil breaks. I open my drawer to find a replacement, but the only two in there are broken as well. With another sigh, I stand up and walk to Mom's office to borrow one from her. On top of her desk is a disorganized pile of printed email conversations. Seeing them now reminds me of last spring when I found an email Dad had sent her about me in this exact same spot; an email Mom wasn't planning to tell me about.

After that, she swore she'd never keep a secret like that from me again. I didn't believe her at the time, but now I think I'm starting to. I wasn't lying when I told her that I'm ready to let go of the anger and resentment I've been suppressing inside me for almost eight years. I genuinely want to move on—now more than ever before.

Back in my room, I sit at my desk and continue working on the practice test. The questions are easier than I'd expected— that is, until I get to the sixth page. As I desperately try to recall material we covered several months ago, I can feel my confidence dwindling.

I slam my fist against the desk in frustration, causing Mom's pencil to roll onto the floor. "Oh, for God's sake," I mumble as I bend down to pick it up. That's when a PowerSchool notification appears on my lock screen.

Grade updated: AP Psychology – B-

I grimace. Considering that my previous average was eighty-seven, I must have really bombed my essay for my grade to dip that badly.

Sure enough, when I open PowerSchool, my essay grade is a discouraging seventy-one. I close the app, but before I return to the practice test, I decide I deserve a break and go onto Instagram to check my feed. I scroll past an album Heather created for a friend's birthday and like Liam's post-victory photo with his lacrosse team. Under his post, the account for The Center for Healthy Living has paired a motivational quote with a rainbow background. I peer at the swirly font: *Recovery is remembering who you are and using your strengths to become all you were meant to be.*

Above the brief caption, which consists mainly of hashtags, something catches my eyes: *Liked by realisaacnielson, jess.k.bishops, and 68 others* Unable to contain my curiosity, I click on Jess' username to see what other accounts she follows. NEDA, NAMI, I Weigh, and Liv Murdoc, a girl who was in treatment with me, are especially interesting.

As I'm scrolling through her posts, like a creepy stalker, something dawns on me. Maybe Jess didn't spend the summer in the hospital because of the accident. Maybe, just maybe, she was at CHL or another treatment program of that sort. That would explain the conflicting cover-up stories, her absence on social media, and even the tan she had when she came back to school. It could be a total coincidence, but the more I think about it, the more plausible my theory seems.

The sudden whirring of a blender interrupts my thoughts. I'm much too distracted to finish the test now, so I leave it on my desk for later and walk downstairs. In the kitchen, Mom is scrubbing the countertop with a sponge while Jamie stands next to her drinking an off-white milkshake.

"When did you get home from school?" I ask.

"Grace!" Mom exclaims. "You're going to spoil the surprise!"

"Will you chill? I already know what you're making me." I glance at the stove, where a Bundt pan containing a flat, light brown cake is cooling. "I thought it would rise more than that."

"It was supposed to," she says. "I must have kept it in the oven for too long."

"Great," I mumble sarcastically.

"Look, I did my best. If you want to try, be my guest."

I shake my head. "I'll pass."

"Then quit complaining. Can you pass me the cooling rack?"

I open the cabinet under the sink and hand her the rack. She flips the Bundt pan upside down and carefully transfers the cake onto the metal crosspieces. It looks even flatter out of the pan, as if someone had stepped on it.

"I'm sure it'll taste great," she says upon seeing the disapproving expression on my face. "So, is there anything special you want to do tomorrow? Other than presents of course."

"Get a tattoo," I say.

"We'll see about that."

"I'm turning eighteen, Mom. I don't need your permission."

"Can I get a tattoo too?" Jamie asks.

"Absolutely not," Mom responds. "What do you have in mind, Grace?"

"I'll show you." I unlock my phone and open Photos, where I've screenshotted a slightly blurry Google Image of my dream tattoo. "I'd probably get it a little smaller, but that's the one I want."

"Very nice," Mom says, sounding surprisingly genuine.

Jamie takes another sip of the milkshake and curiously peers over my shoulder. "What is it?"

"The National Eating Disorder Awareness logo," I say. "Do you know what it symbolizes?"

Jamie shakes their head. "What's that?"

With my gaze trained on the picture, I smile. "Recovery."

20

*'*C *ause girls like you run around with guys like—*
Sometimes I get the feeling she's watching—
No puedo pedir que el invierno perdone a—
I'm radioactive. Radioact—

"Will you please settle already?" I ask impatiently. I press my foot against the brake and slowly turn onto the main road behind a school bus. "You're gonna break the radio."

"I'm not gonna break the radio," Lou says, but she retracts her hand from the dial nevertheless, leaving it on a 2000's pop station.

"And stop playing with the AC. It's freezing in here. If you're so hot, take off your sweatshirt."

In my periphery, I see Lou roll her eyes. "Someone's in a mood," she mutters. "You were the one who offered to drive me, remember?"

"That doesn't mean you're allowed to mess with my car," I say. "Next time, I'm giving Jamie shotgun."

Lou glances behind us, where Jamie is sitting in the backseat with their arms crossed. "What's up with you? You look crankier than your sister."

"I hate school," Jamie grumbles. "It's stupid."

"I'll second that," Lou says. "I found out last night that Mrs. Frickle gave me an F on my essay. An F! And I was actually trying this time. I swear, that bitch has it in for me."

"I got an F on a bio experiment," Jamie adds.

"You did?" I ask, but they carry on like they didn't hear me.

"You know, Kevin says an F is just an A that's missing a leg."

Lou nods in agreement. "Kevin is a smart man. Grace, I think you missed the turn."

"She goes around back so she doesn't have to deal with traffic," Jamie informs Lou.

"Does that work?"

"See for yourself," I say as I pull into the student parking lot. I find an empty spot next to the tennis courts and quiet the engine. "*Et voilà.*"

"I'm impressed."

"And I'm bored," Jamie says. "Can I go now?"

I unlock the door, and my sibling jumps out of the car. While they hurry across the overgrown grass, Lou and I take our time following the paved pathway to the back entrance.

"See you in psych," I say.

"See ya," she echoes.

I walk through the busy English wing, navigating around the groups of students inconsiderately chatting in the middle of the hall. When I arrive at Voices, the first thing I notice is Liam's shirt. It's an offensive neon orange color with *CLEMSON* printed in purple across the front. To his left, Deanna has on a light blue Roger Williams University tank top under a white hoodie—also Roger Williams. I glance around the room, and I'm surprised to discover that almost everyone is sporting college merch.

And then I remember an email I received on Saturday from Aisha, the student body president. I open Gmail and reread her note: *Hey, seniors. This is a reminder that Wednesday is Wear Your College Shirt Day. Let's show some school spirit! - Aisha*

"Dammit," I mumble under my breath. I self-consciously clutch my arms to my chest, worried that my classmates will assume I'm not going to college or I'm taking a gap year like Carla, who's the only other person in the room without college attire.

I don't have a problem with gap years. That said, I worked hard to get into SBU, and now I've missed the one opportunity —other than sharing on social media—to flaunt my acceptance. I sink into my chair and place my head flat against the desk, wishing I could restart the day.

"You okay?" Liam sits beside me and taps my shoulder. "Hello? Earth to Grace?"

"I forgot my college shirt," I mumble.

"That's it? That's what's got you so down?"

"Yes, Liam," I snap. "It's a big deal to me, okay?"

"All right. Sorry I said anything." Liam is quiet for several seconds. "At least you didn't forget your narrative draft," he says finally. "I left mine on top of my printer."

"Bummer."

"Good morning, students!" Miss Bacon greets us. She stands at the front of the room wearing a grey Oberlin V-neck. Great. Even the teachers are participating in College Shirt Day. "We have a lot to do today. To start, please take out your drafts. We'll be breaking into groups of four to peer edit them. I'll let you make your own groups, but if I see you getting sidetracked, I'll have to assign them myself. Make sense?" She looks around the room, where about half of the class are nodding their heads. "All right then. Go for it."

While she situates herself at her desk, the chaotic process of forming groups commences. I end up with Liam, Tommy, and Carla. Neither boy has a physical copy of their draft, so they pull them up on their phones instead. Carla and I look at each other and rolls our eyes.

"It's like they've never heard of due dates before," she says to me. "By the way, are you taking a gap year too? You're not wearing a college shirt."

"No, I'm going to SBU," I respond. "I just forgot my shirt."

"Oh." She sounds somewhat disappointed. "Okay."

"So, who wants to start?" Liam asks. "I nominate Tommy."

"That's fine with me," Carla says, while I nod in agreement.

Tommy glowers at Liam. "Thanks a lot, man," he mumbles, but he opens the document on his phone nevertheless. He uses his thumb and index finger to enlarge the tiny font, and in a flat voice, reads, "I love soccer. I feel most comfortable when I'm on the field. My best memories have come from soccer, like the time I saved a corner shot with my head during premiere play-offs. Or scoring the first goal of the season my fresh—"

"Wait, wait, wait," Liam interrupts. "Hold up. *You* saved a corner shot? With your head? Dude, you're, like, five-four."

"Yes, I saved the shot," Tommy snaps. "Now can you let me read? You're not supposed to say anything until I'm done."

Carla and I roll our eyes again. I'm eager to ask her if she hates peer editing as much as I do, but Tommy has resumed reading, so I hold my tongue. Sharing my writing when it's polished and completed is stressful enough—sharing a rough draft with my judgmental classmates, on the other hand, makes me want to pull my hair out.

Groupwork has never been my strong suit.

As it turns out, my group spends so long critiquing Tommy's poorly-written narrative that I'm spared from having to share mine. When the bell rings, I shove my draft and rubric in my bookbag and follow Liam out the door. We split up at the top of the staircase: him headed to the library; me to Women's Lit. As I'm walking through the hall, I notice a boy talking to Jamie at my sibling's locker. He's tall—I'd estimate around six-three—with messy brown hair that looks like it hasn't been brushed in days. He's wearing a football jersey and black athletic shorts with blue stripes on both sides. I watch as he takes a step closer to Jamie, their faces mere inches apart, and pounds his fist against the locker.

"Oh god." I dart around two girls and hurry over to them. "What the hell are you doing?"

The boy's lips lift into a cocky smile. "You know Janie?"

Next to the boy, Jamie looks so small and vulnerable. Tears are brimming in their eyes. "That's my sibling, you piece of shit," I say and punch him in the face.

It's a light punch—more of a bop, really—but it's enough to piss him off. "Bitch!" he exclaims, clutching his reddening nose. "You're just as psycho as your sister!"

I raise my fist to take another swing at him when someone grabs my arm. When I turn around, Dr. Green stands behind me. "Let's go," she says firmly. "You too, Jack."

"But—but—" Jack starts to protest.

"Now!" she interrupts. "Show's over, folks," she says to the small group of students who have paused to observe the scene. "Go to class." With one hand clamped on each of our shoulders, Dr. Green marches Jack and me to her room and closes the door behind us. "Talk."

"It was her fault," Jack says at the same time I protest, "He started it."

Dr. Green sighs. "You first, Grace."

"He was harassing my sibling," I say. "He's been treating Jamie like crap all year, and no one is doing anything to stop it."

"That's BS," Jack says. "Jamie and I were talking—that's all."

"You punched your fist against their locker," I object. "Ask Jamie, Dr. Green. They'll tell you what happened."

"I could have you suspended for this, Grace," Dr. Green says. "You too, Jack, if what Grace is saying is true."

My stomach sinks. "Please don't do that," I plead. "I'll do anything—just don't suspend me."

"I'm not going to suspend you," she responds to my relief. "But you're both serving detention for two weeks starting tomorrow. Every day after school, you'll report to G-108. Understand?"

"That's not fair!" Jack exclaims. "I didn't even do anything!"

"It's either that or suspension," Dr. Green says firmly. "Your choice."

I don't know if I'm more upset at the unfairness of the situation or relieved that I'm not getting suspended a month before graduation. "Thanks," I mumble.

"You're welcome. Jack? Do you have anything to say?"

"Thanks, Dr. Green," Jack echoes unconvincingly.

"All right, then," she says. "You're free to go."

"Can I have a pass to Women's Lit?" I ask.

Dr. Green takes a green slip of paper out of her desk drawer, scribbles the time and the date at the bottom, and gives it to me. "Jack?"

Jack shakes his head. "Free period."

With the pass in my hand, I follow Jack into the now-quiet hall. He waits until we're several feet away from Dr. Green's room to say to me, "This isn't over. You and that freak are gonna pay for this."

"Keep talking like that, and I'll break your nose for real next time," I respond, surprising even myself with my audacity. "I'll see you in detention."

Before Jack has a chance to retaliate, I quicken my pace and slip into the nearest bathroom. I stand at the sink with my hands against the cold rim and struggle to process what just happened. I don't feel guilty about punching Jack or upset that I have to serve detention. Instead, I'm proud of myself for standing up for Jamie. I doubt I could have done that one year ago. I think I would have been too afraid.

Once my breathing has returned to normal, I raise my head and stare into the dusty mirror. My makeup is slightly smudged and my cheeks are flushed, but otherwise, I'm okay with how I look. I've accepted it.

I wash and dry my hands and toss the crumpled paper towel at the trash can, sinking it on my first try. Before I leave the bathroom, I glance at my reflection one more time: at the flawed face and imperfect body I once would have given anything to change.

And I smile.

When Mom found out about my detention, she was angry—but shockingly not with me. "I'm not saying that what you did was okay," she told me. "You know how I feel about violence. That said, that school has been utterly incompetent at helping Jamie. The poor kid has gone through hell, and what have they done? Jack squat, that's what."

"Have you started looking at private schools yet?" I ask. I take a bite of my hummus and olive sandwich and glance at the clock on the wall: twelve twenty-three. In less than two hours, I'll have to drive back to school for my first detention.

"Only online. There are a few that look promising, but I want Jamie to check them out before I schedule any tours."

"It's kind of like looking for colleges," I say.

"Kind of. I'm not buying Jamie any merch—I'll tell you that much."

"Not even a lanyard?" I joke, to which she rolls her eyes. "Kidding."

Mom picks up an apple slice, then puts it back down on her plate and looks at me. "I hope you know that the only thing I ever want for you and Jamie is for you to be happy," she says. "Grace, over the past few years, I've watched you encounter obstacles most people couldn't imagine facing and come out on the other side. Now Jamie is having to do that too. And even though I wish there was more I could do for them, I know in my heart that they'll be okay. Because if there's one thing raising the two of you has taught me, it's that my kids don't give up. No matter how many times the world knocks you off your feet, you'll get back up and keep fighting every time."

Her encouraging words bring a smile to my face. "Thank you."

"You're welcome. To be clear, though, when I say 'fighting'—"

"It's metaphorical," I interrupt. "I know. I shouldn't have hit Jack."

"You were standing up for Jamie," she responds. "You thought you were doing the right thing, and from what Jamie has been telling me, they feel pretty damn lucky to have you for a sister."

"Jamie told you that?"

Mom nods. "And they meant every word."

After I've eaten lunch and unloaded the clean dishwasher, I retreat to my room to finish writing my narrative. I was finally able to share my draft with my group in class, who, much to my relief, gave me overwhelmingly positive feedback. The only real critique I received was from Liam, who suggested that I consolidate the second body paragraph.

"It's good," he said, "but some parts seem sort of redundant."

Rereading my piece now, I realize that he's right. I delete two sentences, shorten another one, and reword the last so it smoothly transitions to the third body paragraph. By the time I've finished my edits, as well as touched up the rest of the piece, it's twelve past two. So, I turn off my computer and reluctantly head downstairs to prepare for detention.

"Is it that time already?" Mom asks when she sees me lacing up my shoes at the door.

I nod. "Unfortunately. Are you going back to work?"

"Not today. Sam is covering my shift. Should I wait for you to have snack?"

"No, don't bother. I think I'll head over to Lou's when I'm done."

"Well, in that case, I'll see you at dinner. Good luck in detention."

I roll my eyes. "Whatever, Mom. Later."

I grab my keys off the counter and head outside to my car. As I drive to school, my mind drifts to the last—and only time—I served detention. I was in sixth grade, and my history teacher Ms. Martinelli caught me drawing on a classmate's neck with a Sharpie. I spent my lunch period in her room, while she sat at her desk and argued over the phone with her ex-husband about who would take their son to his science fair. In the end, the experience wound up being more entertaining than disciplinary.

I don't have high hopes that this detention will be anything but miserable. The student parking lot is almost entirely full, so I'm forced to settle for a spot in the back near the late buses. Just as I'm walking through the entrance, the bell rings and students spill into the hall. I navigate around them and head downstairs to the basement. I find G-108 between a staff bathroom and a janitorial closet and cautiously step inside.

The room is dark and stuffy, kind of like a cave. Sitting behind the teacher's desk is a cranky-looking man drinking a coffee. I don't recall ever seeing him in my four years at Everett, but then again, I've never seen this room either.

"Um, excuse me?" I say. "Is this detention?"

The man nods. "Take a seat," he instructs in a gruff voice.

I scan the mostly empty room. In the very back, Jack slouches in his chair with his arms folded across his chest. The only other student is seated in the second row by the window and is staring at her lap with her shoulder-length blonde hair covering her face. Even so, I recognize her turquoise halter top and the Vera Wang backpack propped up beside her silver sandals. It's Jess Bishops.

Before I can change my mind, I quietly walk to Jess' row and sit next to her in a squeaky chair. She still hasn't acknowledged me, so I take out my phone.

"Phones away," the man snaps.

"Sorry," I mumble and quickly do as I'm told.

With my phone in my pocket, I steal another glance at Jess. Under the desk, her fingers are flying across her keyboard. *Not fair,* I think. I rest my chin on my hands and stare at the whiteboard, squinting to decipher sentences someone has messily written with a green EXPO market.

I will not throw my e cig at mr lipschitz
I will not throw my e cig at mr lipschitz
I will not throw my e cig at mr lipschitz

It continues like that for seventeen more lines.

"I'm going to the restroom," the man declares. "There'd better be no foolery while I'm gone."

I wait until he's safely out of earshot to turn to Jess and say, "This sucks."

Jess finally raises her head. Since I've only seen her on social media this year, in person, she's a lot different than I remember: her hair is shorter and wavier, other than a little mascara, her face is entirely natural, and she's not quite as thin as she used to be. She doesn't look like a Barbie doll anymore. She looks like a normal girl.

"You're staring," she says.

"Huh?"

"You're staring at me. It's weird."

"Sorry," I apologize. "So, um, what did you do? To get detention, I mean."

"Skipped class a few too many times." She shrugs. "Oh, well. How 'bout you?"

"I punched someone."

Jess' blue eyes widen with surprise. "What? Who?"

"That boy sitting in the back," I say, lowering my voice. "He was harassing my sibling. I wasn't just gonna let him get away with that."

"That sounds like something my brother would do for me. He's so overprotective—in a good way, I think."

"He's in college, right?"

"Uh-huh. community college."

"Where are you going to school?"

"I'm not," she responds. "I'm taking a gap year."

"Oh." Coming from the deputy mayor's daughter, this isn't what I expected to hear. "It seems like a lot of people are doing that. I considered it myself. I mean, it's a good alter—"

"I don't want to talk about it," Jess interrupts. She averts her gaze to her sandals, visibly upset. "And why are you sitting next to me anyway? I thought you, like, hated me."

"I don't hate you," I say. "You hate me. You've been a dick to me since freshman year, and I still have no idea why."

"Sorry about that," she responds, not sounding at all apologetic. "Don't take it personally. It's just how I am."

"You spread a rumor that I was in a psych ward last year," I remind her. "It's kind of hard not to take that personally."

"Well, it was true, wasn't it?" When I shoot her an incredulous look, she sighs. "Okay, so that was a shitty thing to do. But big deal. It's not like you're popular enough for anyone to care."

"Do you think anyone would care if they knew you've been treated for an eating disorder too?" This, of course, is purely speculation, but I can tell by the alarmed look on her face that I'm correct. "That's where you were over the summer, right? You weren't in the ER, like everyone said. You were at a program."

"But I was in the ER," she responds. "Didn't you see the pictures of the accident? My car was fucking totaled."

"So, you were there the whole time then? For three months?"

Jess continues to stare at her sandals. She's quiet for a couple of seconds, and when she speaks again, there's a trace of hostility in her voice. "Even if I wasn't, even if I was at some program or whatever, why do you care? What is it to you?"

"N—nothing," I stutter. "I don't care if you were in a program, Jess. I'm just glad you're okay. I mean, I've been there. I was at CHL for six weeks, so I know what it's like."

"Right," Jess mumbles. Now she's repetitively twisting the silver ring around her index finger. "Will you tell anyone?"

I shake my head. "You know I wouldn't do that."

"You! No talking!" The man lumbers into the room, his fly

still unzipped. "And you," he points at Jess, "put your phone away or I'm keeping it overnight."

With a subtle eye roll, Jess stops twisting the ring and slips her phone in her backpack. When the man turns his back, I try to make eye contact with her, but she looks away. So, with nothing to do to keep myself busy, I spend the rest of detention staring out the window at three hummingbirds flitting around the branches of a magnolia tree. I can just barely hear their pleasant chirps through the thick glass.

After what seems like an eternity, the clock finally strikes three thirty. The man looks up from his computer and grunts, "You're dismissed. Grace and Jack, I'll see you tomorrow. Same time."

"How much detention did you get?" Jess asks as we leave the room together.

"Two weeks," I say. "It could be worse. Dr. Green threatened to suspend me."

"Oh my god. For real?"

"I'm serious." I follow Jess out of the basement exit and to the student parking lot. "So, this is your new car, huh?" I say as she unlocks the door to a silver Mercedes.

"Yeah. My old car was pretty messed up, so my parents bought this one for me once I got out of . . . you know." She starts to open the door, but pauses with one hand on the handle and faces me. "By the way, I never hated you. I just thought you should know that."

I watch her get in the car and start the engine. Several seconds later, she backs out of the spot and speeds towards the exit, running a crooked stop sign in her haste. I wait until she's disappeared down one of the side roads to walk to my car. With warm AC blowing and my mind still marveling over my enlightening conversation with Jess, I leave the parking lot and turn onto the main road to drive to Lou's house. She wasn't in school today—not that I'm surprised. Since her mother passed away, her attendance has been very erratic, and on the days when I do see her, she always tries to act like she's okay. Nevertheless, I know she's hurting. I can tell by the pain in her eyes.

The Jackson's front lawn is in desperate need of mowing, and some of the flowers lining their walkway are wilted. I unlock the door with the spare key they keep under their *Home Is Where the Heart Is* welcome mat and enter the foyer. Like the exterior of the house, the interior is much more disorderly than it was when Mrs. Jackson was around. I kick off my sneakers next to Lou's bright pink flipflops, walk through the eerily quiet kitchen and lounge, and ascend the winding staircase.

Ignoring the *Do Not Disturb* hanger around Lou's doorknob, I open the door. She's sitting at her desk on her laptop. "Hi, Lou."

"Hey, troublemaker," she says. "How was detention?"

"Uneventful," I lie. "I've never been so bored in my life. What are you doing?"

"Going through photos. I have at least a couple thousand on here. Some of them are really old too. Like this one." She ushers me over and points at an image of the two of us kayaking through a swampy river. Lou's lips are pursed into a scowl, while my left hand is in the air swatting at the abundance of mosquitoes surrounding us. "Remember?"

"Oh, yeah. We were spending the weekend at your cousin's cabin in Rhode Island. That was in fifth grade, right?"

"Uh-huh. I can't believe we let that dickhead convince us to go kayaking. I got, like, a hundred bug bites that afternoon." Lou shudders at the memory.

"Me too. I was itchy for weeks. You mind if I sit?"

"Sure." Lou scoots over on her roomy chair, and I squeeze in next to her. She enlarges another photo, this one from

September of seventh grade. We're standing outside of Hubert's Hoagies—a sandwich shop in the Center that went out of business several years ago—and we're both wearing black jeans and My Chemical Romance t-shirts. "Ah, yes. Enter the emo phase."

"That needs to burn," I say. "Look at my eyeshadow. I can't believe I thought that was cool."

"At least you're not wearing a skeleton belt chain," she says as she continues scrolling through the photos. "Oh god. Ready for a cringe attack?"

I exhale dramatically. "Bring it."

Lou double clicks on a photo, and we stare in horror at our twelve-year-old selves, dressed for Halloween as *Twilight*-inspired vampires, lounging on a bench on Lou's porch. Liam sits next to me wearing a full-body hotdog costume and neon green sneakers. Liam and I are cross-eyed, while Lou is mid-bite on a Three Musketeers bar. Her glow-in-the-dark fangs are perched on the arm of the bench.

"You have to delete that," I say.

Lou drags the mouse to the top of the screen and clicks the trashcan icon. "Done. Christ, what a nightmare. Let's just pretend that never existed, okay?"

"Fine with me." I watch her continue to scroll up the file, the years of our lives flashing before our eyes. "You weren't lying about a couple thousand," I joke.

Lou doesn't respond. She's staring at a selfie at the top of the collection of her and her mother in the hospital. Lou is crouching next to Mrs. Jackson's stretcher with her free arm wrapped around her frail shoulders and a strained smile on her face.

"That's the last picture I have of her," Lou says. "She was so weak, she could barely raise her head. And there were all these tubes in her arms and chest. I was afraid to hug her in case I messed something up." Tears well in Lou's eyes, but she brushes them away. "Ma would always say that this was God's plan, but what kind of fucked up God would let a woman die like that? She was only fifty-two, Grace. Fifty-two!"

"I know it's not the same," I say, "but when my dad left, I felt so alone and confused and angry. I wanted an explanation for why he would do that; why he would abandon his family and leave his whole life behind. I wanted answers." I pause and shake my head. "But there are some things that just can't be explained. It didn't matter how much I screamed or cried or pointed fingers; he wasn't coming back. And as painful as it was, I had to accept that. It was the only way I'd be able to move on."

Lou considers this. "Do you still miss him?"

"Of course. I'll probably always miss him."

"Me too. I never thought I'd say this, but I'd give anything to have one more screaming match with her." Lou laughs softly. "Every time I do something that I know would piss her off, I hear her voice in my head; 'Louisiana, why must you be so irresponsible? She was the only person who called me by my full name, you know. I think she did it mostly to get under my skin."

"Your dad doesn't do that?"

"Nah. He used to when I was younger, but not anymore. We've been spending a lot more time together now that Ma's not around. We've started watching old crime shows at night when he gets home from work. We could never do that before because they scared Ma too much. He's also been helping me study for finals. My grades are crap, so I need to get at least Cs if I'm gonna graduate. I can't stay back, Grace. I'd lose my fucking mind."

"You'll graduate, Lou," I say firmly. "I'm not walking across that stage without you. Have you decided what you're going to do next year?"

She nods. "Community college. I thought about it a lot, and I can't leave Pa. Not now anyway. So, I'll live at home and commute there every day. It's only a thirty-minute drive. And what about you? Are you gonna be a Boston girl?"

"I am," I say. "Maybe I'll totally mess up and will have to leave, but at the very least, it's worth a try. That's the only way I'll know for sure."

"And maybe you'll do great and all this self-doubt will be for nothing." Lou closes her laptop and turns to face me. "You don't give yourself enough credit. You're a lot stronger than you think."

"So are you, Lou. You're, like, the strongest person I know."

"You're so full of shit," Lou says, but she's smiling nevertheless. "Just promise me one thing, okay? No matter how many miles are between us, promise we'll never stop being friends."

I place my hand on top of hers and stare into her dark eyes. "You have nothing to worry about," I assure her, meaning every word. "I promise."

21

"My recovery begins with one word: persistence. I soon learned that recovery is a winding road—dammit!" I throw my hands up and accidentally fling my pen across the small auditorium—or, as the theater kids call it, the Blackbox—in the process. It flies through the dimly-lit room and lands next to Tommy's left sneaker. "Crap."

"Nice going, Grace," Deanna says. She's standing a few feet away from me with her narrative clutched in her hands. "Nervous?"

"You can tell?" I joke. "I've never been so anxious about a final in my life."

"Me neither. I'm seriously wishing I'd written about something else, something less personal."

"I know the feeling." I glance down at my piece, my eyes fixating on certain words: *insecurity . . . identity . . . hospital . . . disorder . . .* "Think it's too late to bail?"

Deanna is about to respond when the ceiling lights flicker. "One minute until the doors open!" Miss Bacon announces. "If you have last-minute questions, now would be a good time to ask me. Otherwise, settle into your seats and breathe. You can do this."

"Easy for her to say," Deanna mumbles as we walk to the two rows of chairs positioned in the center of the room behind the microphone. Since she's going first, she claims the chair furthest to the left. "Good luck."

I nod. "You too."

I sit in the fourth chair after Bella and Curtis and skim through my narrative for the umpteenth time. Miss Bacon and the light operator open the heavy double-doors and start to hand out playbills to the crowd that has gathered in the hall. I try to focus on memorizing, but my mind is in a million different places. I'm suddenly reminded of my conversation with Spark at SBU. I could really use an Ativan right now.

Over the next ten minutes, more and more people trickle into the Blackbox. Mom, Jamie, and Kevin arrive with Lou right as we're about to begin. The four of them quickly find empty seats in the back row and sit down. While Lou chats with Jamie and Kevin reads the playbill, Mom averts her gaze to her lap. A few seconds later, my phone buzzes.

Mom: u ok?

Grace: fine. just a bit nervous

Mom: u will be great!

She follows the text with a Bitmoji that says *YOU GOT THIS*.

Although my stomach is still coiled in knots, I smile. I'm about to reply when the ceiling lights dim. Miss Bacon walks to the center of the Blackbox and picks up the microphone. She waits until the room is quiet to address the audience.

"Thank you all for being here. Public speaking, for most people, isn't easy. I've been teaching it for years, and I still get tongue-tied sometimes." Her laugh echoes through the reverberant room. "Over the past year, I've had the pleasure of working with the twenty young adults sitting behind me. Words can't express how proud I am of them for how hard they have worked and how far they have come. For their final project, they were asked to write a narrative about a period of personal growth in their lives. This project integrated their exceptional writing with their public speaking skills and encouraged them to be vulnerable, courageous, and authentic."

It's around this point when I stop listening. I close my eyes, take a deep breath, then place my piece neatly on the floor. I've done everything I can to prepare for this night. Even if it doesn't go accordingly, at least I can say I tried.

"Now I'll hand it over to the students," Miss Bacon concludes. "Please silence your phones if you haven't already, and without further ado, give a warm welcome to our first presenter, Deanna Sherman."

Deanna smooths down her skirt and approaches Miss Bacon, who hands her the microphone. "H—hi. My name is Deanna, and my piece is titled *A Metaphor for My Life*." She clears her throat. "When I was younger, my mom would tell me that it was important to stop and smell the roses. For the longest time, I had no idea what she meant. Firstly, I was allergic to roses." This elicits a couple of chuckles from the audience. "Secondly, why would I want to smell flowers when there were a hundred other, more interesting things I could do with my time? But my mom wasn't really talking about flowers; no, she was talking about stopping and appreciating life."

Once again, I zone out. Deanna's voice becomes a mere murmur in the background, like white noise projecting out of a sound machine. Directly behind me, Becky and Tracey whisper and giggle amongst themselves. I don't understand how they can be so calm and unfazed while I'm a nervous wreck.

I'm briefly brought back to reality by the audience's polite applause. Deanna, looking flustered yet pleased, takes a seat while Curtis assumes his position at the microphone.

"My name is Curtis Henderson, and my piece is titled *One World*."

Curtis' narrative is shorter than Deanna's, and Bella's is even shorter than Curtis'. While Curtis captivates the audience with his strong delivery and powerful story of being a black student in a predominantly white school, Bella loses her place twice and rushes through the second half, talking so quickly that even I, a notoriously fast talker, am unable to catch certain words. In a twisted way, the fact that Bella is struggling makes me feel slightly more at ease. Slightly.

When Bella finishes, she places the mic in its stand and hurries back to her seat. I stand up and shakily make my way to the spotlight, which is brighter than I'd expected. "My name is Grace," I say, "and my piece is titled *Learning How to Live Again*." Wiping my sweaty palms on my black jeans, I take a deep breath and let the words roll off my tongue.

"My story begins with one word: insecure. I've always been insecure. Whether it was genetics, society, or how I was brought up, self-consciousness was a big part of my childhood. Nevertheless, I was a pretty happy kid. I smiled, I laughed, I was praised for being creative and scolded for being impulsive. In fact, it wasn't until high school when my insecurities surpassed everything else."

I realize that I'm staring at my shoes and look up, honing my gaze on an elderly woman in the center of the audience. "High school is hard for everyone, and I wasn't an exception. I had a really tough time fitting in. I was struggling with my identity and trying to figure out who I was and who I wanted to be. I don't remember the first time I looked in the mirror and hated the person staring back at me. What I do remember, however, is how that self-hatred changed my life forever."

"Flash forward two years. I'm a junior now, sitting in a small room with my mom, my sibling, and a therapist. I'm wearing grey sweats, and a hospital admissions bracelet is wrapped around my wrist. My mom is talking to me, but I don't hear a word she's saying. All I can focus on is the tray of food on the table in front of me. I'm paralyzed with anxiety and overwhelmed by the conflicted thoughts racing through my mind."

"Over the next few months, that internal conflict kept getting worse. By February, I'd been in two hospitals, one residential treatment program, and I'd seen more therapists than I could recall. I was becoming fed up with this routine: of lying to the people I cared about; of constantly worrying that I was losing control; of spending each night haunted by flashbacks and each day feeling more dead than alive. As my mom would say: I was sick and tired of being sick and tired."

"My recovery begins with one word: persistence. I soon learned that recovery isn't a line; rather, it's a winding road full of detours, speedbumps, and numerous obstacles I had to overcome. Failure wasn't an option, because I knew if I surrendered to my disordered thoughts, I'd spiral back down the bottomless hole I'd just begun to climb out of. Though the road I was traveling was dark and unpredictable, I regularly reminded myself that with every sunset, there is a sunrise. The ominous thunderclouds that overshadowed my life would eventually part, and in their place, clear blue skies and sparkling sunlight would emerge. I would find better days. I had to."

"My journey continues with one word: hope. It's frightening sometimes to reflect on my past, whereas other times, it's weirdly nostalgic. But no matter how I feel when I think about that period of my life, my experiences have taught me things about myself that I otherwise wouldn't know. I discovered I like writing and plan to write a book someday. I learned that I have a strong will and the courage to conquer any obstacle that stands in my way of freedom. Most importantly, I realized that there's nothing wrong with being different."

"I used to believe my life had no purpose, and that the future wasn't worth living for. Maybe if I'd stayed in limbo and continued to straddle the fine line between relapse and recovery, that would have been how my story ended. But with support and determination, I've chosen a side. I've chosen life. Although there will probably always be ups and downs, one day at a time, I'm learning how to live again."

After my Voices presentation, which Mom spent days raving about to anyone who'd listen to her, the last two weeks of school go by surprisingly quickly. Because my grades—four As with a B in psychology—are high enough to exempt me from my other finals, most of my class time is spent watching movies and signing yearbooks. Lou, who with the help of her father managed to get her grades into the C range, isn't so lucky. Every afternoon, she calls me from her house to complain about how annoying her teachers are and how much she hates studying and how ridiculous it is that the cafeteria stopped selling cinnamon buns when they were clearly the superior snack.

"Now all they have are these shitty shortbread cookies that taste like cardboard," she gripes on Wednesday. "I can't wait to get out of this fucking school. I'm so over it!"

I bite my lip to keep from laughing at her theatrics. "Only

two more days," I remind her. "Lou, we're so close. Isn't it exciting?"

"Three more days for me. I have to go in on Monday to take my British Lit final because Mrs. Carson wouldn't let me take it this week. Dumb bitch."

"I told you you should have taken Voices with me."

"And monologue about my mess of a life in front of fifty people? No, thanks. Honestly, Grace, I have no idea how you did that."

"Me neither," I say. "I thought I was gonna pass out."

"You were the best one too," she responds. "And I'm not just saying that 'cause I'm your best friend. You crushed it, girl."

I blush. "Thanks. Do you want to hang out later? If you're not too busy studying of course."

"Can't. I have a date."

"What? With who?"

"Danielle."

"You mean your stalker?" I laugh. "You'd better give me her address in case I have to rescue you from some torture chamber."

"I'll be fine," Lou assures me. "She actually seems pretty nice. We've been texting, and it turns out we have a lot in common. She just gets me, you know? Like, she understands things about me that most people don't. And did I mention that she's British?"

"You definitely did," I say. "So, is that it with Cassie then? Are you guys really through?"

"Yes." Even over the phone, I can detect sadness in her voice. "We ended things when she got home. We both agreed it was for the best."

"I'm sorry, Lou."

"It's all right. There's no point in wasting time over something that isn't meant to be. It sucks, but life goes on."

"Life goes on," I echo.

"Yeah, well, I should probably go. I need to shower and figure out what I'm wearing, and plus Pa asked me to do the laundry." She groans. "But I'll talk to you later, okay?"

"Okay. I hope it goes well with Danielle."

"I hope so too."

With that, she ends the call. I turn off my phone, slip it in my pocket, and head downstairs to prepare for my appointment with Anna. I'm rummaging through my shoe bin for my navy flipflops when my phone buzzes again—this time with a text.

Katie: hi grace. i was driving by ur house the other day and thought of u. can we hang out this afternoon? id like to catch up.

Grace: i have an appt now but after im free. wanna get froyo at swoop scoops around 3:10?

Katie: definitely. see u then.

I reply with a thumbs up, then walk to the bottom of the staircase and call to Mom, "I'm getting frozen yogurt with a friend after Anna's! I'm not sure when I'll be home!"

"Okay!" she responds. "What do you want for dinner?"

"Don't care. Later."

Back in the kitchen, I slip on my flipflops, retrieve my keys from the blue basket on the counter, and walk outside into the blistering heat. I climb in my car, my exposed thighs sticking to the vinyl seat cover, and start the engine. Warm AC blasts through the air vents.

As I drive through town, I sing along to an alternative rock playlist on my phone. "*Say it ain't so,*" I belt out, coming to a stop at a red light. "*My love is a lifetaker.*"

I was introduced to Weezer last year at my Partial Hospital Program by my ex-boyfriend Isaac, who was a huge fan. He had posters in his bedroom, albums on his bookshelf, and even a signed t-shirt that he'd bought on eBay. And when he found out that they were touring in Manhattan last summer, he was the most excited I'd ever seen him.

I wonder if he ever ended up going to a concert. Other than liking each other's Instagram posts and sending an occasional *happy birthday* or *merry xmas* text, we haven't been in any contact since our breakup. Maybe I'll reach out to him one of these days. Even though I know things will never return to the way they were, it would still be nice to catch up with him. He was a really good friend to me after all.

The sound of a horn behind me jerks me back to reality. Lost in my thoughts, I hadn't noticed that the light had turned green. I hold up my hand apologetically and hastily step on the accelerator before I get honked at again.

As much as I appreciate not having to rely on Mom, sometimes I hate driving.

I arrive at Anna's building with one minute to spare and scan the crowded lot for a vacant spot, eventually locating one near a chain-linked fence. My parking job is subpar, but I don't have time to fix it, so I simply lock my car and hurry inside.

"Hi, Grace," Anna greets me when I arrive at her suite. "Come on in."

She holds open the door, and I enter her office. Plastered to the wall above her chair is a framed photograph of a clear blue lake surrounded by evergreen trees.

"That's new," I observe. "Where is it?"

"Maine," she responds. "My husband and I rented a cabin there for the summer. We're driving up with our girls when they're done with school."

"Cool."

"Do you have any summer plans?"

I stand on the scale and stare out the window as it calculates my weight. "Mom and I are going to Boston to meet with three therapists, but other than that, not really. Oh, and I'm taking another writing program. This one is online though."

"I'm glad to hear that you're still writing."

"I love writing," I say. "Now that I have more time, I think I might finally start working on a book." I take a seat on her couch and cross my legs. "I've only been talking about it for months."

Anna laughs. "It's nice to see you getting excited about something."

"Well, I hope it lasts. I've heard the first few chapters are very trying."

For the sixth session in a row, my weight is steady. Neither Anna or I make a big deal about it, but I can tell that she's pleased.

"Are you meeting with the on-campus nutritionist too when you go to Boston?" she asks.

I shake my head. "She's away then. I'll meet with her during Orientation."

"It sounds like you have everything all figured out."

"Most things," I correct. "I'm still waiting to hear if I got a single room, and obviously I have to find a therapist I like, but other than that, yeah."

"Good for you, Grace. You've worked hard. You should be proud of yourself."

"I just really want it to work out," I say. "I need this, Anna. I need a fresh start."

We spend the rest of the session discussing a variety of topics ranging from food to school to a Netflix documentary about mental illness in teenagers. Mom has been trying to convince me to watch it with her, but since I'm still in the process of catching up on my favorite television series, I keep putting it off.

"You should check it out," Anna says. "It's quite good."

"All right, I will," I agree. "Mom is gonna be happy."

"How are things with your mom?"

"Good. Other than yelling at me for forgetting to take out the recycle, we haven't had a serious fight in weeks. I think that's the longest we've gone since . . . since I got sick, I guess. By the way, it's two fifty-nine."

"Someone is eager to leave," Anna remarks.

"I'm meeting a friend in ten minutes," I explain. "I don't want to be late."

"I understand. Are you ready to move our sessions to every three weeks?"

I shrug. "Sure. Why not? So, the 30th then?"

Anna checks her calendar. "The 30th works for me."

"I'll have graduated the next time you see me," I say.

She smiles. "Yes, you will. I hope the ceremony goes well."

"Me too."

I leave Anna's suite, descend the staircase, and exit through the automatic doors. Since Swoop Scoops is only two minutes away, I don't bother with my car. Parking in the Center is a nightmare anyway. Strolling down Main Street, the weather feels even hotter than it did earlier. I walk on the far-left side of the sidewalk under the colorful awnings of the various retail shops and restaurants. I realize as I'm passing an escape room that although I've lived in this town for eight years, there are still so many places I've never been to and so much I haven't experienced. Now that I'm headed to an entirely new city, the thought makes me a little melancholic.

Swoop Scoops is a small frozen yogurt shop that opened one year ago. With bright green walls embellished with hot pink cartoon owls and a seating area comprised of sparkly silver tables, it's a visual headache. That said, the yogurt is delicious and relatively inexpensive, which explains the overwhelmingly teenage demographic.

"Welcome to Swoop Scoops," a cashier wearing a branded apron and black baseball cap greets me when I enter the shop.

Offering her a polite smile, I find an empty table next to the yogurt dispensers and take out my phone while I wait. Every time the door opens, I glance up, hoping it will be Katie. The first time, it's three toddlers and their mother; the second, it's two giggly preteen girls. I've just looked back down at my phone when the door opens again. Katie, sporting an old soccer jersey and black jean shorts, strolls into Swoop Scoops. She looks better than she did at SBU, more like the Katie I knew on the field. She's even smiling as she approaches the table.

"Hi, Katie."

"Hi," she says. "Thanks for meeting me."

"No problem. I was out anyway. So, froyo?"

She nods. "Definitely."

We select two paper cups with the Swoop Scoops logo printed on the sides and scan the twelve frozen yogurt options. From peanut butter cup to toasted marshmallow to sugar-free vanilla, there's a lot to choose from. After careful consideration, I opt for a fruity combination of strawberry and coconut. At the toppings station, I sprinkle chocolate chips onto my yogurt and wait for Katie by the register.

A couple of seconds later, she joins me with her order—chocolate and mint with mini m&ms—and places it on the scale. Combined, our yogurts weigh an even fourteen ounces.

Once we've paid the cashier, we grab a clump of napkins from a dispenser and return to the table. Katie plunges a pink spoon into the creamy yogurt and begins to mix the two flavors, while I leave mine separate and take a bite of the coconut.

"I used to come here a lot with Kaya and Laurie," she says, referring to the former co-captains of our Varsity soccer team. "They're spending the summer abroad in France. I was supposed to go with them, but instead, my dumb mom basically forced me into an outpatient program. This is my day off."

"I'm sorry, Katie."

"Don't be. It's my fault. I'm the one who screwed up."

"If you don't mind me asking, how exactly did it happen?"

"You mean how did I relapse?" When I nod, she says, "I honestly thought I was prepared for college. I had a therapist in the area, a reliable meal plan, a family friend who lived a block away—not to mention that SBU was my dream school. But when I got there, I realized I was way in over my head. There was so much to adjust to in such a short amount of time, and I didn't know how to deal with it. Then I got rejected from the magazine and the TV channel and two on-campus jobs I'd applied for. I felt like a total failure, which I guess is why I started restricting."

"When I went home for spring break, I promised myself that I'd do better; that I'd get through the rest of the semester without reverting to those bad habits. But the second I came back, it was like I forgot about everything. All my plans and goals and whatever vanished like that." She snaps her fingers. "Then just when I thought things couldn't get any worse, the day after you left, Spark got in trouble and was suspended. I had no friends, no motivation—worst of all, no hope. I started sleeping more and skipping class, and before long, I was barely leaving my room." Katie stares at her melting yogurt with tears in her eyes. "That was the loneliest I've felt in my entire life."

I hand Katie my napkin, as hers is covered in brown stains,

and she pats her damp eyes. "I used to feel that way too," I say. "I couldn't talk to anyone, because I thought they wouldn't understand what I was going through. But I was wrong, and the more I opened up, the better I felt. You're not alone, Katie. I know it might not seem like it at times, but people really do care."

"I wish I'd known that one month ago," Katie says with a sigh. "I hate this disorder, Grace. It ruins everything. A girl graduated from my program on Wednesday, and to celebrate, one of the counselors brought in cannolis. I love cannolis, but I could barely take two bites without my mind going into a full-blown panic."

"I totally get that," I respond. "My mom's boyfriend's birthday was last week, and she made him brownies. I was actually looking forward to them until it was time to eat. That's when I started having second thoughts. But it has gotten better. One year ago, I would have cried myself to sleep. Now, I felt badly about it for an hour and moved on."

"Same," Katie says. "One cannoli won't kill me."

"Were they at least good?" I ask.

"Oh, yeah. They were delicious. Do you remember in seventh grade when we went on a field trip to China Town?" When I nod, she says, "The year I went, it was rainy and cold, and everyone was miserable. But then my teacher took me and a couple of other girls to Little Italy, and we all got cannolis, and somehow, that made the day not suck. It's memories like those that motivate me to get better."

"I know what you mean. I can't wait for the day when I can eat a brownie and not worry about the calories or sugar or anything like that. After all, that stuff never even crossed my mind when I was younger."

"Me neither. You have yogurt on your face by the way."

"Where?" I rub my hand against my chin, but all I feel are a few small whiteheads.

"A little higher. Now to the right. Hold on, I'll get it." Katie leans across the table and pats my cheek with her napkin. "There. That's better."

"Thanks," I say, but Katie isn't listening. She's staring out the window with a distant look on her face. "Katie? What are you thinking about now?"

"I'm thinking about that night in the dining hall," she says, "when you asked me if I was fine. And obviously I wasn't fine, but now that I'm out of that toxic environment, I think I'm going to be. There's still a lot of stuff I'm uncertain of, and this program I'm at is a fucking pain, but at the same time, I have a feeling that things just might work out. Am I crazy to think that?"

I shake my head. "Of course not. There's nothing crazy about having hope."

22

I wake up on the day of my high school graduation to the sound of raindrops pounding against the window. With my blanket wrapped around my shoulders, I get out of bed, open the curtains, and stare glumly at the downpour unfolding before my eyes. The grass is a muddy mess, while on the streets, the sewage drains are overflowing with water. I watch as Felix Hoffman dashes to his car in a maroon suit, holding his briefcase over his head as if that will somehow protect him from the torrential rain.

A sigh escapes my lips. "You've got to be kidding me."

Without bothering to change out of my grey t-shirt and pajama pants, I walk downstairs, where Mom is stirring a thick batter in a bowl at the counter. A frying pan is warming up on the stovetop.

"Good morning, graduate," she greets me. "Your school called an hour ago. The ceremony has been moved to the gymnasium because of the weather."

I roll my eyes. "Awesome."

"Principal Meyers requested that everyone bring as few guests as possible," she continues. "If it's all right with you, I'll ask the boys to stay at home."

"Were they planning on coming in the first place?"

"Of course. We all wanted to show our support."

"Well, it's fine. I don't see why everyone makes such a big deal over graduation anyway."

Mom adds four lopsided spoonfuls of batter to the pan. "It is a big deal. You've worked hard for this. You deserve to be rewarded."

"I guess. I just hate being the center of attention."

"Tell that to Miss Bacon. Has she given you a grade yet?"

"Ninety-four," I say, "which means I'm ending the year with a 3.8 GPA."

Mom smiles. "That's great, hon. If that's not worthy of a reward—"

"It's really not that great," I interrupt. "Aisha, the valedictorian, has a 4.4, so I could have done a lot better."

"Nothing is ever good enough for you, is it?" When I shrug, she says, "Well, I'm proud of you. I hope one day you can be proud of yourself and all that you've accomplished too."

"We'll see about that. How soon will the pancakes be ready?"

"Ten minutes. Why don't you get dressed while you're waiting? We should leave around nine so we're not late."

"That's assuming it'll start on time," I mumble, but I trudge back upstairs nevertheless.

In my room, I lay out the gown on my bed, wriggle into my dress, and stand before my mirror. The dress I've selected is a cream-colored A-line with a lace trim that stops just above my knees. I knew from the moment I saw it on the clearance rack at Macy's that I wanted it. Not many things make me feel beautiful, but for whatever reason, this dress does.

After several more seconds of vainly admiring myself, I reluctantly pick up the hideous bright yellow gown and pull it over my dress. Then I grab my cap off my dresser and walk to the bathroom to fix my hair and apply makeup. I return to the kitchen just as Mom is transferring the last pancake from the pan to a platter. Kevin stands next to her sipping a mug of coffee, while Jamie sits at the table on their phone.

"You look nice," Kevin says to me. "Very official."

"I think she looks like a banana," Jamie pipes in.

"You're kind," I respond sarcastically. I take the pancake platter from Mom and place it in the center of the table between the honey and syrup. "Are we gonna eat or do you guys need a minute?"

"I'm ready," Kevin says. "My stomach has been grumbling since I woke up. Kira?"

Mom, who's scrubbing the messy countertop, sets down the sponge and nods. "Let's eat."

Fifteen minutes later, as Mom and I drive to school in the steadily pouring rain, I feel the nerves start to set in. When I check my reflection in the sun visor mirror, my face is noticeably paler than usual. I wish I'd chosen a different shade of eyeshadow, preferably one that doesn't make me look like a corpse.

"Why did you get me purple eyeshadow?" I ask Mom.

She frowns. "When did I do that?"

"On Christmas. It was in my stocking, remember?"

"Oh, right. I don't know. I thought it would like nice." She pulls into the crowded parking lot and squeezes into a corner spot. As she's reaching for the umbrella in the backseat, she asks, "Are you all right? You seem on edge."

"I'm fine," I say. "I'm just a little nervous—that's all."

"Ah. If it's any consolation, I imagine everyone is feeling that way."

"It's not, but thanks, I guess. Were you nervous at your ceremony?"

"I didn't go to my ceremony. I was actually on a ferry heading to Martha's Vineyard with my best friend while it was happening. School got out late that year, and we'd booked our trip months in advance. We figured there was no point staying around town when we could be relaxing on the beach and eating Chilmark Chocolates instead." Mom smiles at the memory. "I think that was one of the best summers of my life."

"Better than Reykjavík?" I ask.

Without a moment of hesitation, she shakes her head. "No. Nothing compares to Reykjavík."

Mom gets out of the car and opens the umbrella, then walks over to my side so I won't get wet. Using the large canopy to shield us from the rain, we follow three of my gown-clad peers and two middle-aged women into the school. Inside, Mrs. Hawkins sits behind a rectangular folding table distributing pamphlets.

"Welcome to graduation," she greets us cheerfully. She hands Mom a pamphlet and points to the gymnasium, where a steady flow of people are filing in. "Have fun!"

"Thanks, Jeannette," Mom responds. "Are you coming, Grace?"

I take a deep breath. "I'm right behind you."

It's pandemonium in the gym. Packed with four hundred students, eight hundred adults, and a couple dozen frazzled volunteers desperately trying to control the situation, I feel anxious simply standing in the doorway.

"I don't think I can do this," I tell Mom.

Mom steps to the side as Matt and Tommy dart past us, their sneakers leaving muddy footprints on the hardwood floor. "Don't be ridiculous. Of course you can. Look, there's Lou." She points at the bleachers, where my friend is standing next to a slender girl with short brown hair. "Go say hi. I'm going to find a seat . . . somewhere."

While she disappears into the crowd, I walk over to Lou and the girl. "Hey," I say. "When did you get here?"

"A few minutes ago," Lou responds. "This is Danielle by the way. Danielle, this is Grace."

"Nice to meet you," Daniella says in a distinct British accent. She removes her right arm from around Lou's shoulder and extends her hand.

I shake it. "You too."

"Can you believe this?" Lou asks, gesturing to the chaos surrounding us. "This was not what I had in mind when I pictured graduation."

Danielle coughs into her elbow. "My dad tried to convince me to stay home. He's worried I'll get sick, but I told him I'd take that chance. I didn't want to miss this."

"Did you bring your mask?" Lou asks.

"What mask?" I ask, but both girls ignore me.

"My doctor said I don't have to wear it anymore. My dad is just being his usual paranoid self." Suddenly, her handbag buzzes. Danielle takes out a glittery purple phone and glances at the Caller ID. "Speak of the devil. I'll be right back."

"So, what's the deal with the mask?" I ask Lou once Danielle is out of earshot.

"I didn't tell you?" When I shake my head, she says, "Danielle is in remission from leukemia. It's been years."

"Oh." Several follow-up questions immediately pop into my mind, but before I have a chance to ask any of them, Principal Meyers taps the microphone.

"Can I have everyone's attention?" He waits until the gym is quiet to continue. "Thank you all for your patience. We're about to begin, so please find a seat. And be careful—the floor is wet."

Before we part, Lou hugs me. "We did it," she whispers in my ear.

Although the strong scent of her vanilla perfume is making me dizzy, I lean into her embrace. "Yes, we did."

Once everyone is seated—or, since there are at least thirty chairs too few, standing in the back of the gym—the ceremony begins with The Pledge of Allegiance. Then the senior acapella group, One Note Stand, sings *The Star-Spangled Banner*, while their parents hover around the makeshift stage filming the entire anthem.

"Thank you, One Note Stand, for that performance," Principal Meyers says when the song is finally over. "I'd now like to invite our valedictorian up to the stage, Bianca Santos."

"Wait, Bianca is the valedictorian?" I whisper to Matt, who's to my right. "Where's Aisha?"

Matt shrugs. "No idea."

"I'm not actually the valedictorian," Bianca says into the mic. "Aisha Farooq was supposed to be here today, but she's sick, so I'll be reading her speech for her. When she texted me this morning and asked if I'd take her place, I was super flattered. Aisha is, without a doubt, the smartest person I know. If anyone deserves to be a valedictorian, it's her. So, Aisha, this is for you, girl."

Bianca clears her throat. "I'd like to start by congratulating every graduate in this room. I know that it hasn't been an easy road for most of us, and that in varying ways, to varying degrees, we've all had to overcome adversity at some point in our adolescence. For me, that adversity came at age twelve when I moved to America. I was a scared and insecure Pakistani girl who barely knew any English. My parents enrolled me in an all-girls private school, where I was the only student who wore a hijab. So naturally, I stuck out like a sore thumb. Part of me was tempted to ditch my hijab, because I thought if I looked like the other girls, maybe they would be kinder to me. Maybe they would accept me. But I wasn't brought up to change myself for anyone else. I stayed true to who I was—and I have to this day. I'm still Pakistani, and I'm still insecure, but I'm no longer scared."

I glance behind me at the audience, who seem unfazed by the self-assured Latina girl delivering a speech about being a shy Muslim. When I return my attention to Bianca, her dark red lips are set in an unwavering smile. Her voice is strong and steady, like she's done this a hundred times before. I admire Bianca's confidence. Even after taking Voices of Our Generation, which, as Miss Dixon predicted at the beginning of the year, ended up being a good experience, I doubt I'll ever be able to speak comfortably in front of an audience. It's just not who I am.

Bianca concludes Aisha's speech several minutes later by declaring, "From this day forward, we must believe in ourselves so that we can fulfill our goals and achieve our dreams. Here's to the next chapter of our lives. Congratulations, graduates."

The audience applauds as she walks back to her seat, still smiling. Principal Meyers waits until the gym is silent again to say a few words of his own. Then the vice principal takes her turn, then the superintendent, and lastly Dr. Green, who, for some odd reason, was voted Teacher of the Year.

By the time Principal Meyers announces that it's time to hand out diplomas, I'm so bored that my nerves are almost entirely gone. Had the ceremony been held outside, we would have lined up behind the stage like we'd practiced during last week's rehearsal. Because of how little space there is in the gym, however, Principal Meyers calls us up one at a time instead.

"MacKenzie Aaron . . . James Abernathy . . . Elizabeth Anderson . . ."

I sigh. When I thought this morning couldn't get any longer, it just did.

"Evelyn Dunn . . . Matt Durham."

Matt, wearing his trademark cocky smile, saunters across the stage. Like everyone before him, he takes the diploma from Principal Meyer and shakes his hand. Once their grips are locked, Matt faces the audience and tilts his head forward and to the side, as if he's at a photoshoot.

"Yay, Matty!" Mrs. Durham calls. When I turn around, she's standing up and enthusiastically waving her arms over her head. On her lime green t-shirt, printed in glittery letters, are the words: *Team Matt, Proud Mom*

The principal patiently waits until Matt has concluded his charades and left the stage to glance back down at his cheat sheet of names.

"Grace Edwards."

And just like that, my anxiety returns. I take a deep breath and, with my heart pounding in my chest, approach Principal Meyers. He smiles kindly at me and extends his hand. His skin is damp—whether from sweat, moisture, or a combination of both, I'm not sure—but I pretend I don't notice.

"Well done, Grace."

"Thank you," I say.

I take my diploma from him, and he turns my tassel. As I'm leaving the stage, I quickly glance at the audience. Mom, who's sitting in the third-to-last row, has her phone in her hand and a proud smile on her face. When she sees me looking at her, she mouths something that I can't make out.

"What?" I mouth back.

She tries again, and this time, I understand what she's saying: "I love you."

I realize as I'm settling into my stiff chair that I'm smiling too. I uncurl my fist and stare down at the tightly-rolled scroll. A red ribbon is looped around the center, holding it together. Part of me is tempted to undo the ribbon and open it right now so I can be sure that this is real; that I've really made it. After all, it wasn't too long ago when the thought of coming back to school —much less graduating with actual goals for my future—seemed next to impossible. But, if there's one lesson the past few years have taught me, it's that anything is possible if you just try. And I've done more than just try. I've conquered.

THE REST of the graduation ceremony is a blur. After all four-hundred-and-thirty-six graduates have received their diplomas, the marching band walks laps around the seating area playing an upbeat tune that echoes through the reverberant space. Then Principal Meyers informs us that the rain has stopped, and we can head outside to take pictures. The second the words have left his lips, there's a mad dash towards the exit. It seems that everyone else is as eager to escape the stuffy gymnasium as I am.

The weather is surprisingly mild considering how hard it was raining just hours earlier. While most of my peers and their parents follow the paved pathway to the lawn where the cere-mony was supposed to be held, I separate from the crowd and tromp across the muddy grass to the vacant courtyard. I take off my gown and fold it into a lump, then place it on the damp brick ledge and sit on top of it. With a gentle breeze rustling my hair and dress, I gaze at the small garden that the environmental club had planted two years ago. Once barren, leafy vegetable plants and colorful flowers now proudly protrude from the dirt.

As I'm watching a monarch butterfly land on a tomato vine, I realize that life is similar to this thriving greenery. Because no matter how many times difficult circumstances threaten to decimate it, it always grows back stronger and livelier than before.

Life can be hard. But then, it can also be beautiful.

ACKNOWLEDGMENTS

I used to think that writing was a solo career and that when it came to publishing my books, I could do it all on my own. Looking back, knowing what I do now, I realize how very naïve and inaccurate that thinking was. I can say with one-hundred-percent confidence that I wouldn't be in the place I am today without the many incredible people who helped me along the way.

Thank you to my mothers, Mom and Mama, who are the best parents anyone could ask for. Not only have you been the biggest fans of my writing; you were there for me when I was at my worst and never gave up on me. I attribute a great deal of my professional success and personal growth to your unconditional love and support.

Thank you to my superb team of editors. Thank you to Karin Stahl, author of the memoir *The Option*, Cindy Rodriguez, teacher and author of *When Reason Breaks,* and Kari Karp and Bailey Francis, teen librarians at Noah Webster Public Library and Lucy Robbins Welles Library. Thank you, as well, to best-selling author Michelle Wildgen for writing my blurb, which put a huge smile on my face. All of you took time out of your busy schedules to help me, and for that, I'm grateful.

Thank you to Kate Conway, author of the best-selling *Undertow* series, for designing my epic cover for the third time. I'm constantly in awe of your talent and appreciate the mentorship you've given me since I reached out to you three years ago asking for advice. Little did I know how much good could come out of a simple phone call.

Thank you to my treatment team for continuing to guide me through recovery. With the world in such a dark and unpredictable state, the reliability and familiarity of your support is something I cherish now more than ever before.

Finally, this series wouldn't be what it is without you, the readers. Thank you to everyone who read my books, listened to me talk, came to my events, and contacted me online. Every time I get a message, I remember why I decided to write *Changing Ways* in the first place. Knowing that I'm making a difference and helping people who are battling the same demons I was not too long ago is the greatest gift I could ask for and has had a monumental impact on my own recovery. So, thank you. For everything.

ABOUT THE AUTHOR

Julia Tannenbaum is the author of the *Changing Ways* trilogy, which she started writing when she was seventeen years old. She's an advocate for mental health awareness and often incorporates her personal struggles into her fictional work.

Tannenbaum is currently pursuing a Creative Writing and English B.A. at Southern New Hampshire University. She lives in West Hartford, Connecticut with her family.

Website: wackywriter.com
Facebook: writerjuliatannenbaum
Instagram: julia.tannenbaum
Twitter: julia_tann